EXODUS '95

KFIR LUZZATTO

PINE 10

CONTENTS

Pine Ten, LLC

205 N Michigan Avenue

Chicago, ILL 60601

First publication: May 2017

ISBN: 978-1-938212-39-0

CHAPTER 1

Portofino, Italy, July 1995

The evening was beautiful, as July evenings can't help being in Portofino. An assortment of elegantly dressed guests of mixed ages and nationalities populated the veranda of the Hotel Splendido. Dan Ze'evi sank into one of the luxurious armchairs provided by the hotel for its guests, deep in thought, fantasizing about how his business trip would fix all of his company's problems. Little wonder then that a stranger's unexpected question failed to register.

Coming out of his reverie, he lifted his gaze, expecting to see a waitress pushing drinks at him as before. Instead, there was an elegant young woman before him, who was anything except a waitress. *An heiress is more like it,* he thought. She was slim and medium height, with auburn hair and piercing green eyes.

"Are you waiting for me?" she asked. She was so beautiful, and he wanted to say yes until it hurt.

"I'm afraid not unless you're a middle-aged businessman in disguise who has shaved his mustache," he responded instead, surprised at his own uncharacteristic wit.

She flashed a smile at him, wiggling the tip of her nose as a bonus. "You're Dan Ze'evi, right?"

He felt the smile leave his lips. "How do you know my name?" he said, jumping to his feet in a late show of politeness.

"I'm waiting for Andrey Leskov, too," she said. "He called to say he was running late and would arrive in Italy tomorrow. He asked me to seek you out and make sure that you got the message."

"Oh...do you work for him?" he asked.

"You could say that."

"Doing...?"

"I don't think that we should talk shop tonight. Not before Andrey arrives," she answered.

Her long hair was arranged into a casual ponytail. Her girl-next-door look, free from any noticeable makeup, made her an unlikely candidate for a Leskov business representative.

"Are you allowed to say your name, or is that off-limits too?" he asked after a brief silence.

"I am Claire Williams," she said, blinding him with another smile and offering him a hand to shake. "Nice meeting you, Dan."

"The pleasure is all mine..."

"I hope not," she said, making it sound like she meant it. She sat beside Dan, and he sank slowly back into his armchair, searching his head for something to say to keep the conversation going.

The house musician had taken over the piano and was singing old Sinatra songs. A couple who looked like royalty on a honeymoon was dancing like pros. Dan looked around. He was out of his element and would never have spent the kind of money that the Splendido charged its guests had it not been for Leskov's invite. But since his host was footing the bill, he could be grand, he reminded himself with a chuckle.

"Would you like a drink?" he asked.

She waved the waiter over without answering and ordered lemon vodka. Dan opted for another whiskey sour, an ill-advised choice for someone not used to drinking. *Pretty good stuff,* he thought with appreciation after gulping down his second one. He seldom drank much, but he had to keep his hands busy with something because Claire's presence made him nervous. Something was wrong with his hands—he couldn't figure out what, but they were sweating.

Dan wasn't a self-conscious person, as a rule, but he had never been more aware that his belly was starting to show a hint of a bulge. Though he had shaved that morning, the feeling of the bristles on his face made him wonder if his appearance was unkempt. And he suddenly realized that his jeans were old-fashioned and his sneakers were worn down at the heels. He had felt at ease until Claire had come along, but she had somehow managed to make him feel ill-suited for their elegant surroundings. The second drink had helped that. But now, he was woozy and in danger of making a fool of himself by throwing up on the floor.

"I...I need some fresh air," he gasped.

Claire took a step back and nodded. "I expected that you would by now," she said. "Come with me."

The fresh air on the balcony did wonders for Dan. His head cleared a bit, and the glass of ice-cold water that Claire had brought him from the bar sobered him some more.

"You shouldn't be drinking if you're not used to it," she said, sounding either reproachful or amused—he wasn't sure which.

"It's that evident, eh?"

"Uh-huh," she agreed, nodding for emphasis.

"I'm okay now," he said. "Embarrassed, but otherwise okay."

"Are you up to walking?" she asked.

"I think so."

"Then let's take a walk down to the garden. The path that leads to the harbor is steep, but it's a beautiful evening, and it would be a shame to waste it."

"Good idea," he said, getting up. He was still a bit uncertain on his feet, but he hid it as best as he could.

They walked down the path until they reached the garden's edge, where stone steps led down to the harbor. There, she stopped.

"Let's catch our breath here for a moment. It's a magnificent view," she said.

"It is..."

"Your accent is what, German?"

"No, Israeli. Hebrew is my mother tongue."

"So, tell me about yourself."

Dan paused, considering how to present himself in the best possible light. "I'm an electronics engineer," he said at last. "I design underwater communication equipment...for divers, you know?"

"I don't, really. I'm a mountain girl myself. But go on," she urged him.

"I have this small company in Tel Aviv...in Israel. It's only a couple of other guys and me—and this year, I decided to go to CeBIT'95 last March in Hannover, Germany."

"I've heard about CeBIT. It's a big electronics fair, isn't it?"

"Huge. I spent a small fortune—for me, at least—but I didn't get much out of it and went back home rather low-spirited. Then, out of nowhere, Andrey Leskov's representative came last month and said he wanted to invest in my company. I gather he's rich."

"Oh, yes. He's rolling in it."

"How is he? As a person, I mean," Dan asked.

"You know, I think you need to form your own opinion. Andrey may impress different people in different ways."

"Am I imagining it, or are you avoiding answering my questions?"

"You are imagining it," Claire said flatly. "We need to go back now. Tomorrow'll be an early start, and you need to sleep it off."

She turned her back to him and strode back up the garden path.

"Hey!" Dan called after her, "Slower, please. I'm still a bit shaky on my legs."

Claire stopped ahead to wait for him. "Be careful not to break a leg. Tomorrow is your big day."

"You didn't tell me anything about yourself," Dan said when he reached her.

"That's correct," she said and started walking again.

CHAPTER 2

New York City, January 1995

Claire almost missed his figure, standing in the dimly lit hallway. Mr. Jones—Jack, as he had begged her to call him—looked even smaller and frailer than she remembered from the last time they had met a few days before.

"Oh, I'm sorry, Jack," she said as he tugged at her heavy winter coat sleeve. "I didn't see you. I'm so absentminded these days..."

The old man smiled a quick, sad smile that seemed to express his resignation at being unnoticeable. "Will you come up for tea later?"

"I have some work to pick up..." she began, but the imploring look in his eyes made her stop. "But I guess I'll be back by five o'clock. Five okay with you, young man?" she asked, trying to lighten the atmosphere.

"I'll be waiting for you," he said, nodding. He let go of her sleeve. Even holding the cloth looked like a painful deed for his hands, which age and arthritis had deformed without mercy.

"I'll be there," she said, trying to sound as enthusiastic as she could manage.

Mr. Jones nodded again and shifted his gaze from her face to the floor. Claire nodded, too, but more to herself than to him. She opened the door and walked out into the frosty morning.

Claire had met Mr. Jones for the first time five months earlier when she had moved into the old building where he lived. The building was in bad repair, with the heating system breaking down more often than not—but the rent was cheap, and its location in a safe part of town made up for its many flaws. It was a perfect fit for Claire, who kept odd hours at the advertising agency where she worked as a graphic designer. The agency was only three blocks away.

Mr. Jones lived in the attic, two floors above Claire's flat, which the owner had converted into a tiny apartment. She had had a long tea session with Jack not long after moving in and had heard the story of his life—or, as she later discovered, the least interesting part of it—and how he had happened to end up so far away from his native Ireland. She liked the old man—he was eighty-seven years old—and he had made no secret of his fondness for her. He often waited for her in the hallway to catch her on her way to work, giving her oranges or peeled apple quarters. That always brought up fond memories of her mother, who used to wait for her at the door back home in Colorado to ensure she would take a bite on her way to school.

Mr. Jones' apartment, which seemed carved out of another dimension, had a kitchen that doubled as a living room, an ancient sofa next to a small window, and a bedroom to which one acceded through a door squeezed between the couch and a wood fire stove. When Mr. Jones opened the door for Claire on that winter afternoon, the kettle was already starting to whistle with perfect timing. She took off her coat, which he laid in an orderly manner on the sofa, and he motioned her to sit at the table. After a few words of welcome, he placed tea and butter cookies before her, and they drank in awkward silence.

"Your place is really cozy," said Claire, to make conversation. "I see that you still keep the wood for the stove outside the apartment, near the log with the ax. Are the neighbors still coming up to split wood for you? I'd like to do that too. This January is colder than ever. Do you have enough wood to get by?"

Seeing that her prattle wasn't getting any reaction from Mr. Jones, she stopped and waited. "What's on your mind, Jack?" she asked after a while.

He looked at her with watery blue eyes for a few seconds before speaking. "Tell me a bit about yourself, Claire," he said at last. "How did you wind up in New York?"

Claire didn't like to talk about herself. She took a deep breath, suddenly aware of the smell of incense. It came from a candle burning before the portrait of a severe-looking woman in her sixties that Claire knew was Jack's late wife. "Well," she said eventually, "after my brother's nineteenth birthday, when he decided to enlist in the army, there wasn't much left for me to do in our hometown. I'd been taking care of him—of both of us—since my mother died, but at that point...our hometown felt too small for me...and there were other reasons, too."

Claire didn't feel like expanding on those and was happy Jack let it go.

"And your father?"

"He died six years before my mother. Skiing accident."

"I'm sorry to hear that. I didn't know. You're from Colorado, right?"

Of course, you didn't know, Claire wanted to say. *How could you?* She hadn't expected that she would have to bring up unhappy memories at afternoon tea. She wished she could change the subject.

"Yes. I'm from a small mountain town. Our family owned a hardware store that kept my brother and me going. I sold it, and the house, and I managed to get through design school with my half. So now, here I am, almost twenty-seven years old and struggling to get by. But I'm not complaining—I've been on my own since I was eighteen. I'm used to it."

She spoke matter-of-factly without a hint of bitterness. Mr. Jones nodded in appreciation as if she had just recounted some commendable accomplishment.

"You're strong, Claire. You're doing fine, and you'll be all right."

"Do you think so?" said Claire. She felt a strange need for his approval. She had been forced to become an adult too young and sometimes missed a parent's support. Jack's fatherly demeanor made him a good candidate for a shoulder to cry on, she thought, if she should ever indulge in self-pity.

"I'm sure of it. I think I'm a good judge of character. You're a good person...perhaps too good," Jack said, choking on the words. He lowered his head in embarrassment.

"What's the matter, Jack?" Claire asked apprehensively.

He kept silent for a few more moments, then lifted his head and pursed his lips. "I'm old, Claire, and I don't have much time left," he said.

"Oh, nonsense!" she rebuked him. She tried in vain to find something to say that wouldn't sound too much like a cliché. He shook his head and struggled for more words as if wanting them to linger in his mouth.

"No, I mean it," he said at last. "My days are numbered. I can feel it in my bones. My body is getting ready for it and is warning me...How considerate of it," he added with open sarcasm. He made an effort to smile.

Claire felt a lump in her throat, and her fingers instinctively took the old man's thin hand. His bones felt as fragile as a bird's wing, and she held his hand in a gentle grip for fear of breaking them.

"Don't worry," she said, immediately regretting the stupid words.

"Oh, I'm not afraid of dying," he said, and she knew that he meant it. "I'm about ready to go, and I have nothing to hang on to life for. But I'm scared of dying alone. I'm terrified at the thought that I will die here, all by myself, and nobody will know—nobody will care…"

His voice broke, and he swallowed as if to regain composure.

"You told me that you have a daughter," Claire managed, relieved that she had recalled that detail from an earlier conversation.

"My daughter," said Mr. Jones with a sigh. "She is busy with her life, and there is no room in it for me. She's ashamed of her father, of my poverty."

"Don't say that!" said Claire, her voice breaking, "I'm sure she's not ashamed of you. There's nothing to be ashamed of."

"Claire," he said, this time speaking without hesitation, "will you sit with me while I die?" She turned with a jerk to face him, her eyes wide. "Please? I know it's a huge favor to ask of you, but it won't be for nothing…"

"I don't want anything," Claire said quickly.

"But I want to give you something—something truly important. It's nothing tangible. It's not money. It's knowledge that has immense value for the right person. I want you to have it. I don't want it to be lost when I die."

He gazed at her intently. As she hesitated, he said, "Please," again, in a low, pleading voice.

Claire couldn't find the courage to reject his gift, whatever it was. She swallowed, putting on a brave face.

"I'll take it. Thank you, Jack."

CHAPTER 3

Portofino, Italy, July 1995

The phone by Dan's bed jerked him out of his sleep with a high-pitched trill, at odds with the calm atmosphere of the hotel. Dan cursed it and answered, trying to speak clearly from a pasty mouth.

"Hello," he managed.

"Mister Ze'evi, this is Vadim, Mister Leskov's assistant. Can you be ready in twenty minutes?"

"I don't know. What time is it?"

"It's well past nine. Mister Leskov wants to see you at ten."

"I'll be quick, but I need coffee."

"I'll have some sent up to you. I'll wait for you by the reception desk."

Dan climbed out of bed with little vim, brushed his teeth with his eyes still closed, and splashed water on his face to try to clear his head. He had a severe headache but didn't have the time to do much about it. *To hell with Vadim,* he thought and jumped into the shower. The running water helped a little, but soon, an imperious knock sounded at the door, followed by a "room service" call.

He gulped down his coffee, shaved, and dressed without

paying too much attention to the result. Claire was waiting at reception with a man whose shaved head, black shirt, and twitching biceps made him look like a thug.

"Vadim," he said.

They shook hands briefly, and then Vadim strode out, saying over his shoulder, "We must get moving. You took too long."

"It took me exactly twenty-two minutes," he whispered to Claire, but she shrugged and offered no comment.

Outside, a shiny, black Mercedes waited by the entrance. Vadim climbed into the driver's seat, and Claire took the passenger seat beside him. Dan had no other option than to sit alone in the back, which he did in a huff, feeling excluded. They drove out of Portofino along the beautiful coast until Vadim took a left turn up a hill. Five more minutes brought them to a high iron gate that led into an enclosed garden.

Vadim touched a remote control, and the gate opened before them. A sloped, winding path led up to a graveled esplanade before the beautiful façade of one of the most elegant villas that Dan had ever seen. It looked like an eighteenth-century or earlier building, with generously sized windows and balconies. It was located in a stunning, perfectly peaceful setting with ancient trees and well-kept gardens. Vadim stopped the car near the entrance, switched the engine off, and hurried out.

"Wait here," he ordered as they entered the cool, dark foyer. He strode away, disappearing through one of the doors at the end of a long corridor.

"Is this Leskov's house?" Dan asked, speaking in an undertone. To raise his voice in this impressive building would feel inappropriate, like being noisy in a mausoleum.

"One of them," Claire answered, returning the whisper. "He has many."

"And this Vadim character...is he the chauffeur?"

"Not exactly. He's an aide or something, I think."

"I don't like him. He's...shady? Is that the right word?"

"Your English is quite good," said Claire. She gazed into the dark corridor throughout these exchanges and didn't look at Dan as she spoke.

"Meaning?"

"Meaning that you're asking too many questions and speaking too much. I suggest that you do more listening and less talking for now."

"You make it sound as if we're in a mafia setup. Granted, this investment is important for me and my company, but if I don't like the people or the deal, I can simply walk out."

"I wish it were that simple. It isn't, and stop babbling."

Dan opened his mouth to demand an explanation for this last cryptic comment when a door he hadn't noticed before opened near them. Vadim stepped out of it.

"Mister Leskov will see you now," he said, moving aside and gesturing for them to come in.

CHAPTER 4

Dan and Claire walked into a room filled with beautiful antique furniture. A huge, ultra-thin TV screen took up an entire wall and surprisingly didn't overwhelm its surroundings. A man stood looking out of the French windows that led to a small veranda, his back to them. When the door opened, he turned around and extended a hand for Dan to shake.

"Ah, Mister Ze'evi," he said, "or can I call you Dan?"

He didn't wait for Dan's response, turning to Claire.

"Hello, my dear. You look charming as usual. I'm glad to see you."

"Thank you, Andrey," said Claire.

Andrey Leskov was a small man, almost half a head shorter than Claire, but he dominated the room. He sported a short, black beard and a net of deep wrinkles that started at the corners of his eyes, like those of a man who had lived for a long time in the open, squinting a lot against the sun.

"Please sit down," said Leskov, pointing to chairs that were disposed in a semicircle before the screen. He spoke with a heavy Russian accent but didn't seem at all self-conscious about it. "I'll show you a short movie about Leskov Industries."

The movie seemed meant to glorify Leskov himself more than his industries. For five minutes, Dan watched the downright ridiculous tale of how Leskov had created his first industry from scratch while roughing it in the tundra and eating dirt and how the early success had led to a chain of ambitious projects that made him rich. Whatever Leskov needed, it was not ego.

"Quite impressive," Dan said dutifully as Leskov switched off the screen.

"And you haven't seen anything yet, my friend," said Leskov. "Champagne!" he cried, and a maid in an old-fashioned traditional black-and-white uniform wheeled a cart with bottles and crystal glasses into the room.

"I can't drink this early in the morning," said Dan as Leskov handed him one of the glasses the maid had poured.

"You drink," said Leskov, pushing the glass into his hand so that Dan had to take it or let it fall on the floor.

"I don't have a problem with champagne any time of the day," said Claire cheerfully, taking a full glass off the cart.

The maid disappeared, leaving the cart behind, and Leskov lifted his glass. "To our deal," he said and drank.

Dan held the glass in his hand but did not drink. "I'm flattered and, of course, happy about your interest in my company, but I am not sure what the deal is. Isn't it a bit early to toast?"

"Nonsense. The deal is one you can't reject. It's too good for you. The deal is simple—I'm buying 51 percent of your company for two million dollars."

"But..."

"Wait! That's not all. If the project I'm interested in goes well, I'll give all the shares back to you, and you can keep the money. It doesn't get better than that, right?"

"I...I don't understand," said Dan. "Your employee never said anything about a project."

"Look here, Dan. Your little company...I'm sure it's great. But I'm not interested in running it, okay? You can keep managing it, but I have a specific project that I need to bring to completion in Egypt. And I need you to be involved because of your...particular knowledge."

"In Egypt? I don't understand. Is that a project involving divers?"

"You could say that. Yes, you could. But I can't reveal all the project details before you're on board—I'm sure you can appreciate that. So now we shake hands on the deal and drink our champagne."

"I'm a bit confused. I don't know. I mean, I'm not alone in the company, you know. I own 75 percent of it, but I have two partners. I need to go back and talk to them and see if they agree."

"No time for that," Leskov said, cutting him short. "Your partners are already aware of the deal and are selling their shares to me. You have a majority interest in the company, so you're getting a nice sum right now."

"But how? I left Israel two days ago, and they knew nothing. Are you sure?"

"Am I sure? *Am I sure?*" Leskov paused, eyes flashing and lips trembling with anger. "Claire, take Dan back to Portofino so he can talk to his friends about their little company. Okay, Dan? You talk to your friends and come back tomorrow to sign the deal. Vadim will give you a copy of the papers. Go now. I'm busy."

Dan got up, unsure of how to react. "But what happens if I don't like the project you want me to participate in? Or if I don't have the skills needed for it? I need some more information."

"Oh, you have the skills, let me assure you. And you will like it —because if you don't like it, I'll have your nice little company shut down, and you will never find an investor again. Now go!"

Dan left his head in turmoil. Claire followed him, unruffled. As the door closed behind them, he turned to her and spoke in a whisper.

"How rude can the man be? And what is this? It sounds like something out of a bad movie..."

"Oh, boy. You may be a bright engineer, but you're stupid! Keep your mouth shut and cool down if you don't want to lose your chances on this. Andrey may sound rough sometimes, but he knows what he's doing."

Vadim appeared from the end of the corridor as if out of nowhere. He handed Dan a manila envelope. "You take papers," he said and turned toward the entrance door and the car. Dan and Claire followed.

Dan kept silent during the trip back to the hotel. He was annoyed that Claire had taken liberties talking to him as to an underling. He wasn't used to people telling him to shut up, but he had counted to ten and stopped himself from telling her off then and there. He would pick the right time for it.

CHAPTER 5

New York City, January 1995

"Let me tell you a story, Claire. You need to know all the details. Thirty years ago, I was a professor of archeology. While on sabbatical in Moscow, I was recruited by the KGB. Bear with me," he added when Claire tried to speak. "What I'm going to tell you is not easy to digest. I received KGB training and became a dormant agent back in Dublin."

"Wow!"

"Yes. Then, in 1970, I took a position at Cairo University. The KGB had a lot of interests there, and I worked under the authority of their top man in Cairo, by the name of Andrey Leskov, who is now a billionaire."

"Wait a minute, you make my head spin. What were you doing there?"

"I did real research, and at the same time, I made connections with important people and obtained information that my bosses wanted me to get."

"So, how did you wind up here?"

"You know your Bible, right?"

"Bible? Like everybody else, I guess."

"Are you familiar with the Book of Exodus?"

"Yeah, sure."

"As you know, Moses had a magic staff that allowed him to free the Israelites from the pharaoh's slavery. That staff is a most precious relic that was never found. Until I found it."

"Wow again! How?"

"Through a chain of documents and a lot of research. Leskov knew about my research and was most anxious to put his hands on the staff, but I knew he would take it away from me for his own purposes. So I placed it in a booby-trapped box, and with a pretext, I went and hid it in the desert."

"So, where is it now?"

"As far as I know, it's still in a cave in the desert where I put it. I couldn't return to Egypt after betraying the KGB, so I managed to come to America, where I assumed I'd be safe. Then my wife died, and my life took a downturn, and now here I am."

"Why are you telling me all this, Jack?"

"Because the staff is worth millions, and you can recover it and sell it to Leskov and live a good life—not as I did. If I die and take this information with me, the staff will be lost, perhaps forever. I want to pass the torch on to you. Will you take it?"

"Let me get this clear. You are suggesting that I should recover the staff and sell it to this Leskov person?"

"It's more complicated than that, but that's the essence."

Claire's countenance became dreamy, and she remained silent for a while.

"You know, Jack," she finally said, "I keep telling myself that I would do anything to get away from this drab life, day in and day out, slaving at that desk, without any prospects. Only I can't think of a way out. So if this staff is my lifeline, of course, I'll do it."

Claire watched with amazement as Mr. Jones hopped around her, fiddling with a big box and the cables that connected it to what looked like some sort of control. He was visibly excited and more vital than she had ever seen him.

"I'm almost ready, Claire," he said. "Now, when I turn on the light, keep your eyes open. Relax in that seat, and don't worry about the light flashes."

"Yes, but...what is all this, Jack?"

"Let's recap. I told you you need a key to open the box without blowing it up. In fact, you need two keys—an external one and an internal one. What I'm going to give you now is the external key. This code generator generates the internal key," Jack explained, showing a small device to her, "which I will explain later. Opening the box requires first using the external key, which allows the lid to be lifted, exposing a keyboard embedded in a glass cover that seals the staff. Once the keyboard is exposed, you have one minute to key in the internal key, missing which the box will blow up. If you use the correct internal key, you can lift the glass and get to the staff."

"That sounds complicated."

"It isn't, really. The internal key is a simple eight-digit code generated by this device. The external key is more complicated because it is a graphic representation of the shape of the external dial when you correctly turn its ten keys. By separating the two keys, we ensure that nobody can open the box safely without your help."

"How can you give me the eternal key—with a projector?"

Mr. Jones put the control box down and came to sit on the chair facing her. He placed his thin hand on Claire's arm in a comforting gesture.

"All right. Let me explain," he said. "I don't want you to worry. This machine is rather ingenious. The KGB scientists designed it to impart information that cannot be extracted from an operative when captured. After I'm through impressing it on you, you'll recognize the correct pattern when you see it, but you won't be able to reproduce it or describe it to anybody. That's information that can't be taken away from you."

"But, wouldn't it be simpler if you just gave me a picture? What if I forget it and can't recognize it when I need it?"

"There is no way that you are going to forget it. And if I gave it to you, your life wouldn't be worth a dime the moment Leskov put his hands on it. This way, you make the rules."

"You're full of surprises, Jack. First, you turn out to be a professor, then you tell me that you've sold your soul to the KGB." Claire paused, and her expression softened, making it clear she wasn't rebuking him for his past. "I wonder what you'll be telling me next..."

"You've got pretty much all the dirt on me. Now, stay still, and let's get to work. This will take time."

Claire had sat more patiently than she knew she could through her "impression" despite the annoyance the flashes caused her. Jack had become assertive and vivacious, and the metamorphosis had left her speechless for a while. It was clear that he knew what he was talking about. Yet he wasn't delusional, not a bit—and she was sure of it.

In the days after the first impression, she had grown convinced that there was substance to Jack's story. Every day after work, she would climb the last flight of stairs leading to his door, and then she would sit in the only comfortable chair, and Jack would flash patterns before her eyes. The last time they followed the same routine, Jack looked tired and older than he had looked for days.

"This one?" he asked.

"No."

"And this one?"

"Yes, that's the one," she would say, and she was right every time.

"Let's see if I can trick you. I'll show you a sequence of almost identical patterns. You have five seconds for each. Just say yes or no. Ready?"

Claire nodded, and the images started rolling before her eyes.

"No. No. Yes. No. Wait a minute...no. Yes."

Jack turned the projector off and sat beside her.

"You're ready, honey," he said, speaking with evident satisfaction. "You're tuned to a T."

"You make me sound like some sort of instrument."

"Clockwork, that's what you are," Jack said, smiling tiredly. "You haven't missed even a single one in all our tests. You're ready."

"You're confident, but I don't feel so ready. This pattern...it looks like...like...I can't describe it. It has dots, straight lines, and curved lines...I mean, I'm a graphic designer. I should be able to define it."

"No, you can't. That's how it works. And that's why you're ready. We're almost done here. One last session to fixate all the information I gave you—a very long one, I'm afraid—and that's it. With your impression and the information I gave you, you'll be able to continue without my help." He hesitated and then continued in a lower voice. "But be careful, please, extremely careful. These people are ruthless, and the stakes are high. And I won't be able to help you from up there—or rather, down there, more likely," he added, grinning.

"I will, don't worry," said Claire. She swallowed a lump that had formed in her throat and fought the tears that were forcing their way out.

"No more gloomy talks," said Jack, getting up. "Let's have tea."

"And some of that Scotch I brought you the other day, too."

"A toast...hmm, why not," said Jack. "It can't be bad for my health," he added, smiling wistfully.

. . .

Claire fought to keep her eyes open against the strange lights that blinded her.

"What's happening to me, Jack? Am I dreaming? I feel strange..."

"No, Claire. You're doing fine, don't worry. You're okay. Close your eyes, don't force yourself to see."

"I have...thoughts that are not mine...and I can't see clearly. What have you done to me?"

"Nothing, sweetie. Nothing bad, I promise."

"But why do I feel so...different?"

"You are different now, thank God. I've given you the strength to do the right thing. You won't remember it when you wake up, but it'll be with you when you need it."

"But why, Jack? What have you done to me?"

"The best I could. That's what I've done. Quiet now. Relax now. Deeply relaxed. Good girl. You're doing fine...keep breathing slowly...just like that..."

CHAPTER 6

Portofino, Italy, July 1995

"Why didn't you say anything? Why did you nego-tiate behind my back? I don't believe it!"

Dan was venting his frustration to Ben, his partner and friend of many years. He had waited until the late afternoon to call home from his hotel room, trying to calm down but only managing to nurture his anger with every minute that passed.

Ben was the realist, the one who understood finance. Dan, in contrast, was the dreamer, developing new products that were every diver's dream. His diving computer and communication apparatus were arguably the best on the market. He had an inner urge to create and would have done it even if nobody wanted them. And they were pretty close to a point where nobody wanted their products. Not because they weren't good—they were excel-lent—but because they were too expensive. Unless they managed to raise funds to mass-produce them, only a few wealthy people would be able to buy them, which had led Dan to the current predicament.

"Dan, be reasonable!" Ben pleaded. "It's not personal. We will all benefit—you even more than us because you're selling more shares and getting more money. And we were sworn to secrecy by Leskov's man. Otherwise, the deal was off. What could we do?"

"What could you do? You could have told me. Anyway, I have a mind to turn him down, so it doesn't matter."

"Turn him down? And say goodbye to two million dollars?"

"Yes, yes! He wants 51 percent of the company, meaning that we lose control. If he wakes up on the wrong side one morning, he could shut the whole operation down."

"Dan..." Ben's voice dropped to a murmur. "If we don't do this deal, the company is doomed anyway. It won't see the end of the year. We don't have enough money to go for more than a couple of months. I keep telling you that, but you're only interested in developing and developing. You talked us into going to CeBIT'95 to look for deals, and we spent pretty much all our reserves on it. We're broke, Dan. This Leskov is our company's lifeline. Are you still there?"

"I'll call you back," Dan said finally.

"When?"

"I don't know. I'll call you back."

He hung up and sat on the bed with a heavy heart. He knew that he had no choice, but Leskov had behaved like such a thug. He worried that the so-called "project" could turn out to be something illegal. But he also had a responsibility to the company and his friends—and Ben was right. They would go under in no time without Leskov.

A knock on the door brought him out of his musings. Claire was on the mat, looking contrite and tense at the same time. All the way back from Leskov's house, they had sat in silence, Dan fuming but unable to speak before Vadim. He had gotten out of the Mercedes at the hotel, slamming the door, waiting for her to get out and apologize to him for her rudeness. Instead, she had given him a quick glance and walked away without a word. That had made him even madder. He'd been convinced she was in Leskov's corner.

"May I come in?" she asked.

Dan shrugged and moved aside. Claire stepped into the room and closed the door behind her. "Are you mad at me?" she asked without preamble.

"I'm mad at everybody," said Dan, shrugging again. "I find out that my friends and partners are playing me, together with Leskov and you. Of course I'm mad."

"That's pretty childish of you, you know," Claire said severely, glaring at him. "What have I done besides helping to keep your company afloat? And from what I've heard of the deal, it sounds like you're hitting the jackpot, so what's your problem?"

"Why did your boss send you to me?"

"I have no boss. Just because I'm a woman, you take it for granted that I work for Leskov, right?"

"Don't you?"

"I don't. I cooperate with him on this project, but he doesn't own me. I'm a free agent. So leave me out of your tantrum."

"I'm sorry, you're right," said Dan. "I'm pissed off, but I have no right to take it out on you. I apologize."

"It'll take more than that to make me accept your apology," said Claire, now looking mollified.

"What do you want me to do, beg?"

"Take me out to dinner," she said. "I'm starved, and the restaurants in the harbor serve amazing fish."

Dan hesitated. Was she manipulating him? Was she on a mission to convince him to sign that contract?

"But on one condition," she added. "No shoptalk at dinner. Agreed?"

"Agreed," said Dan. He was feeling better already.

"I'll be down at seven," she said. Before he could think of a response, she was gone.

CHAPTER 7

Made wiser by the previous night, Dan refused the offer of an aperitif and instead chose sparkling mineral water. Claire, in contrast, was sipping her second dry martini, which didn't seem to have any effect greater than water on her. She wore a flimsy, canary-yellow dress, simple but elegant, and seeing her waiting for him at reception had sent Dan running back up to his room to replace his eternal jeans with his only dressy black trousers, above which a polo shirt at least looked decent.

"I owe you an explanation," he said hesitantly.

"About what?" she asked.

She was gazing straight into his eyes, making him feel vulnerable. It was almost as if she was controlling him with her eyes. He tried to keep control of the conversation.

"About lashing out at you. I shouldn't have," he said. *I sound too meek,* he thought, mentally kicking himself.

"You don't owe me anything," she said, brushing it aside. "As I said before, now that you're taking me to dinner. I could tell that you were upset."

"This is not an apology. It's an explanation. I was more than upset, but not at you—at my partners and Leskov. After you left, I sat down and thought about it all. I probably shouldn't say this to you, but I'm past caring—if we lose this deal, my company is sunk. Still, it is my baby, and I am being asked to give control of it to a Cossack like Leskov, who doesn't care a bit about it. I realized that I'd rather see the company shut down than hand it to someone who doesn't understand it, but I have my partners to think about, too." He paused.

"And?" she prompted him.

"I'm going to sign the deal. I don't have much choice."

"You are a good man, but you're not disciplined. You remember that I said 'no shoptalk,' right?"

"Yes, sorry. I just wanted to straighten this out between us."

"You've done that. Now let's move on," she said, unsmiling. "I'll need some vital statistics from you."

"Like what?"

"Like, did you always live in Tel Aviv?" she asked.

"Most of the time. I was born there."

"Your English is excellent for an Israeli. Did you study abroad?"

"That's because my mother is South African. I grew up bilingual. And then, after my military service, I went to study in England. I was only twenty-one years old and had already gone through the bloody '73 war. I needed a change of scene."

"How was it? The war, I mean."

"Bloody, as I said. Still, although I can think of better ways to grow up, it made a man of me. I went into the army as a teenager, barely out of high school, and two months later, I found myself in the middle of a battlefield. If you're catapulted into a war like I was, don't throw yourself to the ground and whine about your bad luck. You do what you have to do. But I don't like to talk about that time much."

She gazed at him for a few moments with what he thought was admiration, and then she went on.

"And what do your parents do?" She shot questions at him between sips, and he had to look away because watching her sensual lips work was confusing him.

"They're both retired. My mother was a high school teacher, and my father was a bank manager."

"Brothers?"

"No. Sole child." He gave her a side glance. "So, where is your lamp?"

"Lamp?"

"The one you shove in the prisoner's face to extract confessions."

"You're hilarious," she said, but her face expressed the opposite. "I wouldn't need to ask all the questions here if you responded a bit more generously. Talking to you is like having a conversation with a telegraph pole."

"I'm sorry. I guess that comes from being a Sabra. That's what they call native Israelis," he explained.

"Oh, yes, the Israeli prickly pear thing. Thorny on the outside but sweet and soft under the skin." She gave a little laugh. "Are you sweet and soft inside?"

"That's not for me to judge, but I think I'm okay. A fair one."

"Well, then, I guess I'll have to dig under that thick skin to find out," she said, smiling.

"Be careful handling those thorns while you do it, though," said Dan, smiling back.

"No, I'm serious. You don't know it yet, but if the deal goes through, we will have to work together on this project—so give me a glimpse of what lies below that skin."

"I'll do my best. Keep asking."

"Girlfriend?"

"Not lately. I've been too busy working day and night for the past two years. I don't have much time for anything else," said Dan. Claire mused for a moment before responding.

"Can we be open with each other? Can I ask questions

without insulting you? Without bringing those Sabra thorns upon me?"

"I don't take offense unless some is meant. Go ahead and ask."

"Are you gay?"

Dan gawked at her, speechless, trying to understand if she was serious or joking, but her countenance convinced him she meant it. He burst out laughing. "Of course not!" he said. "I'm not gay. What a notion!"

"Look, I don't care what your preferences are, and I don't mind either way. It's just a matter of getting to know you, so if we end up working together, I can factor that in. If you're not gay, that's fine by me, and vice versa. It's just that two years without a girlfriend, for a healthy male your age, sounds a bit...unusual."

"I said 'no girlfriend,' not 'no sex.' I get plenty of that, but without getting involved. I'm thirty-nine years old and want a mate for life, so no convenience girlfriends for me. Not anymore."

"Fair enough. Do you think you're attractive?"

Dan let out a little laugh, attempting to hide the growing uneasiness with her direct questions. "I never give much thought to that, but I assume that women find me okay," he said at last.

"Yes, you are okay," said Claire, nodding, which made Dan laugh again with embarrassment. A straight talker himself, Dan did not object to directness. Even so, she seemed to be a little weird where social interactions were concerned.

"What are you doing?" he asked.

"Getting to know you. Getting into your head as much as possible, so I have no surprises."

"Are you a shrink?"

"No, I'm a simple country girl."

"I bet..."

"I am. Let me tell you a bit about myself."

"And about time too..."

"I was twelve years old when my father went skiing and never came back. That was when my world changed from a comfortable,

30

sheltered life into a collision with reality. That's when I learned to brush bullshit aside and look life in the eye. And I also learned that life is complicated enough as it is. That's why I'm a straight talker, which sometimes gets people disoriented."

"You could be a Sabra yourself," said Dan. "We should get along."

"We'd better because—" Claire stopped midsentence. Her face looked suddenly disoriented. She dropped her glass on the table and got up.

"Where am I?" she murmured in a barely audible voice.

Dan got up as well, surprised and worried by her behavior. "What's the matter? Are you feeling well?"

Claire didn't answer; instead, she turned and gave him her back. She stood there silently for a long minute and then walked the few steps separating their table from the harbor to face the water. Dan watched her, ready to run to her if anything else happened, but she soon turned back toward him. In a kind of slow motion, she returned to the table. She motioned him to sit down, and then she closed her eyes. After a few seconds, she opened them again and straightened herself up in the chair.

"I felt dizzy," she said.

"I worried that you might take a dip in the water," said Dan.

"The water?" said Claire, furrowing her brow.

"When you stood by the harbor."

Claire looked worried. After a while, she sighed deeply and asked, "Do you mind if we go back to the hotel? I'd like to lie down."

"Of course. No problem," said Dan, signaling the waiter to bring them the bill. "But I'd stay away from alcohol for a while if I were you."

CHAPTER 8

New York City, January 1995

Howard Kowalsky cleared his throat to attract the attention of the young woman seated in the meeting room of the law firm of Dell, Kowalsky & Priebus. He had been reading the document he held in his hands for the third time, and she had let her attention wander around the room.

"Miss Williams," he said, "as you know, our firm specializes in acting as escrow agents—I assume that's why you came to us—but I must say that this escrow agreement is, how shall I put it...most unusual."

"Is there a problem?" Claire asked.

"No, no. No problem. It's just that I want to be absolutely sure that you and I fully understand the provisions of the escrow. We don't want to make mistakes in executing our fiduciary duties."

"I appreciate it."

"So," Kowalsky continued, "I am going to read the main details of the agreement to you. The escrow fee is two thousand dollars, which covers you for the first year from today. Should you require an escrow extension, the fee for a further twelve months will be thirteen hundred dollars. It's all here in the agreement."

"That's quite acceptable," said Claire.

"Let's proceed, then. Our firm will hold in escrow for you a sealed envelope containing a card with a four-digit PIN code written on it, along with this gadget," he added, picking up a small device from the table. "I understand it is a code generator. Is that correct?"

"That's correct. Please be careful when handling it. It's a single-use device, and that little button, if pressed, activates it."

Kowalsky replaced the device carefully on the table, consulted the document, and continued.

"We are not to know the pin code. Please go to that table at the corner of the room. You will find there a card, a pen, and an envelope. Please write the pin code on the card in big, legible numbers and place it in the envelope without showing it to me, along with the code generator. When you're done, please seal the envelope. We will sign the sealing flap later to ensure its integrity until it's time to open it."

Claire approached the table, wrote "2012" on the card in clear handwriting, placed the card and the code generator in the envelope, sealed it, and returned to her seat.

"Now, for the instructions that you conveyed to us. Please make sure that they are correct. We are to open the envelope when you call and ask us to do so. We will ask you to give us the PIN code and compare it with the one you just wrote. Correct?"

Claire nodded in assent, and Kowalsky continued.

"If the pin code is correct, we are to activate the code generator and read the code it shows to you over the phone, right?"

"Yes, an eight-digit code."

"And then dispose of the code generator. How?"

"Any way you like. It doesn't matter how, but you can't keep it."

"All right," said Kowalsky, making a note on the back of the agreement. "So here's the part that I find slightly confusing and need to clarify. It relates to what we should do if the PIN code you give us over the phone is incorrect. If you give us a pin with the number five as the first digit, we are to tell you that we cannot disclose the code to you over the telephone and that you will have to come here in person to get it. Correct?"

"You got that straight," said Claire, with a sigh.

"But if the first digit of the pin you give us over the phone is the number seven, you want us to read out to you the sequence of eight numbers mentioned in paragraph eight of the agreement. I don't get it, Miss Williams."

"You don't have to," Claire said with open annoyance.

"I don't mean to be inquisitive, but I want to make sure that there is no mistake here, and if something doesn't make immediate sense, I feel it's my duty to double-check."

"What doesn't make immediate sense to you, Mister Kowalsky?" Claire asked, this time patiently.

"Of course, I know nothing of the purpose of all this, and I don't need to. But I surmise that the code generator is needed to gain access to something at the appropriate time."

"So?"

"You said that the code generator is a single-use device, which I infer you haven't used yet. Hence, you'll get the code only when we activate it in the future."

"I hear you."

"From which, I also infer that the code given in paragraph eight is not a correct code for anything. That's what I don't understand. I can't see the utility of being read a code that you know is incorrect and which anyway you already have."

Claire's countenance changed from severe to amused and then back to serious.

"You are sharp, Mister Kowalsky," she said, "but you are also right. Why I do what I do is none of your business. Can we get on with it?"

"Please bear with me a little longer. The agreement doesn't

cover one more situation. What should we do if the PIN code you give us is wrong but doesn't begin with a five or a seven?"

"Then you'll know it's not me calling you, in which case you should simply hang up."

"Hmm...I'll make a note at the top of the agreement. We'll need to initial it."

"Fine with me. I just want to get going. I've got things to do."

"As you wish, Miss Williams. Please sign here. And here," he added with a sigh.

It all felt quite unusual to Howard Kowalsky, but curiosity was a lousy counselor in his line of business, and he seldom indulged in it. Still, he would need some time to put all this weirdness out of his mind.

CHAPTER 9

T el Aviv, Israel, August 1995
Claire walked past customs and into the Tel Aviv Ben Gurion airport's arrival area, dragging her voluminous suitcase. She scanned the crowd waiting for their passengers to come out and almost missed Dan, who looked different from the man she had met in Portofino only three weeks before. Perhaps it was due to his worn-out blue jeans and T-shirt, or maybe he looked more confident in his natural environment, but the difference was noticeable.

Sometimes, Claire thought that Leskov behaved irrationally. Why did he have to send her to Israel without instructions more specific than the simple "Keep an eye on him" he had muttered in response to her questions?

"But what am I supposed to do? What should I look out for?" she had insisted.

"Just make sure that nothing happens to keep him from coming with us when we are ready," Leskov had said. "Keep him happy."

"Oh, well, now I know exactly what to do," she had said, but the sarcasm was lost on Leskov. "Good," he had said, which was the end of the discussion.

Claire had a disturbing feeling that when Leskov said, "Keep him happy," he meant something in particular. In the few days she spent at the Leskov Industries headquarters in Moscow, she saw how he lavishly paid beautiful girls to keep his visiting business associates "happy." The thought that he might be placing her on the same level as those entertainers enraged her.

He's just a stupid Cossack, and what he thinks doesn't matter, she told herself, brushing the thought aside. She had made a habit of caring only about a few people who mattered to her. Whatever opinion Leskov had of her was of no importance.

She waved to Dan, and he waved back, smiling his childish, captivating smile. He waited for her to navigate through the mass of passengers, who were hugging and kissing families loaded with balloons and flowers and blocking the passage.

Dan was ambivalent about Claire's visit. On the one hand, he liked her, but on the other, he resented having her as a sort of supervisor who was coming to audit his company for an unspecified period of time. That was Leskov's way of doing things all right—signaling to Dan that he didn't trust him by having someone look over his shoulder.

True, after signing the agreement, Leskov had become all friendly and promised him great things, bringing in more champagne, caviar, and oysters, which he had not touched. He refused to tell him anything about the project that he wanted Dan to pursue. "You have details when time comes," he ruled in his Russian-inflected English. The contract that Dan signed had a provision requiring him to acknowledge that he would have to take part in a project in Egypt, the details of which would be secret until the project's starting date or until such a time when a Leskov Industries representative would instruct him. Dan's terms included refraining from inquiries of any kind into the project before that date.

"Hey!" he said when Claire finally managed to get past the family reunions.

"Hey to you," she answered. "Thanks for coming to meet me."

"It's nothing...Here, let me take your bag."

"Thanks. Please, let's go. This terminal is only a trifle hotter than blazes."

"You haven't been outside yet," said Dan. "You have no idea what hot means."

Dan had parked his car quite far from the terminal, and they had to walk under the midday sun to reach it. Dan looked at Claire with admiration—even when sweaty, she looked beautiful and fresh.

"Turn on the AC, will you?" she urged him.

"I would, but...I'm afraid that it's not working."

"What? Are we in the dark ages?"

"No, it's just my old Ford. The air-conditioning breaks down every other day."

"But why don't you fix it, for God's sake?"

"I meant to but didn't have the time. I had to deliver some equipment to a client, which comes first. But if you open your window, that will help," he said, making it clear that the heat was no big deal to him. Claire didn't share that view.

They drove with both front windows open, which only slightly alleviated the heat and made conversation impossible until they reached the Tel Aviv Hilton.

"I can't park here," said Dan. "Why don't you check in and get some rest? I can come to pick you up and take you to the office when you're ready."

The bellboy had taken charge of the bag, and Claire—who couldn't wait to get out of the furnace that was Dan's car—already stood beside him.

"I don't feel like doing much work today," she said.

"Fine by me. Dinner?"

"Dinner would be nice," she said, smiling for the first time.

"I'll pick you up at seven. Meet me in the lobby."

"Okay," she said.

Dan nodded and drove away.

The early evening weather was oppressive, as August weather always is in Tel Aviv. The humidity made the air seem thick enough to cut with a knife. Dan had found a parking spot next to the hotel entrance, so he was a few minutes early, but Claire was already waiting for him in the lobby. She wore a simple, above-knee, light blue dress that made her look younger than her business attire. She had clearly been working on her hair and wore light makeup, like a girl ready for a party. Dan approached her unhurriedly, adjusting to her new, softer look.

"Hi, you're early," he said.

"I hate it when people I meet are late. I am always on time if I can help it."

"Noted," said Dan. "Do you have any preference for food?"

"I'm omnivorous," Claire said. "Take me somewhere good."

"I've made a reservation at a small restaurant in Old Jaffa, famous for fish and seafood. Exceptional dishes with a great view of the harbor and the old city."

"That sounds good,...and romantic. Is that where you take your dates?"

"What? No. It's just that I like the food there. I often take visitors from abroad there," Dan said, confused. The woman had a way of making conversation that was disorienting at times.

"Visitors. I see. That means me. Take me there, then."

They made the ten-minute drive to the restaurant with open windows, so conversation was out, and they kept silent except when the car stopped at a red light. "You know you owe me for ruining my hair," Claire said, but the light turned green before Dan could respond.

The restaurant was small and already busy. The head waiter escorted them to a small table with a perfect harbor view. With cocktails in their hands, they studied the menu and ordered.

"So..." said Dan, leaning back in his seat.

"So here we are," said Claire.

"Yes, I'm not complaining, mind you, but I wonder why."

"You know why. Leskov wants me to study your company and report to him, so I'll do that. My first recommendation will be that you get a proper car. With functioning air-conditioning."

"Hmm...no offense meant, but I don't see what qualifies you to audit a tech company. You're a graphic designer, if I'm not mistaken."

"Ah, the Sabra's thorns. I was wondering when they would sting. You don't understand how Russian billionaires like Leskov work. They need to work with people they can trust, which is more important to them—particularly to Andrey—than the formal qualifications for the job. I'm not supposed to understand how your equipment works, just what makes you and your company tick."

"I see..."

"Can't we leave that for the morning? I thought you were going to show me a good time tonight."

"Isn't that what I'm doing? Look how nice this restaurant is," said Dan.

"I hear you. The place is gorgeous," said Claire, taking a sweeping look around, "but I wish you'd check those thorns with the cloakroom for tonight." Claire's expression suddenly changed from amused to worried. "That man!" she exclaimed in a husky whisper.

"What man?" Dan asked, puzzled.

"The one at that table outside who's speaking with the head waiter."

Dan looked in the direction she had indicated. "What about him?"

"He was in the lobby of the Hilton today."

"Plenty of people were," Dan said mildly.

"Yes, but I saw him there," Claire said.

"And how's that a crime?"

"He kept gazing at me there, and also now, I caught him doing it."

"And how's *that* a crime? You may not have noticed it, but you can make a few good men stare at you. I should think you'd know that by now."

"Yes, but...he didn't look at me that way. I can't explain."

"I bet you can't. Let's eat," he said as a waiter placed two plates diffusing delicious smells before them.

Claire nodded, but her furrowed brow betrayed tension.

As the evening unfolded and Dan poured more Golan Heights Chardonnay into Claire's glass, she relaxed and let the conversation flow. The man at the far table got up and left, and she relaxed again. Dan drank more than his usual measure, which wasn't more than a couple of sips, and started to feel a bit dizzy.

"Are you trying to get me drunk?" Claire asked as he refilled her glass for the third time. "Because I can take much more than this bottle."

"No, no. It's just that I'm driving, so I can't drink anymore—and someone has to work on this bottle."

"This is good stuff. Pour on," she said, giggling. It was the first time Dan had heard her giggle, and for a moment, she looked a younger and less refined version of herself, perhaps as she had been in her teens.

After dessert, Dan paid the bill, and they got up to leave. "One moment," said Claire. She walked up to the head waiter, who turned his attention politely to her.

"I hope you enjoyed your dinner, miss," he said.

"Yes, thank you. I wanted to ask you: Who is the man who sat at that table over there, the one you were talking to before?"

"Mister Hamid? He's a good customer. An old customer. Do you know him?"

"I'm not sure. That's why I'm asking."

"He's a visa officer at the Egyptian consulate."

"Oh, then I must have confused him with somebody else. Thank you," she said, and with a nod to Dan, she went to the door.

"You're persistent, you know? Don't you ever let go of something?" Dan asked, shaking his head.

"Not until I'm satisfied, I don't."

"Are you tired, or would you like to stroll a bit to digest?"

"I'd prefer to go back to the hotel now. It's been a long day."

They walked to the small parking lot, and Claire stopped abruptly as it came into view. Even from a distance, they could see Hamid perched against a black Mercedes with a diplomatic registration plate, smoking.

"I told you," Claire exclaimed. She took an angry step toward the Mercedes, but Dan grabbed her arm.

"Hey, chill out! What's the matter with you?" he whispered.

"I...I'm sorry," said Claire, relaxing a little. "I'm overreacting, but it bothers me...that man."

"He's not following you. He's enjoying a smoke after a good meal."

"Maybe."

"Why would anybody stalk you here in Tel Aviv? Nobody knows you but me."

"It's just...I guess I'm making a big deal of nothing, but something about that man isn't right," Claire said. She chewed on her lower lip.

"I agree; he looks out of place. He's too well-dressed for my liking. But he's a diplomat, so I assume he has to dress like that," Dan said, attempting a joke.

"No, it's not that…"

"Forget it. Let's go to the car and ignore him altogether, okay?" Dan suggested.

"Okay."

To reach Dan's car, they had to walk past the Mercedes. They walked in silence, looking straight ahead. Claire's nervousness was contagious, and by the time they reached the parking lot, Dan had grown edgy as well. Perhaps that's why he thought the little smirk and imperceptible nod Hamid gave them as they passed by him was sinister.

CHAPTER 10

Tel Aviv was a surprise to Claire. She hadn't known what to expect, but the vibrant, modern city that didn't sleep surprised her. She hadn't expected the ultramodern, high-rise towers scattered between old, plain apartment buildings. And the Bauhaus area near her hotel gave a unique aspect to the city. She liked to walk around in cities she was visiting for the first time, and walking in Tel Aviv felt safe, although she had to do it after dark because of the heat. Even then, ten minutes outside made her long for a shower.

On the second evening of her stay, a Tuesday, she had refused Dan's offer to take her out again for dinner. He had seemed relieved, and that had irked her for some reason. But she needed time alone to process everything that had happened in the past few weeks and prepare for what was in store for her. Since her teen years, she had learned to manage loneliness well and had grown to cherish her quiet time.

That evening, she had had a reasonable dinner at her hotel and was now strolling along the beach promenade. The breeze coming from the sea took away much of the humidity and made the heat almost bearable. The promenade was deserted, and only a couple walked before her, hugging and talking loud enough to be heard from a distance. A black figure she hadn't noticed startled her as it detached itself from a nearby stone bench and approached her.

"Miss Williams," said the man. He was tall and lean, and Claire immediately knew who he was: Hamid, the Egyptian.

"Who are you? How do you know my name? What do you want?" she said.

"Please don't worry, Miss Williams. I'm a friend," he said, speaking unctuously. He spoke in good English but with a heavy Arab accent, making the *P*s sound more like *B*s.

He was blocking her path but had made no menacing moves. Not yet.

"Go away! If you don't go away immediately, I'll scream!" she said, trying hard not to sound panicky.

"That's uncalled for, Miss Williams. I just want to speak with you."

"Well, I don't want to speak with you," she retorted.

"I am approaching you on behalf of a common friend, Miss Williams—the excellent Mister Bshari."

"I'm not interested."

"Please, Miss Williams, hear me out. Mister Bshari is keen on completing the transaction you two discussed in New York. He is willing to improve his offer. This is what he charged me with telling you."

"I have nothing for him. Tell him that. And get out of my way or else."

"Miss Williams..."

"I know your name. I'll go straight to the police."

"That would be a futile exercise. I have diplomatic immunity, and I haven't done anything wrong. Strolling along the promenade is not a crime. Be reasonable, Miss Williams."

"I am always reasonable."

"Then, please tell me you will at least consider the offer."

Not in a hundred years, but no harm in telling him that I will, she thought.

"I will think about it," she conceded.

"Then I wish you a good night and a pleasant continuation of your stroll," said Hamid. He made a slight bow and backed away from her.

Claire turned away. Her heart was beating fast, but she managed to walk with dignity, not letting him know she was running away from him. She headed back to the hotel to get a drink and pull herself together. She struggled with whether she should call Dan and tell him about Hamid. On the one hand, it would vindicate her, and he would stop thinking that she was hysterical, but...

I can't tell Dan. He'll freak out, she realized. Dan was already too nervous about the project, and telling him about Hamid meant also telling him about Bshari and the staff. No, she had to keep it to herself. But was Dan in danger, too?

Should she tell Leskov? No, that would be even worse. With his suspicious mind, Leskov was sure to see some sort of conspiracy about it. Then, it would have meant telling him about her contact with Bshari. *I'm on my own,* she thought. But then, that was old news to her.

The third day of Claire's stay was mercifully dull. Dan had taken her to a port outside of Tel Aviv where a client of his—one of the few he had—was using his communication equipment for divers who did underwater maintenance. She had watched people putting on gear that looked like something out of a science fiction movie, but she had understood little of what they were doing with it. She was happy when Dan called it a day and drove them back to his office.

They had been in the office for nearly an hour, Dan busy with some electronic gadget and Claire fiddling with papers that lay in random piles on a desk. She dropped a list of purchase orders she had been faking to read on the table.

"Are we done here?" she asked.

"You tell me," he answered.

"Let's see...today, I've heard a lot of technical terms that went straight over my head. I saw one of your clients using your company's equipment, and now I've gone through mountains of paper. I think I'm done. How on earth can you spend your life in this smelly basement?" she asked.

"This smelly basement, as you call it, has been my lab, workshop, and office for years, and I love it. There were times when I slept here more often than at home. This is where I developed my best products."

"I don't doubt it. Andrey called me this morning," she said, changing the subject.

"And you gave him a report?"

"Yes. But he called to say that we are ready to go. We need to be in Cairo in five days, and tomorrow, I have to go to Moscow to give him the full face-to-face report of my visit. You and I will meet in Frankfurt and take a flight to Cairo from there. So this is my last evening here. It feels like I haven't seen much of the city."

"Unless, of course, spending hours shopping counts as sightseeing..."

"I haven't spent hours shopping! Well, just a little while, perhaps. I'm not sure how to use my last few hours here."

"Actually, I have a couple of ideas. What about a midnight swim? The Hilton Beach is perfect for it. We could have an early dinner, then go to an Irish pub I like, to kill some time, and around midnight we would be ready to go for a swim."

"That sounds like a plan, except I'm a lousy swimmer."

"The waters at the Hilton Beach are shallow, and there are no dangerous currents at this time of the year. You'll enjoy it."

"All right, but that means I must buy a swimsuit. I haven't owned one in ages."

"Apropos of swimming and diving, what equipment do I need to prepare for our Cairo trip?"

"Nothing. We will get everything we need there."

"I don't like that. I know I can rely on my equipment, but if I have to dive with equipment I don't know, that's a problem."

"Don't worry. You'll get an opportunity to inspect and approve whatever equipment you need. Besides, getting gear into Egypt is not so easy—you'd need permits, and Andrey doesn't want to attract attention."

"I still don't like it, but as long as I get to approve the equipment..."

"Anything you'll need to use," she confirmed.

"All right. So I'll see you tonight. You can get a taxi outside. You know where the taxi stop is," said Dan.

Claire nodded in assent, got up, and grabbed her bag. "How thoughtful of you to point that out to me," she said, making a face. "Pick me up at seven," she added and left.

Dinner at the Romanian eatery that Dan had picked was quick and tasty, and Dan and Claire reached the Irish pub, not far from the Hilton, just after ten o'clock. The pub was quiet, except for four Aussie engineers on a business trip who appeared to have invented a new drinking game. Dan and Claire joined them for a few rounds and then left for the hotel.

In the hotel lobby, Dan led Claire to the elevators. "Go change and bring a couple of large towels with you. I'll get my swim trunks from the car and change in the lobby bathroom. I'll meet you here in fifteen minutes."

Claire nodded, and the elevator doors closed. Dan walked to his car, picked up his swim trunks, and went to the lobby bathroom to put them on. He felt excited. In the past, he'd often gone for a late-night swim, but he hadn't in a few years. He'd been surprised that the idea had popped up in his mind. He had always associated night swims with courtship and sex, which, of course, were out of the question now.

Claire walked out of the elevator, wearing a beach outfit over her bikini. She moved with grace, like a dancer.

"I'm ready," she said, handing him the towels to carry.

The beach was only fifty yards away, and at almost midnight, nobody was around. Dan walked north, away from the hotel's strong lights, and when they reached a stretch he liked, he unfolded one of the towels and spread it on the sand.

"Let's sit for a while before we go in," he said.

"It's soothing...the sound of the waves, I mean," said Claire from beside him.

"Yes, it is. I often sit on the beach just to listen to it. It aids thought."

"You know, you may be thinking too much for your own good," she said. "Don't you ever let your instincts drive you? Do you always have to bring out the engineer?"

"Wow. Do you always ask this many questions of everybody?"

"You are not 'everybody.' You're my partner in the job we're going to do in Egypt."

"Speaking of which, what *is* the job that we are going to do in Egypt?"

"You'll have all the details soon."

"But..."

"Let's go in," Claire said. She got up and took off her beach dress, revealing a tiny bikini that took Dan's breath away. "Promise to stay close to me," she added. "Remember that I'm no good at swimming."

"Don't worry, you're safe with me," said Dan. He got up and took off his T-shirt and jeans, remaining in a pair of swimming trunks.

Treading gingerly, they walked into the sea, stopping as Claire gave a little cry and grabbed his arm.

"This is too deep," she said nervously. "The water's up to my chin."

"You're standing on firm ground; nothing to worry about," he comforted her.

"Yes, but...the waves are pulling me. And...what is *that*?"

A white globe was floating near Claire's shoulders.

"It's a jellyfish. Better move aside a little," said Dan.

He spoke in a low, reassuring voice, but Claire shrieked loudly and threw her arms around Dan's neck, clinging to him like a life-saver. Dan backtracked toward the beach until the water only reached up to his navel, and the jellyfish was no longer in sight. Claire had surprised him by instantly turning from a strong, determined woman into a defenseless, almost childish girl.

"It's okay," he said, "it was nothing."

Claire did not speak but raised her head and gazed into Dan's eyes. Dan felt dizzy, inebriated by the feeling of her body against his, and, almost against his will, he felt something stirring in him. *It's the alcohol,* he thought, unable to convince himself. Claire had slackened her grip, but her arms were still around his neck, and she gave no sign of moving away from him. Dan's brain had stopped making any rational thoughts, and his head moved forward, his lips almost touching hers. It almost felt like he was watching somebody else doing it, someone he had no control over.

"No!" Claire said at last. She pushed him away.

"I'm sorry," Dan said. He knew he was blushing and hoped the moonlight wouldn't let it show. "I didn't mean..."

"Forget it," said Claire without looking at him. "My fault. I shouldn't have..."

They were back to the beach, and Dan silently handed her the clean towel. She dried herself off and then gave it to him.

"Let's forget that this happened, okay?" she said. "No harm done."

"I was just...I meant to comfort you because you got scared.

There is nothing else to it. Nothing to forget, except my lousy idea to take you to the beach without accounting for the jellyfish."

"Good," said Claire. "That's the spirit. Let's go back to the hotel. I need to take a shower, and now is not soon enough. I have an early flight tomorrow and must catch some sleep."

They walked back to the hotel in silence and parted at the elevators with a brief good night. Despite his attempt at nonchalance, Dan felt terrible about the whole event and also a little abashed. But he was practical, and since he had no way to fix it, he decided to put it out of his mind. On his way out, Dan noticed a tall, lean man in a black suit speaking with the night guard. Hamid was probably a frequent guest at the Hilton, but he thought it was lucky that Claire was not there to run into him again, or she would get little sleep that night.

CHAPTER 11

Lufthansa's flight to Cairo was as comfortable as they come, but Dan wasn't enjoying the business class's attention. He hated being kept in the dark without the ability to plan ahead. He was an engineer, and planning was his second nature. Right now, he was uptight, and his stomach was in nervous knots. This was his first visit to Egypt if one didn't count his time in the Sinai desert during the '73 war. It would also be his first face-to-face meeting with his past enemies. He didn't know what to expect.

In sharp contrast, Claire, who sat beside him, was enjoying herself.

"Why the long face, Engineer?" she teased him.

"I'm thinking. I've never been to Egypt before, and I don't know how they will receive me as an Israeli. I wonder..."

"Fasting isn't going to help you any, you know? Your brain works better if you have food under your belt."

"I'm just not hungry. Have you been to Egypt before?"

"Nope. My first time, too, but that's not stopping me from enjoying the trip. In fact, I'm rather excited."

And excited she is, Dan thought, *like a child going to a Luna*

Park. It wasn't the first time he had wondered about the transformation possible in Claire, from a matter-of-fact, no-nonsense person to a lighthearted, childish girl. He found it puzzling...and charming.

"I hope we'll be able to make time to see the pyramids," she added, radiating as if this was a vacation.

"Speaking of which, what is our schedule?" Dan asked. "All I know is that someone will meet us at the airport."

"That's all you need to know right now."

"Do you know more than I do? Tell me."

"Not now. Not here."

"Why did they send you to meet me in Frankfurt? Did Leskov think that I wouldn't board the plane?"

"He knew that you would follow instructions. After all, he owns you now...your company, I mean. I didn't realize that traveling with me was an ordeal for you."

"No, no! I didn't mean it to sound like that. Your company is great. It's just that all this secretiveness is starting to irk me. I'm not used to it."

"We are engaging in an important business operation, and secrecy is a virtue. Besides, Russians are secretive by nature, and Leskov is no exception."

"I'm starting to see that."

Dan fell back into thought. He had a bad feeling about the so-called "operation," but Claire's presence and outlook somehow mitigated his misgivings. *Is she playing games with me?* he wondered.

He turned his face toward the window to keep her from seeing the expression on his face, which he worried might betray his thoughts. She touched his arm to get his attention, and he turned toward her, relaxing his facial expression as much as he knew how.

"Tell me, how good is your knowledge of the Bible?" she asked directly.

"The Bible…fair, I assume. I had to study it in school, but it's not my strong suit. Why?"

"Oh, I was just curious."

"Hmm…should I believe you?"

"Sure. And after that most satisfying meal, I'm going to take a nap. I suggest you do the same," said Claire. She turned to one side, giving him her back and pulling the blanket to her head.

Going through immigration and customs was an unnerving experience for Dan, who unreasonably expected to be arrested at any moment. In reality, passing inspection turned out to be a smooth and reasonably fast process. Retrieving the bags was an altogether different story, and they had to wait forever by an old and squeaky conveyor belt before the baggage showed up.

In the arrival hall of Terminal 2, the noise was deafening. They stood, scanning the mass of people until they spotted a sign, scribbled and misspelled on a piece of cardboard, which said, "Mr. ZIVI." It was held by a small man with a mustache, dressed in a black suit that seemed two sizes too large for his body.

"That must be our man," Claire said, brightening up and hurrying toward him.

Seeing them approach, the man lowered the cardboard sign and addressed Dan. "Mister Zivi?" he asked, and when Dan nodded in assent, he continued, "*Ahlan wa sahlan*. Welcome to Cairo. *Ismi* Saleem, I your driver today. I take you Shepheard Hotel. Please give me your bag," he added, and took Dan's bag, ignoring Claire altogether. "*Min huna.*"

Claire and Dan looked at each other and burst out laughing. Dan shrugged, took Claire's bag, and followed.

"Don't you dare tip him," she hissed to Dan.

"I wasn't planning to. It's all paid by our boss, remember?"

"Well, don't," she said firmly.

. . .

The car was a black limousine that surprised them by being clean and not sticky like everything else they had touched since entering the terminal. The trip from the airport to the hotel was mostly spent in silence, watching the chaotic traffic. The tangle of diverse vehicles, camels, and oxen made progress almost impossible. The most useful thing to have in Cairo was a car horn, and everybody was making much use of it, creating a deafening clangor that defeated the car's closed windows.

"Who's this Abusir person we are going to meet?" asked Dan, emerging from his thoughts.

"Karim Abusir is Leskov's agent in Cairo. He is the one who will help us organize for our task. He'll meet us at the hotel."

"But what *is* our task? You said you would explain when we got off the plane."

"Later."

"Later when?"

"Just later. Be patient," said Claire, sounding exasperated.

"I didn't know I could be as patient as I have been already. My patience is running out, okay?"

"I understand. Just a little longer, and we're there. Please?"

"As if I have a choice…"

"You do. You could go back to the airport, jump on a plane, and get out of here."

"Sure," said Dan, laughing a small, bitter laugh.

"Perhaps you should," said Claire, turning serious. Then she hastened to add, "No, I didn't mean to say that."

"What did you mean? What are you not telling me? Am I going to get into trouble here?"

"No, no, I'm sorry…I shouldn't have said that. Please forget what I said. It was stupid of me."

Claire now sounded upset and nervous, as he had never seen her before. He stared at her, and she turned her face toward the window to avoid meeting his gaze. It wasn't the first time since they had met that Dan had gotten the feeling that he was in trouble, but it had never felt as ominous as on this trip from the airport toward the unknown.

CHAPTER 12

Mahmood Bshari was a patient man because he had to be. He waited for word that his targets had arrived, enjoying the safe anonymity afforded by the noisy casino of the Shepheard Hotel. He knew that the reception clerk could be trusted to send the signal. He was paying him an extravagant sum every month to make sure that he would be reliable. Only the month before, that receptionist had been instrumental in obtaining some pictures of a French company's vice president, which the man had very much preferred that his wife did not see.

He only wished his underling, who stood beside him clad in the hotel uniform, could be a little brighter.

"Have I been clear, Rafik?" he asked for the third time. "Be sure to make no mistakes."

"I understand, sir. I will stay close to the man and be sure not to lose him."

"And should he come near me while I speak with the woman?"

"I'll approach him and tell him that he is needed at the telephone booth, that there is a message for him."

"Have you checked that the others are waiting outside by the car?"

"Yes, they are waiting and will not move," recited Rafik.

"Did you make it clear to them that they are not to go for a smoke or to eat or anything?"

"Yes, I explained it twice, and they understood."

"Good. Good, *mumtaz*," Bshari murmured to himself. Waiting was beginning to unnerve him, and he wondered why the Europeans took so long.

"*Ahlan wa sahlan*, welcome, Mister Zivi..."

"Ze'evi," Dan corrected the reception clerk, who smiled condescendingly and continued undeterred. "Mister Abusir left a message for you, Mister Zivi. The message says that he is detained by unexpected business and won't be able to meet with you tonight. He humbly apologizes and says he will meet you tomorrow morning at nine for breakfast. Meanwhile, these are your keys—you are in room 302 on the third floor. And these are your keys, miss, room 405 on the fourth floor. I hope you will enjoy your stay with us," he concluded, and with a snap of his fingers, he summoned a bellboy for their bags.

When the elevator stopped on the third floor, Dan grabbed his bag and motioned for the bellboy to stay with Claire. "So what now?" he asked.

"I'll freshen up and rest a bit, and then perhaps we could have dinner in the hotel...I'm too tired to think about going out for food. What do you say?"

"You're right. The hotel restaurant looks to me like the safest bet. Seven o'clock in the lobby?"

"Deal," she said, and the elevator's doors closed.

The day had been hot, and the evening hadn't brought much relief from the humidity, but Dan donned a light jacket over his best trousers and took the elevator to the lobby well before seven o'clock to people-watch.

He did so for a while, strolling through the spacious lobby. When he glanced through the entrance door, he saw Claire talking to a man just outside. She appeared angry, and the man seemed trying to soothe her. He put a hand on her shoulder in a familiar fashion, and they moved aside, disappearing from Dan's view.

This stranger piqued Dan's curiosity. He was middle-aged and definitely an Egyptian, but it could not be Abusir who wasn't coming. Claire would have some explaining to do at dinner, including why she was keeping him waiting when she knew he hadn't had anything to eat on the plane and was probably famished.

His thoughts turned to Claire. Despite her secretiveness, he liked her. Perhaps he liked her more than he was willing to admit. True, she always seemed to be toying with him, but maybe that only enhanced her attractiveness. He felt like a player in an unde-clared game—a game that was fascinating because of its undefined rules. She seemed to like him too, though, or at least that was the feeling that came across—but then she was unconventional all over, and perhaps that was her way with everybody.

Tired of walking around, Dan sank into one of the lobby armchairs facing the entrance, ready to catch Claire as she walked in, but the time passed with no sign of her. He walked to the door twice and looked outside to see what she was up to, but she wasn't in sight. When the lobby clock chimed eight, Dan got up, his patience now tried to the limit. He wasn't in the mood to eat alone in a restaurant. Instead, he took the elevator back to his room and ordered room service. She would have to get dinner for herself, but she had asked for it.

A moody dinner only stoked Dan's annoyance. Claire should be made to understand that there was a limit to what he was willing to take from her. He got up and dialed her room. The phone rang, but there was no answer or option to leave a voicemail. Dan tended to cool off after a while, so he wanted to express himself while still angry. He found some writing paper in a drawer and sat down to compose a short and pungent note, which he put in an envelope and inscribed, "Ms. Claire Williams, Room 405." At the reception desk, he addressed a clerk who looked like the twin brother of the one who had checked them in.

"*Masa' alkhayr.* Good evening, sir. What can I do for you?" the clerk asked courteously.

"Will you please have this note delivered to room 405?" said Dan.

"Of course, sir," said the clerk. He consulted the computer before him, then furrowed his brow and looked up. "But, excuse me, sir, the room number is wrong. Room 405 is not occupied," he said.

That was puzzling to Dan. "I was sure 405 was her room number," he said. "Can you please check what the right number is? The room is in the name of Miss Claire Williams."

"I already did, sir," said the clerk, looking embarrassed.

"And...?"

"And we don't have a Miss Williams in the hotel, sir. No guest of that name."

CHAPTER 13

New York City, January 1995

Claire let herself into Mr. Jones' apartment with the key he had given her just as he came out of the bedroom with a battered suitcase that he placed beside another at the door. He straightened himself up with an effort, panting a little.

"Going somewhere?" Claire asked, lifting an eyebrow.

"No, no. Come in. Take off your coat and sit down," said Mr. Jones. He pulled back a chair and sat down heavily in it. "That almost exhausted me. I'm no longer a youngster of seventy," he said, producing a forced smile.

Claire took off her coat and then sat next to him. "Couldn't that have waited for me?"

"Some things...must be done," said Mr. Jones, gasping between words. "The suitcase on the right contains things that I want my daughter to have—a few photographs and some of my late wife's things that I didn't have the heart to throw away. I bet she will, but at least that will weigh on her conscience, not mine."

"Are we getting all gloomy again, young man? You're still strong and will run this operation for the two of us."

"Yes, all right, but listen: The suitcase on the left is for you. I've placed a letter in it that confirms that the items in it are yours, and—"

"Jack," said Claire, trying to sound reproachful, fighting back the tears.

"And we have stuff we need to get rid of, like the projector. It's in that bag over there." He pointed to a grocery bag waiting by the sink. "I've taken it apart so nobody can figure out what it is. You can dump it in the trash outside. But please do it today, will you? It must not be found here."

Claire nodded, too saddened by Mr. Jones' practical preparations to speak.

"Now tell me, how did it go today?"

"Not so hot, Jack. I went again to see Leskov's New York representative, but he said he had no news for me."

"I don't like it. I was sure mentioning Moses' staff would bring Leskov running to America. It doesn't feel right."

"He said that Leskov Industries is a big outfit and that getting through the system takes time. He promised to call me as soon as he hears back from Russia."

"I don't like it," Mr. Jones repeated.

"I'll take out the garbage," said Claire. She needed to get away from the oppressive atmosphere of the room, even if only for a few minutes. Mr. Jones nodded, and Claire put her coat back on, taking the grocery bag outside to the trash bins.

A man in a black overcoat walked up to her.

"Miss Williams," he said with a heavy Arabic accent.

"Do I know you?" she asked. She had no recollection of having met this man.

"Not yet, I apologize. My name is Mahmood Bshari, and I would like to talk to you about your visit to Leskov Industries."

"Are you with Leskov?"

"No. Not at all. But I am interested in what you have to offer. It's quite cold out here. My limo is parked here. Can we talk?" he asked, pointing to a nearby stretch limousine.

"Mister Bshari," Claire said patiently, "this is New York City, and you don't go with strangers into their limos in this town. So no, thank you."

Bshari nodded in assent. "Forgive me; I'm a foreigner here. Then perhaps I can buy you a cup of coffee, and we can talk? That Starbucks over there would be convenient."

"Why don't you tell me here what you want? Someone's waiting for me who will wonder what has become of me by now."

"I promise to be quick," said Bshari. Claire was too curious to say no, so she nodded and walked toward the coffee shop with Bshari by her side.

With a cup of hot coffee in her hands, Claire eyed her interlocutor. He was middle-aged and had keen, piercing brown eyes that peered at her from above a bristly mustache. He took a sip of his coffee, lowered his cup, and moved it aside. "What do you know about Moses' staff, Miss Williams?" he asked point-blankly.

His directness startled her. She lifted her gaze from her cup and tried not to betray her emotions.

"Well, I know a little. For instance, I know it is on display at the Topkapi Palace in Istanbul, but I've never seen it."

"That's Turkish bullshit, Miss Williams, and I believe you know it. The Turks have a mania of grandeur and tell you any lie they can come up with to feed it. But no, the staff is not in Istanbul."

"Okay, so it's not there. But why should I care?"

"Miss Williams, I want to be open with you. I know what you have been discussing with Leskov's representative in New York, and I also know that you have not reached an understanding. I have my sources, as you can see. I surmise that Leskov is not interested, but I am. *Insha'Allah*, we can reach an understanding that would benefit us both."

"Mister Bshari, I'm not sure I know what you're talking about..."

"Listen, Miss Williams, this is my number," he said, pushing a business card at her. "When you are serious about this, give me a call. I want to make it worth your while. But don't wait too long. My offer won't be open forever."

"I see," Claire said.

"Good," said Bshari. He got up and left, leaving a pensive Claire behind.

CHAPTER 14

Cairo, Egypt, August 1995
　　Claire's disappearance left Dan numb with apprehension. He had been sitting before a switched-off TV set, trying to figure out his next step, when a knock on the door brought him to his feet with a jerk.

"Who's there?" he asked through the closed door.

"Message for Mister Zivi," came a voice from outside.

Dan put his eye to the door's peephole and saw a young man in a hotel uniform holding an envelope in his hands. He opened the door, and the young man handed the envelope to him without a word.

"Thank you," said Dan curtly.

Dan closed the door and glanced at the envelope that bore his name but revealed no clue about its origin. He tore the envelope open and unfolded the paper with familiar handwriting—or at least it looked much like Claire's, but he hadn't seen enough of it to be sure. The note was short.

Dan,

The man who brought you this note is reliable. He will ask you to follow him immediately. Remember what I told you in the taxi coming in. Don't wait.

Claire

Dan read and reread it, but there was nothing more that he could learn from it. He went to the door. The young man was waiting outside.

"What's your name?" he asked him.

"I am Rafik, sir. Please, sir, take your bag, and let's go."

"Where is Claire? I want to talk to her."

"That's not possible right now, sir. We don't have time."

"I can call her. Give me her phone number."

"Sir, please." Rafik's demeanor was nervous, and Dan started to feel it, too.

"What's going on?" he asked.

"Sir, we must go now. It's dangerous to stay. The miss told me to bring you, but I'll have to leave you and go if you don't come now."

Dan eyed the lean young man and felt that the urgency he was conveying was real. Refusing to go with him could mean he would not find Claire, and he was lost without her. He was in some kind of danger—he had no idea of what danger, from whom, or why—but strange things were happening in the hotel.

"Okay. Come in while I pack. It won't take me a minute."

CHAPTER 15

Mahmood Bshari was rather pleased with himself. His hands-on management of the affair was paying off. While he meditated on what lay ahead, he watched his guests enjoy themselves at the party he was throwing at his spacious Zamalek residence in the exclusive district of central Cairo encompassing the northern part of Gezira Island, situated in the Nile River. Only a tiny proportion of the approximately six hundred guests were Egyptians. The rest were Europeans and Americans, businessmen and diplomats, with solid representation from Persian Gulf countries.

Anybody who was somebody in Cairo had gotten an invitation, and few had waived the opportunity to attend one of Bshari's opulent feasts. A live band played Western music, and a few couples danced next to where Bshari stood. The others were busy conversing and stuffing themselves at the buffet and off the trays of the never-ending canapés.

"You see, Muhammad," said Bshari, speaking to his aide who stood dutifully beside him, "now that Miss Williams is cooperating, I am sure that beating Leskov to the staff will be easy. Did I ever tell you how much I dislike Leskov?"

"No, sir," said Muhammad. His boss had these spells when he felt the need to confide in somebody, but his choice of confidants was limited. On the other hand, Muhammad had little interest in the stories he heard from him but was an expert at nodding and making a showing of interest good enough to satisfy Bshari.

"We have been enemies since 1973. At the time, Leskov was a potent KGB officer stationed here with the Russian advisors. I was a lieutenant, a young pilot, and an aide to Rais Mubarak, then Commander of the Air Force. You were a toddler, so you can't remember. Leskov attended High Command meetings and always did his best to humiliate me and other young officers."

A well-dressed young man approached Bshari and spoke in Arabic, interrupting his monologue. "They're on the 6th of October Bridge," he said.

"Good. Get Miss Williams now," said Bshari.

Five minutes later, the young man returned with Claire in tow.

"You look beautiful, my dear," said Bshari with an appreciative smile. "Is your room comfortable? Do you have everything you need?"

"Skip the niceties, Mahmood," said Claire.

"Oh-oh, are we sour? Your Israeli friend will be here in a minute, and I need you to be radiant and happy when he arrives—remember?"

"I'll do my part," said Claire dryly.

"*Mumtaz*. Excellent. That's all I need," said Bshari. "Here he comes if I'm not mistaken."

Dan walked toward them through the crowd, guided by Rafik. He gaped at Claire, who had switched on her smile. "Hi, Dan," she said.

"What...what is this place?" he burst out.

"I'll explain, but first, let me introduce you to Mister Mahmood Bshari, our host."

"*Ahlan wa sahlan*. Welcome, Mister Ze'evi," said Bshari, putting out a hand. Dan shook it. "Claire and I worried about your safety back at the hotel, and I told her to bring you here as my guest. I have more rooms than I need, and I'm more than happy to have you."

"Yes, but..."

"Tomorrow, we can talk about the future, but tonight, please just have fun and enjoy the little party I have organized for a few of my friends."

"But..."

"Rafik, take Mister Ze'evi's bag to his room. It's the one next to yours, Claire," he added, then he turned again to Dan. "Claire will show you when you tire of the party and want to go to bed. Please feel at home in my humble place."

"Let me get you a drink," Claire said, taking Dan by the hand and pulling him. "You look like you need one."

Dan followed Claire without resistance, his head in turmoil, as she cut through the crowd and piloted him toward the bar. "Whiskey sour, right?" she asked. "And a dry martini for me," she said to the barman.

"What the hell's going on? What is all this?" Dan asked between clenched teeth.

"Drink up your medicine and then take me to dance," Claire said under her breath, still behaving like she was enjoying herself.

Dan gulped down his drink. He realized that he indeed had needed it and wondered if he was turning from an orange juice drinker into an alcoholic. Claire drank her martini and then towed Dan to the esplanade, where a few couples were dancing to Dean Martin's "Everybody Loves Somebody." As soon as they reached the center, she put her head on Dan's shoulder, and they started to dance. Her body was pressed against his, but Dan's mind was racing from one anxious thought to another, and he was in no condition to enjoy it.

"Why did you come here, you fool?" Claire hissed in Dan's ear. "And put on a happy face as we speak."

"Because your bloody note said so, that's why! And because

you had taken off without telling me anything. What else could I do?"

"Can't you read? Or are you thick?" Claire's tone was furious, but she kept her voice down and her smile up. "My note said, 'Remember what I told you in the taxi. Don't wait.' Didn't I tell you that you had better go back to the airport and get the hell out of here? What wasn't clear? And keep smiling, I tell you! Stop looking like your belly aches."

"You wrote that the man who brought me the note was reliable—what was I to think? I was worried crazy, with you disappearing and the hotel telling me you had never existed. I didn't know what else to do."

"Did you expect me to send him to you with a note saying that he was *not* reliable? I should've known that men can't take hints. Now we're stuck!"

"What do you mean 'stuck'? Your friend Bshari can stuff his hospitality. Let's get out of here and back to the airport."

"Yeah, try it and see which armed guard will stop you first," said Claire, sounding bitter.

"Do you mean to say that we are prisoners here?"

"Now, you've got it. Good for you! I'm supposed to be working with Bshari. And you too."

"How on earth did you get here? And why did you go away without telling me?"

"Think, Einstein. What do you do when Bshari tells you to get into that car or else, and he backs up his invitation with two goons with guns?"

"That's what happened? That's what they did to you? I'd like to bash his head in," said Dan, his anger rising.

"So do I. You'll have to get in line. But meanwhile, we need to stay friends with him."

"How?"

"I told him that Leskov is a liar and a thief—he was quite receptive to that—and that I wanted to take his offer all along, but

Leskov kept me almost a prisoner and threatened us. It looks as though he bought that, although I'm not sure. Anyway, I told him that we would cooperate with him and be much happier working on the project with him than with Leskov."

"Talk about presence of mind...but what *is* the project? It's time you told me."

"I will, but not here. When we are alone, somewhere people can't hear us. And don't look like a puppy that has just been kicked."

"What will Leskov do now?" he asked.

"I've been wondering that too. As soon as he learns that Bshari has us, our lives won't be worth a dime to him unless..." Claire left the sentence hanging.

"Unless what?"

"I haven't figured that part out yet."

CHAPTER 16

The time was past two a.m., and the guests had left. Dan and Claire sat in a corner of the garden, watching the waiters clean up the feast's debris. The evening was beautiful and had cooled off slightly, but he was in no mood to appreciate it.

"All right," he said, "now explain."

Claire sighed and turned her attention from the waiters to Dan.

"It all goes back to Moses," she said.

"Huh?"

"You remember how the Bible tells of the wonderful things that Moses did with his staff? Like hitting the rock and having water gush out so the Israelites could drink in the desert? And there was some other stuff about a snake, which I don't quite remember right now."

"Yes. What is this, Bible class?"

"No, but you need to concentrate on the staff. It played a big part in the Israelites' departure from Egypt, as told in the Book of Exodus. The staff embodied the power God had bestowed upon Moses, and he used it to part the waters for their escape and for pretty much everything else he needed to be done."

"Okay...an interesting relic, but what does that have to do with anything?"

"People have searched for Moses' staff throughout the centuries, and now we believe that it has been found thanks to research done by an archeology professor. Well conserved in an elaborate preserving sheath, or so I've been told. Leskov wants it, and Bshari wants it, but not for the same reason. Leskov thinks that the staff holds a secret to its powers, and he wants it to study it to learn that secret."

"He must be insane!"

"He may be, or he may not be. I don't know. It is all so weird that I wouldn't rule out it actually has magical powers. But Leskov is devious, and you can never tell his real intentions. He is so egotistic that he probably cares more about showing the world that he was instrumental in recovering the staff than about its real powers."

"That makes sense. But what is in it for Bshari?"

"Bshari wants the staff for another reason—if Leskov gets it, he will likely go public and make a big deal about it. The staff would corroborate that the story in the Book of Exodus is true, and Bshari's heart is set on preventing it. He's a nationalist Egyptian and a follower of those who maintain that the Book of Exodus is no more than a children's fib invented to belittle the splendor of ancient Egypt. By telling of a man who was able to beat the mighty Egyptian army using only a wooden staff, it makes the pharaoh look silly, I think. He will do whatever it takes to find the staff first and have it studied to disprove its origin or, better yet, to destroy it."

"So Bshari doesn't have all his marbles either. But where do you and I come into this?"

"You'll understand in a moment. As I told you, an Irish professor found the staff after years of research and a chance finding of a chain of documents that led to it. That professor was in Egypt, doing research at Cairo University and working for the KGB at the same time. Leskov was the KGB's top person in Egypt at the time of the discovery—and here's where the plot thickens. The professor had second thoughts about giving the staff to the KGB, so he used KGB technology to place it in a booby-trapped explosive box and then hid it."

"An explosive box?"

"Yes. Nobody can open the box without the correct key. Attempting to force the lock will set off the charge and destroy the staff, killing whoever is around."

"And this professor has the key?"

"No, the professor is dead."

"So this is a fool's errand unless the professor has hidden the key in some place where it can be found," said Dan.

"The key was found. I have it."

"How did you get it?"

"It's a long story. I'll explain later, but for now, let's concentrate on the box."

"Okay, so where is this box?"

"I don't know. Only one person knows its location."

"And who is that?" Dan asked.

"You."

CHAPTER 17

Sinai Peninsula, October 1973

Breathless, Dan dropped himself behind the low dune that stood in his path. He was too tired to keep going. His right leg, which he had severely bruised when escaping from the burning tank, hurt with a pulsating pain. He refused to look at it for fear that seeing the severity of the wound might debilitate him. He lay there, taking short breaths, almost panting—and his mind raced back in time, desperate for an ordinary memory to hold onto. He remembered his childhood in Tel Aviv, his simple, almost spartan home, and his parents, who avoided luxuries of any kind as if they were sins but ensured that he lacked nothing. The 1960s and '70s were austere times in the Jewish state, and people made do with simple pleasures.

His uncomplicated environment reflected well on his social life, which revolved around simple but rewarding pleasures. There was no liquor at high school parties—nor, God forbid, drugs—and taking a guitar to a campfire on the beach counted as a top amusement. Dan couldn't count the times he had ended up making out at some private spot on the beach or in a nearby garden with one of the girls who had sat singing wide-eyed by the fire. *How naïve we were back then,* Dan thought. The reality of war had shattered the perfect world he had thought he was living in.

"Dan," called Zigi from his left, forcing him to return to the present. Zigi had been a crew member in his second tank, the one before the last. Together with Dan, he had been assigned on the spot to another M48 as a loader despite his protest that he was a gunner. But that hurried assignment had been just his luck because the gunner and the commander had been killed by a Sager missile less than an hour later. The tank blew just as he limped away from the wreckage. Zigi had called his name, and they had run away together without thinking, talking, or planning. Two other men from another damaged tank had followed them into the solitude of the surrounding dunes. The four of them had been together for a few hours without seeing anybody else.

"Dan," Zigi called again. "I'm out of water. Do you have any left?"

"I have some," said Dan, taking his canteen from his belt. "Just a little, okay?"

Zigi nodded, drank with quick, small, measured gulps, and then handed Dan's almost empty canteen back. They both turned their backs to the dune and watched the ground around them. The other two soldiers had thrown themselves onto the ground in the open, too tired to drag their bodies the remaining distance to the foot of the dune. *A sorry crew we are,* thought Dan. They were all regulars. Dan was the oldest, and his nineteenth birthday was in five months, but he felt old and tired. They all looked to him as their leader for no particular reason, and he resented the imposition. He only wanted to close his eyes for a while and rest. But he couldn't let the others know how powerless he was, or they would lose hope.

He waved his hand to signal the others to join him, and they dragged themselves over with slow, painful movements. When they all got together, Dan searched for something to say: anything that would elicit a trained response and give the feeling of order and organization. Their eyes were riveted on him, waiting for reassurance or an order, and they weighed on him more than he thought he could bear. The silence was absolute, and Dan felt on the brink of panic. Then, a sound infiltrated his attention.

"Vehicle! All down!" he ordered. They all crawled closer to the back of the dune, trying to blend in to avoid discovery by the soldiers in the vehicle.

"Ours?" Zigi asked. Dan listened.

"I can't tell by the noise," said Dan, frustrated. "It sounds like a truck, and it's standing now. I'll have to go and see. You all stay here." He began to crawl toward the top of the low dune.

He crept, advancing inch by inch and trying not to let too much sand into his battered Uzi shotgun. The sight that awaited him at the top froze him. He crawled back to his men the short distance and waved to them, urging them closer.

"Egyptians!" he whispered, adding a warning hand gesture when the others were close enough to hear. "Four or five of them in a BMP-1 vehicle. I saw three of them, I think, maybe four, go into some kind of hole, maybe a cave or something. They were carrying a big box, perhaps ammunition. This may be our opportunity. If they left only one soldier to guard the vehicle, we could kill him and steal the BMP-1. Agreed?" Everybody nodded in assent, and Dan continued: "We must move fast before the others come back. Come after me," he ordered, crawling again toward the top of the dune, this time with more purposeful movements.

Having reached the top, Dan surveyed the area. The BMP-1 had stopped about three hundred feet before what looked like a cave opening. Only one soldier guarded the vehicle, and he had stepped down to smoke a cigarette, leaving his gun perched against it.

Dan turned to the eldest of the two soldiers, who looked more steadfast than the others.

"What's your name?" he asked.

"Avi."

"Okay, Avi. Cover me," he said. "I'll circle around and try to take him down without noise, but if he sees me and reaches for his gun, shoot him, clear? I'm counting on you. If you fail me, I'm a dead man."

"Don't worry," said Avi, "I'm a good shot."

Dan nodded and started to circle to his right, but someone in Dan's party made a noise, and the Egyptian threw the cigarette away, taking a step toward his gun. Avi fired three times and killed him, along with Dan's hope to go unnoticed. Dan ran to the BMP-1, climbed on its deck, positioned himself behind the PKT machine gun, and aimed it toward the cave.

"Come, quick!" he shouted to his men.

The unmistakable noise of Kalashnikov's shots made him turn around. Two Egyptian soldiers were running toward the vehicle, shooting at him. Dan squeezed the trigger of the PKT and swept back and forth until both soldiers fell to the ground. His men reached him and climbed inside. Dan then turned the machine gun toward the cave's opening and let out several rounds.

"Stop! Hold your fire! I'm Irish, I'm neutral," came a desperate shout from inside the cave. The man was speaking English without a trace of an Arabic accent.

Taken by surprise, Dan stopped shooting, and an uncanny silence replaced the gunfire as its echo died away.

"Who are you? What are you doing here? Come out with your hands above your head!" Dan commanded, responding in English.

"I'm coming. Don't shoot."

A small, middle-aged man came walking with hesitation into the light. He took a few steps and squinted against the sun as if to see who his interlocutor was. He stopped midway to the BMP-1.

"I'm Professor Jones of the faculty of archaeology of Cairo University. I'm here doing research. I'm not a fighter, and you don't have any business shooting at me."

"Doing research in the middle of a war? Are you nuts, or do you think I'm stupid?"

"No, I'm telling you the truth and can prove it. I have documents to prove my identity and a permit from the Regent of the Sinai Peninsula to do my work."

"Dan!" Zigi shouted, pointing toward the cave. A uniformed figure had appeared behind Professor Jones. It ran at incredible speed toward the wadi, one of the ravines common to the Sinai desert, which ran behind the rocky formation from which he had emerged. Instinctively, Dan turned the machine gun toward the running man. Before he could pull the trigger, his men fired several shots, and the figure disappeared, tumbling down the wadi.

"You tricked us!" Dan yelled at the Irish professor, turning red in the face.

"I didn't, I didn't! He threatened to shoot me in the back if I told you that he was there. What choice did I have?"

Avi intervened. "Don't worry. "I'm pretty sure I got him. He won't get far."

"All right. Let's get the hell out of here. Zigi," Dan said, "you watch this so-called professor, and if he makes a false move, shoot him."

They organized in the vehicle without wasting time, drank from the water jerricans, and familiarized themselves with the equipment. Dan had seen a BMP-1 before and knew how to drive it, but the question was which way to go. Then he realized that they had the answer: the professor.

"Where are we?" he asked him. "What is this place?"

The professor slapped a little bag that hung from his side. "Here," he said. "If you allow me to open my bag, I have an English map. I'll show you."

Dan studied the map. The area where the professor's finger pointed was definitely the right one. They were far away from the Israeli lines as he knew them, but they had fuel, water, and some canned food, and for the first time since abandoning his damaged tank, he felt optimistic again.

"Zigi, take a look at this map. I'm sure I know which way to go."

"If you're sure, that's good enough. I'm useless at reading maps. I couldn't find my way with a map in the middle of Tel Aviv. You drive. I trust you."

Again, all the burden to get them to safety was placed on his shoulders, but he felt confident that he knew what to do this time. He turned to his prisoner.

"You sit tight, Professor," he said, trying to sound reassuring. "And if you don't give us trouble, you stand a good chance of making it out alive and back to Ireland in one piece. Boys, we're in business!" he told the others as he switched on the engine.

CHAPTER 18

"Yes, I remember Professor Jones. How could I forget him? That was the weirdest thing that happened to me during the whole war. We were together only for a few hours before we reached our lines, and I turned him over to the military police, but I remember him well. He was the kind of absentminded professor who would ignore a whole bloody war around him if it got in the way of his research. I often wondered what had become of him. I kept his map as a souvenir, and I must still have it somewhere in my house—but I haven't looked at it for years."

"He remembered you too. He had a fond memory of you. He said that he owed it to you that he got back alive. The army sent him back to Ireland, and after a short time, he left with his wife for America. That's where I met him."

"And you say he's dead now?"

"Yes, he died earlier this year, peacefully, of old age."

"How come he never went to retrieve the staff himself?"

"I asked but couldn't get a straight answer. He said that returning to Egypt was not an option for him, that he'd had his fair share of excitement and needed to keep a low profile because of his former involvement with the KGB. But I think some additional reason kept him from getting the staff himself, which he didn't want to confess to me. Perhaps something else he did in the past that he wasn't proud of. But he was always evasive when I tried to dig deeper."

"Well, we won't find out now. So he gave you the key. Do you have it on you?"

"You could say that."

"But isn't that dangerous? Can't Bshari or Leskov steal it from you?"

"No. Jack—Professor Jones—made sure of that. I'll explain someday, but for now, it is sufficient to say that they can't take it away from me. Without me, they will never be able to open the box, and without you, we won't find the cave where the box is hidden. Do you see what a precious pair we are?"

"So that's why Leskov took an interest in me. It had nothing to do with my company..."

Claire put out a hand and touched Dan's arm. "No, it didn't. I'm sorry," she said.

Dan felt a pang of sadness, followed by rage. He had been made a fool of. All this time, he had believed that his engineering exploits had finally paid off. Now, he understood that he had been a pawn in a game. He felt cheated and almost violated.

"You and Leskov were laughing at me the whole time, then," he said, not trying to hide his bitterness.

"I'm sorry," Claire repeated emphatically. "But no, I wasn't laughing at all. It's true that you weren't approached because of an interest in your company, but the things you do are amazing! Even I can see how sophisticated your products are. And Leskov wasn't laughing either. He physically can't laugh," she joked, managing to bring a little smile to Dan's face.

"Yeah, yeah..."

"You were essential to us. What would you have said if I had come to you and told you that we needed you to help us find a cave in the Sinai desert—asked you to forget about your struggling company and come to Egypt with us? How would you have liked that?"

"I would have told you to take a hike."

"Exactly. That's what we thought, too. I'm sorry for the little white lie we had to use, but we thought you would get a big enough reward to keep our conscience scrubbed clean."

"One thing I don't understand is, if you were working for Leskov..."

"With Leskov," she corrected him.

"Have it your way. But how did Bshari come into the picture?"

"Bshari and Leskov go back a long time. They are rivals for personal reasons. I understand that their rivalry goes back to the '73 war or something like that, but I don't have too many details. Bshari became rich thanks to his ties with the Egyptian ruling cast. Now he has a tentacular organization in Europe with head offices in Germany. He even has someone who infiltrated Leskov's organization and spies for him. The moment he heard about the staff, he jumped on a plane and came to see me in New York. At first, I blew him off because I had already approached Leskov's representative in New York City, but after a while, it looked as though Leskov had no interest in the staff. That was weird because Jack knew that Leskov always wanted to get his hands on the staff, and he thought that Leskov would be thrilled that we were handing him an opportunity to retrieve it. When I didn't hear from him for a couple of weeks, I decided he wasn't interested. That's when I called Bshari back, but then Leskov himself came to meet me. Bshari didn't take it too well, but there was little he could do about it."

"It sounds like you got yourself—and me—into quite a mess."

Claire sighed. "I'm sorry. I sincerely am, and I would undo it if it were possible—but it isn't."

A few waiters had come to clean near them, so they moved away, speaking in whispers.

"So, what happens now?" Dan asked.

"Now, we play ball with Bshari and work as a team to find the staff."

"And what happens after we find it?"

Claire placed a soothing hand on Dan's shoulder.

"My arrangement with Bshari was the same as the one I have with Leskov. When we find the box, and I open it, they will pay me 2.5 million dollars. So, to your question, I get my money after we find the box, and we live happily after," she said.

"Sure. And Leskov, who is a vindictive thug, will torpedo my company, so I'm left with nothing—if he doesn't kill me, of course. And I have a good mind just to take Bshari on a wild goose chase."

"I wouldn't do that. If Bshari thinks we're playing him, there's no telling what he'll do. He's no less dangerous than Leskov. As long as he keeps us prisoners in this gilded cage, he has us in his power. We must play it straight and hope that he'll do the same. Whatever happens with your company, I'll make it up to you. Promise. I'll have enough money to make you happy, too."

"So, you're saying that I should just trust you?" Dan said, a look of disbelief on his face.

Claire gazed into Dan's eyes for a long minute, then lowered her eyes and bit her bottom lip. She shook her head as if to signify that she had no answer.

"I can't give you assurance, and I can't say anything that will convince you to trust me, but you should," she said at last. "We're in this together, remember? Whatever happens will affect us both."

He *wanted* to trust her despite all his doubts, which were many.

Claire had watched him in silence as thoughts raced through his mind, peering into his face as if trying to read inside his head. "Give me your hand," she asked at last.

"Let's make a pact—a solemn promise to look out for each other," she said.

"What is this, the Girl Scouts?" Dan objected.

"Call it what you like—a solemn promise is a solemn promise. Ready? I promise," she said, and Dan realized she was serious.

"I promise too," Dan said, "although I feel like a stupid teenager playing games."

"Well, don't," she said.

She didn't let go of his hand, and he closed his eyes, feeling a little embarrassed. She passed her warmth on to him, and it gave him comfort. Right then, he knew that she meant what she was saying. When she finally let go of his hand and got up, he opened his eyes and knew he needed no more assurances.

CHAPTER 19

Dan climbed into bed at four a.m., feeling the fatigue of the long day. He had lingered under the shower in the private bathroom annexed to the room, which was larger than his Tel Aviv apartment. The satin bedsheets felt slippery against his bare skin. Sleep was a necessity, but the strange situation he found himself in kept chasing it away.

I'm in a satin bed like you see in the movies, in the house of an Egyptian millionaire who kidnapped Claire and me, he thought. *How am I expected to sleep?*

His thoughts oscillated between resentment toward himself for missing the opportunity to get away and apprehension at what the future had in store for them. He toyed with the idea of trying to escape, but he knew that he wouldn't undertake anything without Claire—and she had made it plain that getting away was out of the question.

I wonder what my life will look like when this is over...if it will ever be over. He tried to imagine a quiet new life, with plenty of time developing new products and toys. That was something he had learned during the war—when the going was tough, he would fantasize about something distant and pleasant. He would build an imaginary world where only good things happened to him because he was in total control. But this time, every image that he tried failed to soothe him.

A light knock on the door, followed by the door opening, brought him back to full alertness. "Who's there?"

"It's me, Claire. May I come in?" she whispered.

"Yes, of course. What's up?"

"I can't sleep," she said. "Did I wake you up?"

She closed the door behind her and gingerly tiptoed in the semidarkness toward the bed.

"No. I can't sleep either," said Dan.

She approached the bed, and Dan looked at her with appreciation. She had dressed for the oppressive heat of the August night, wearing yellow shorts and a white T-shirt that emphasized her firm, round breasts. Dan tried to keep his eyes away, but they were a magnet to him. *They are...perfect.* He finally managed to look away, grateful for the dim light that hid where his attention had gone.

Claire sat on the edge of the bed, facing him.

"Tomorrow's going to be a busy day," said Claire. "We should get some sleep."

"So why don't you?"

Claire didn't answer immediately.

"Are you crying?" he asked, and Claire nodded and sniffed.

"I'm sorry," she said at last.

Dan moved in the large bed and came closer. He put a hand on her arm, unsure how to react.

"It's all right," he said in an attempt to reassure her.

"No, it's not all right," she said in a low voice. "I wish I were back in New York, working at my old job, even if I could only buy a hot meal every other day. I'm not the strong girl that you may think I am. I try, but—oh, I don't know!"

She no longer tried to hide her tears now, and Dan panicked. "Come here," he said at last. He instinctively knew that getting too intimate with her was a bad idea, but he had to find a way to stop the flow of tears. As she climbed onto the bed, he wondered whether this was another way of manipulating him, but having her close felt too good for him to worry about it. They sat in the middle of the bed with their backs against the wall. He put an arm around her shoulders. She relaxed and let her head rest on his chest.

Claire snuggled a little closer to him. "I'm starting to see the inside of the Sabra. You're okay, Engineer," she said, this time smiling, close enough to Dan's eyes for him to see her face even in the semidarkness of the room.

Dan said nothing, feeling lame. *I'm not going to make a fool of myself again as I did at the beach. I don't care if she seems to expect it. I misread her signal once before, and that was enough. I'm not doing it again. Not now, not here.*

Claire wiped the tears that had stopped forming at the corners of her eyes, sniffed a little more, and continued.

"You know, I have learned to be self-sufficient since I was a little girl. As I told you, my father died on the day of my twelfth birthday. He went skiing and disappeared in an avalanche. They never found him. I had to be strong for my mother, but she never recovered from the blow and died six years later. Cancer."

"I'm sorry. It must've been hard on you."

"It was, but it also taught me to be self-reliant. Enough with that now. Let's try to catch some shut-eye, or we'll be miserable tomorrow. I'll go back to my room and let you sleep in peace."

"If you go away, I'll start thinking again and will never get to sleep. Let's slide down and close our eyes."

"Can try that..."

"Let's."

They lay in bed, facing one another, without touching, eyes closed. "Good night," said Claire.

"Night," said Dan.

Claire closed her eyes and fell asleep after a few moments. Dan was not so lucky.

CHAPTER 20

Morning came too soon. Dan shook his head to chase the mists of sleep away and watched Claire, still sleeping. Her face looked relaxed, and she rested peacefully.

Dan got up carefully to avoid waking Claire. Brushing his teeth and washing his face helped restore some vitality. He dressed and sat on the bed, caressing Claire's hand. She stirred and opened her eyes. "Hey," she said. She blinked a little and pushed herself up with her elbows, then to a more erect position against the cushions.

"Good morning," said Dan, smiling at her. "It's after eight o'clock, and I think you should get up and organized. I don't know how puritanical these Egyptians are, but they may be less than happy to find that you have been sleeping in my bed."

"Oh, screw the bloody Egyptians! Who cares what hurts their stupid sensibility?" said Claire, but she kicked away the bedsheets and jumped out of bed.

"I don't care about them, but I do care about breakfast. We ought to scare some up. How long will it take you to get ready?" asked Dan.

"Knock on my door in ten minutes," Claire said before walking out.

The door had barely closed when the phone by the bed rang, giving Dan a jolt. He picked up the phone and heard a voice with a strong accent. "Mister Ze'evi?" it said.

"Yes?"

"Sabah alkhyr," said a deep, throaty voice. "We have some breakfast for you. Please walk down the stairs and go to the first door to your right. The morning dining room. Mister Bshari would like to see you in one hour."

The timing made Dan wonder whether someone had been spying on them. All he said was, "Okay, thanks."

"Shall I also call Miss Williams, or will you tell her?"

"I'll tell her," said Dan, again feeling that his interlocutor knew too much about what went on in his room. He ran through their night conversation and relaxed when he realized they had said nothing harmful. Even if their room had been bugged, it didn't matter.

Breakfast was rich, like everything else in that house. Dan would have felt pampered had he not known he was a prisoner in a gilded cage. Still, not knowing who was watching them, Claire and Dan tried to sound cheerful. He even commented at one point how much he was looking forward to working with Bshari, but a nasty look from Claire checked him before he went too far.

Rafik came into the dining room and guided them to a study as soon as breakfast was over. Bshari awaited them in one of the several imitation Louis XV armchairs that dotted the room. He had furnished the study with expensive bad taste, obviously designed to show visitors how wealthy its owner was. It was beyond nouveau riche—embarrassing and vulgar, with huge paint-ings portraying European noblemen and mismatched Italian majolica scattered around.

"Ah, *sabah alkhyr*. Good morning, good morning!" Bshari welcomed them without getting up. "Please sit. Did you sleep well?"

"Fairly well, if not for long," said Claire. Dan only nodded.

"All right. Now, Mister Ze'evi, where is it?" asked Bshari.

"Where is what?"

"Please don't play games with me, Mister Ze'evi. You know very well that I am talking about the staff."

"Oh. I can't tell you exactly where it is because I don't have the coordinates. I have a general idea of the area where it is hidden if nobody has moved it during all these years. I think I can retrace my steps to the cave once I get to the Mitla Pass. At least, I hope so."

"You hope so? Mister Ze'evi, pardon my directness, but much is at stake here. We can't base our operation on hope. I need answers from you." Bshari hadn't raised his voice, but his brow was furrowed, and he looked seriously irate.

Dan knew he had to appease him. "Listen, Mister Bshari," he said. "All this happened twenty-two years ago, and I never gave it another thought until recently. I am pretty sure that I can find my way around once in the area, but it may take some searching. You'll have to be patient with me."

Bshari sighed. "I guess that what you say makes sense. Tell me, is it in an easy place?" he asked. "I mean, can we pull it with robes?"

His heavy accent confused Dan. "Robes? I'm not sure that I'm following you," said Dan.

"Ropes. Cables. Can we take the box out with them, or do we need special equipment?"

"I don't know. It's in a cave. I saw it going in, but not where they placed it. Or, at least, I saw them taking a long box in, but I can't guarantee what was in it."

"I see. We'll need to plan on getting you to the Mitla Pass then. I'll call you when we are ready to go. Meantime, I hope that you will enjoy my home."

Bshari made an imperious dismissive gesture, and Rafik opened the door. Taking the hint, Dan and Claire got up and left.

"Come to the garden," Claire whispered. She sounded frightened, and Dan wondered what could have happened to scare her. *Claire must have seen something I missed,* he thought, walking a little faster. Claire managed to keep a calm countenance until they reached the garden, where they could speak without being overheard. She guided Dan to a stone bench with enough shade from the house to save them from the baking-hot sun. She turned her head to make sure that nobody was within earshot, keeping a straight face that did not betray her emotions.

"Dan, I'm freaking out," she said in a whisper.

"What's the matter?" he asked.

"I just realized that Bshari doesn't need me. He must be planning to get rid of me."

"What do you mean, 'doesn't need you'? Without you, he won't be able to open the box."

"I don't think he wants to open it. I think he wants to make sure that it's the right box, and then he will be happy to blow it up. He needs you for that, but not me. I am an inconvenience to him. Why pay good money for something that you want destroyed?"

"Then you should demand payment upfront. If he pays you now, he will have little to gain doing harm to you."

"You're right. I'll try to get him to agree to that, but I have no leverage."

"What do we do then?" he asked.

"We play along for a while, and at the first opportunity, we escape and go back to Leskov."

"Why Leskov? Why don't we just run away? We can cross the border into Israel in many places."

"Even if we manage to escape, we will never have peace as long as that box is not retrieved. If not Bshari, Leskov will be after us. But if Leskov gets the box, Bshari will probably give up. I think he's more pragmatic than Leskov and not as vindictive."

"You're right. We're in deep trouble either way," said Dan.

"Yes...but keep smiling," said Claire.

CHAPTER 21

Bshari's study looked like a command post, with a large map of Egypt and the Sinai Peninsula spread out on a table. It had taken him only a couple of hours to summon Dan and Claire back. As soon as they walked in, he lifted his head from the map with a crocodile smile.

"We have a plan in place," he said. "Listen carefully. To get to the Mitla Pass, you must take the Cairo-Suez Road and cross the Suez Canal in the tunnel. The problem is the checkpoint outside Suez City, where the road splits, and you must go north toward the tunnel. We would be in big trouble if they inspected our vehicles and found weapons. The army would immediately think that we are members of the Muslim Brotherhood, and you would be lucky if they threw you in jail alive. So we can't go through the checkpoint."

"But what do we need weapons for?" asked Dan.

"Do you really think that Leskov will not react to your defection? The area is sure to be swarming with armed Leskov men—assuming he knows about the Mitla Pass. Does he?"

Dan considered for a moment which answer would serve him best. Bshari didn't know that Leskov had never discussed the staff with him, but instinct told Dan that he should let Bshari believe that Leskov was breathing down his neck.

"You're right, he does," Dan said at last, "but just like you, he doesn't have any more details."

"That's why we need weapons, and heavy ones at that," concluded Bshari. "Anyway, this is how we overcome the problem. We do a bypass, leaving the Cairo-Suez Road three miles before the checkpoint. You see this high area here?" he said, pointing his finger to the map. "It belongs to the Ataqah Mountain and has some accession routes. You will climb it before the checkpoint and go down after the checkpoint. In this way, you can cross the Cairo-Suez Road without inspection. Then, you'll drive straight north and join the Ahmed Hamdi Tunnel Road. It's a long way, and the mountain roads are not good, but with Allah's help, it will get you to the tunnel with your weapons. Clear?"

"I think the plan is pretty straightforward," said Claire.

Dan nodded.

"Good," said Bshari. "You will have two Jeeps and four men with you. You two will ride in a Jeep driven by Rafik. He's in charge."

"Aren't you coming with us?" Claire asked.

"I will, but not in the Jeeps. As soon as you cross the canal, Rafik will send me a radio message, and I'll come straight to the other side. It's only a two-hour drive to the Mitla Pass, and you'll wait for me there."

"There is one more thing that I wanted to discuss with you, Mahmood," said Claire casually.

"What is it?"

"My money. I would like you to make the deposit now before we leave. Once you retrieve the box, I want to get away immediately to avoid running into Leskov."

"I'm afraid that this will not do," said Bshari, looking grave.

"Why not?"

"We don't have time. I can wire you the money later."

"Claire is going to share the money with me, and it would help my memory if I knew that the money was already in the bank," Dan intervened.

"What is it? Don't you trust Mahmood Bshari?" said Bshari, suddenly menacing.

"There is no question of trust," Claire said. "It's just a business issue. We may have to leave in a hurry after we get the staff."

"Listen, you two!" Bshari almost shouted. "Mahmood Bshari is a man of his word, a man of honor. I don't know if you are of your word. If we find the box, you get your money. If no box is there, you get no money. Clear? No money now!"

"I see," said Claire, sounding resigned. She didn't insist. "When do you plan for us to leave?"

"You need to cross the roads when it's dark because it is all plain terrain; otherwise, they may see you from miles away. But you don't want to drive through the mountain in complete darkness because the roads are dangerous. That's why you need to leave in two hours. Rafik will wait for you in the garage. If you need any gear you haven't brought with you, let Rafik know immediately."

"We'll see you at the Mitla Pass, " Claire said.

"*Insha'Allah*, I'll see you there, and may Allah be with you," said Bshari, avoiding her eyes.

CHAPTER 22

Karim Abusir had been dreading the moment he would have to call Leskov to report that the visitors had disappeared. But that moment had come. He had raised Cain in the hotel, interrogated, threatened, and then pleaded with the manager on duty, but to no avail.

"I know that you made reservations for those guests," the manager had said, "but they didn't show up. I should be charging you a no-show fee, and instead of being grateful that I'm not doing it, you come here with all kinds of complaints."

Karim knew that he was being lied to. "But my driver brought them here and saw them go into the hotel," he had said in a feeble attempt to convince the manager to change his story.

"Well, I know nothing about it, and, as I said, they never checked in. If you will excuse me now, I have many other matters to attend to."

Before becoming Leskov's man in Cairo, Abusir had made a career selling refrigerators. He was a good salesperson and had soon risen to be the marketing manager of the small company at which he had worked, which had provided a modest but comfortable living. When Leskov Industries bought his company, he showed the new boss around Cairo. Leskov had liked him and his broad knowledge of the city and its people, and he soon found himself appointed as Leskov's personal local business affairs representative. The job came with a handsome salary and a light workload. Karim realized early on that to keep his position, he needed to show a blind devotion to Andrey Leskov, which he found easy to fake. He had considered himself a lucky man, but his luck seemed to have run out.

He picked up the phone and stared at length at the receiver before finally dialing Leskov's private number. He listened for five beeps, unreasonably hoping that there would be no answer, but at the sixth beep, he heard a click and then Leskov's impatient "Yes?"

"Andrey...this is Karim."

"Yes, Karim?"

"I must report a problem...with the two individuals that I was to meet...the man and the woman..."

"Yes? What is the problem?"

"They...they have...disappeared," he said, speaking with difficulty.

"What do you mean 'disappeared'?"

"I mean, they are not at the hotel, and I don't know where they are."

"I don't get you, Karim."

"I know that they were at the Shepheard—my driver took them there—but when I went to meet them this morning, the hotel claimed that they never existed. I don't know what to make of it. It could be that they took off or that they were kidnapped. I'm at a loss..."

The silence that ensued was thick and loaded with significance. It lasted so long that Karim almost spoke up to ask whether Leskov was still on the line, but knowing his boss, he kept quiet. When Leskov finally spoke again, it was not to yell at him as he had expected. "I'll leave for Cairo as soon as my private jet is ready," he said instead. "I'll let you know when to pick me up from the airport."

Then, the line went dead.

CHAPTER 23

Driving from Cairo along the Cairo-Suez Road was a simple and uneventful affair. Rafik stopped the Jeep three miles before the checkpoint and waited for the second one to join them. He got out and went to speak to the other driver.

"I guess this is where we leave the road," said Dan, turning back to Claire in the backseat. "Rafik left his Kalashnikov in the car. We could grab it and steal the Jeep," he added, speaking urgently.

"There is no magazine in it," Claire pointed out. "That's why he left it unattended. Besides, have you seen the others? They are a bunch of cutthroats. They won't hesitate to shoot us if we make a false move."

"But time is running out. We must do something," said Dan.

"I know—"

Claire cut her answer short because Rafik was climbing back into the Jeep. He switched on the engine and left the road without a word of explanation. Two minutes later, they started to climb up a narrow dirt road. Rafik drove at a slow speed, but even so, he raised a trail of dust. The second jeep kept at a distance to avoid it.

When they reached the summit of the hill they were climbing, the engine started coughing and spluttering until the Jeep came to a halt. Rafik jumped out and raised the hood. The second Jeep approached, and the other three joined him. A long and loud conversation in Arabic ensued, sometimes sounding like an argument. After a while, they lowered the hood and tied a thick rope between the two vehicles. Rafik climbed back behind the wheel and pushed the gearshift into neutral.

"What's happening, Rafik?" Dan asked.

"The fuel pump is dead. I told that stupid mechanic to change it, and he said he had fixed it. May Allah take revenge on him."

"So, what now?" Claire asked.

"Now they'll tow us to a place where we can wait for them to return with a new pump. It's only a mile or so away."

"Marooned on a mountain. Perfect," said Dan with a sigh, but nobody else had a comment to make.

The mud building where they would spend the night had been a police post decades before. Only God—and perhaps some Cairo bureaucrats—knew why someone had decided to place it there to guard a secondary road through which nothing of importance would transit. The entrance door was gone, the walls not blackened with soot bore Arabic inscriptions, and the only furniture left was a metal table hand-painted in gray paint. A second, smaller room had a barred metal door and some dirty straw on the floor, making it look like a prison cell, which was probably its original function.

Claire had thrown herself to the floor and sat on her sleeping bag with her back to a corner. She lifted her gaze toward Dan, shook her head, and raised her eyes to the ceiling. "I'm miserable," she said. "I'm not built for this kind of heat. I don't know how you manage."

"I'm used to it," said Dan. "Still, today, it was a bit too much for me. But it's cooling off now. Temperatures drop in a matter of minutes in the desert at night, and it will soon be cold."

"Are we going to sleep here?"

"I don't see that we have much choice. I'd rather sleep outside than beside our smelly friend Rafik, though, if not for the cold. We could try to overpower him and get away now," he said. "What do you think?"

"He's big and strong, but we might do it together while he sleeps. We could tie him up, but then what?"

"Then we could try to get to the checkpoint, or to stop a car on the road and go back to Cairo, or even walk all the way to Suez and go to the police," said Dan.

"He never lets go of the Kalashnikov. I bet he'll go to sleep with it. It's too risky," said Claire.

"Right. We may have to find a better opportunity, but I'll keep my eyes open. If he lets go of that gun..."

"Shh," she admonished him, glancing nervously toward the door.

"He's outside, gathering twigs for a fire. Don't worry. Let's hope that he finds enough wood to make coffee."

Rafik returned empty-handed just as Dan seated himself on the floor beside Claire. "There's no wood around here," he said. "I'll have to bring the gas stove from the Jeep."

"How long do you expect we'll have to wait for help here, Rafik?" Dan asked.

"The other Jeep should have gotten to Cairo by now, but the shops are closed at this hour. They'll need to buy a new fuel pump and come back here. I think they will be back tomorrow around noon. Replacing the fuel pump takes half an hour, but we will still have to wait until evening to move."

"All right," Dan said. "Then we'd better make ourselves comfortable while we wait."

Rafik gave him a quick glance, shrugged, and went out, returning a few minutes later with a portable gas stove and a finjan for boiling water. Without a word, he kneeled beside the stove, ignited it, and started brewing coffee. They drank in the dubiously clean cups silently, too tired for conversation.

"I think I'll go and crash on that straw inside," said Dan, finishing his cup. "What about you?"

"I'll sleep in the Jeep to guard the equipment," said Rafik. "There may be Bedouins around, and they will steal everything in sight."

"I'll sleep right here," said Claire. "I got used to this corner."

"Good night, then," said Dan. He got up, grabbed the sleeping bag he had dropped on the table, and walked into the cell. Two minutes later, he was fast asleep.

A scream jerked Dan wide awake. "Stop! Stop it!"

It was Claire's voice. Underneath, Dan could hear sounds of struggle.

Dan jumped to his feet and ran to the rescue, only to discover that someone had locked him in using a chain and a padlock. He grabbed the bars with both hands and shook the door, but the chain kept it tightly closed. The shouts had stopped, and now he only heard muffled sounds and panting. Peering through the bars, his vision adapting to the faint light cast by the moon through the door, he saw Claire lying on the floor and Rafik stooping over her, fighting to open her blouse as she fought back.

"Stay still!" he ordered, slapping her hard with the back of his hand.

Claire started to cry with low, short whimpers, and Dan shook the bars with all his strength, creating a loud noise. "Stop it, you son of a bitch!" he cried.

Rafik let go of Claire and picked something up from the floor. The object turned out to be a dagger as long as his arm. He approached the barred door and showed it to Dan. "You keep your mouth shut, or I'll give you some of this," he said, hitting the bars with the knife for emphasis. Dan let go of the bars and took a step back just in time to avoid being hit across his fingers.

Claire had exploited this interval to get up, and now she stood by the metal table, shaking. "Please," she said, whimpering.

Rafik grinned viciously and approached her, placing his dagger on the table. With a swiftness that surprised both Rafik and Dan, she went for the blade, lifted it above her head, and brought it down on the side of Rafik's neck, cutting his carotid. Blood came gushing out, and Rafik rolled his eyes to the ceiling and collapsed. He was dead before he hit the floor.

Claire dropped the dagger to the floor, turned to Dan, and approached the bars. Dan gaped at her in shock, unable to believe what he had just seen. "Claire..."

"Not Claire," she said, speaking in a deep, masculine voice. "Jack. Jack Jones. Good to see you again, soldier."

CHAPTER 24

Dan opened and closed his mouth but couldn't find words to speak. Claire was still standing before him, smiling. His head swam, and he felt too faint to keep standing. Grabbing the bars to keep himself from falling, he slid to the floor and sat there, gaping.

"You're in shock,...understandable," said Claire. Watching her full lips move and hearing them speak in Jack's voice was too surreal for Dan's brain to register. He kept gaping while Claire continued. "But there is an explanation for all this. First, let me find the keys and let you out."

Dan watched as Claire turned Rafik's body over and searched his pockets at length, trying to stay out of the pool of blood that had formed on the floor around his body. At last, she said, "Aha!" and got up, dangling the keys triumphantly. Dan watched apprehensively as she approached and unlocked the padlock. The chain fell to the floor, and the barred door squeaked open.

"You need something strong," said Claire, still speaking in the manly, unnatural voice that scared Dan so much. "I'll go and see if I can find anything."

She went out and returned after a couple of minutes, holding a bottle of Scotch in her hand. "I found this in Claire's bag. Good girl!" She unscrewed the cap, took a liberal gulp, and offered it to Dan, who took it and drank some. He shuddered as he felt the heat run through his body, lowered the bottle, and lifted his eyes to look up at this person who looked like Claire but spoke like a man.

"What are you?" he asked.

Claire took hold of his arm and lifted him up. "Let's go sit on your sleeping bag—it's cold here," she said softly.

Dan allowed her to guide them inside the inner room. Claire took another sip from the bottle and offered it to Dan, who shook his head.

"I assume that you have heard of a condition called multiple personality disorder?" said Claire. "It is now also referred to as dissociative identity disorder."

Dan was having trouble thinking of the person before him as Claire. She didn't sound like her and even moved differently. *I have to keep calm until I understand what is happening*, he thought. He took a deep breath. "I've seen a movie about it once. *Sybil* or something. It's like having several different people living in the same body, right?"

"More or less. A person with a dissociative identity disorder has two or more different personality states—the scientific term for a separate personality is *Alter*—and each of those Alters takes control over the person's behavior at some time. Each Alter may have distinct traits, personal history, and way of thinking about and relating to their surroundings. An Alter might even be of a different sex, typically have a separate name, and have distinct mannerisms or preferences. Blood tests may even show different hormone profiles as well."

"So Claire is sick, and you are one of Claire's Alters?"

"In essence, yes, but usually, the disorder is a mental disease. Claire is not mentally ill. Her Alter was induced artificially by me."

"You son of a bitch!" Dan cried. He jumped to his feet, immediately shaking with rage.

"Sit down, please," said Jack. "I did it for Claire's good—there are things you don't know. You must trust me."

Dan kept standing. "Everybody wants me to trust them," he said, "and I don't feel I can trust anybody."

"That's a dangerous attitude, my friend. Your situation requires you to make informed decisions about who you can and can't trust, and the price of a mistake can be your life. First, let me assure you that you and I have the same aim: Claire's welfare—or at least, I assume you wish Claire well."

"Of course," said Dan.

"All right, then let me explain. While I was at the KGB Academy, I learned how to create a split personality. It involves using drugs and hypnosis to induce a certain state in which memories, data, and commands can be installed in a person's head. In a sense, it is like a posthypnotic command, only much more complex. To get the result, I had to induce much deeper and longer states of hypnosis than needed with simple hypnosis. That's why sophisticated drugs had to be developed specifically for this procedure. Claire put herself in my hands and allowed me to hypnotize her. The poor, trusting thing," said Jack with a sigh.

"Is it reversible?"

"Yes—it requires conditions and skills but can be undone."

"Why did you do this to her? Why didn't you tell her and get her permission? She trusted you, and you betrayed her trust."

"I wish life were that simple. I knew that she would refuse, so I didn't tell her. I had no choice. I did it for Claire. I love her more than my own child," said Jack. He paused as his voice choked a little. "Imagine what would have happened tonight without it," he continued. "Claire can't hurt a fly, and she wouldn't have been able to cut that animal's throat. I, on the other hand, had no qualms about doing it. You both may owe your lives to me."

Jack took another gulp from the bottle of Scotch and looked at Dan with a pensive expression as if seeing through him. Then he continued. "Besides, allowing me to go on living in Claire's body is

KFIR LUZZATTO

not such a bad thing. I've had a difficult life and a lot of bad luck, and with all I'm doing for Claire's future, I deserve some happiness. I didn't want to simply disappear now that the end was near. Am I a bad person for wanting to stay alive?"

Dan remained silent. He didn't know what to say or react to what sounded like crazy talk.

"So, soldier, I will need some help from you. With information."

"What information?"

"What is now resident in Claire's brain are my character traits and memories of what Claire and I did together, but I don't have any older memories. Those could not be passed on to her."

"I don't understand."

"I'll give you an example. I have a perfect memory of what Claire and I discussed—well, almost perfect. Some of it is blurred, but I've got the essence. So I remember perfectly how you and I met during the war, as I told it to Claire. But I have no *real* memory of that encounter, just what I told her. So you see, I may need you to fill me in on details now and then."

"But how did all this start?"

"Claire and I planned this together—not the Alter thing, no, but the rest—Leskov and the staff, and how she will make enough money to keep her comfortable for the rest of her life."

"So, you were there, watching her all the time?"

"Not at all. As a rule, the switch of personalities happens under stress. It's a fight-or-flight response. One second I wasn't here, and the next, I was. Thank God I was quick to appreciate the situation and to react."

"So you are not with us when...when Claire is Claire? You don't remember what happens to her when you're not... 'switched,' right?"

Jack leaned back and lifted an inquisitive eyebrow. "Why do you sound embarrassed? Are you and Claire...?"

Dan's mind went back to the previous evening and their

cuddling together in his huge bed. *You would like to hear juicy details, wouldn't you, you dirty old man,* he thought, but he only said, "Let's say that I like her very much and leave it at that."

Jack nodded in comprehension.

"I understand...You shouldn't worry. I don't see you when I'm not in command, just as Claire won't remember anything that has happened since we switched. You'll have to fill her in, just as I will rely on you to update me in the future when we switch again. The only other time I saw you was at a restaurant near water. I switched for a moment and realized I was about to blow it, so I quickly calmed myself and let her switch back. I don't know what caused it, and it only lasted a couple of minutes."

"Oh, so that was it...I wondered. Claire was worried by that short loss of memory. She'll be happy to know that nothing was wrong with her—except, of course, that everything is wrong." Dan was only starting to appreciate the complexity of Claire's situation.

"You will have to tell her at some point, but I wouldn't tell her about me immediately. It might freak her out, to say the least, and knowing about me would do her no good anyway. She and I can't communicate—not directly, that is. Moreover, if she knows about me and keeps worrying that I might switch, that in itself could trigger a switch. Stress often does that."

"But how am I going to explain all this to her? I mean, the last thing she'll remember is that Rafik was trying to rape her, and she was fighting him off. All of a sudden, Rafik will be dead, and she won't remember a thing."

"It's simple. Tell her she fainted, and you managed to break out and kill the bastard. That'll account for the gap in her memory."

"You have all the answers, don't you?" said Dan, without appreciation.

"I certainly hope so. What I don't know and need you to explain to me is this setup. Why did Leskov send you into the desert with that animal? I assume that you are on your way to the staff."

"Yes, indeed we are, but that wasn't Leskov's doing. Rafik was Bshari's man."

"Bshari? I don't understand. Before I...when I was still working with Claire on this, we had an understanding with Leskov. I know that Bshari wanted us to find the staff for him, but we refused."

"It's a long story, but the gist of it is that we came to Egypt to do the job for Leskov, but when we got to Cairo, Bshari kidnapped us. Claire made him think we were happy getting away from Leskov, so now Bshari believes we are working with him of our free will. Regardless, I assume that Leskov is looking for us right now. Quite a mess, isn't it?"

"That's not good," Jack agreed. He fell into thought. "That's not good at all. That wasn't the plan. Bshari is bad news."

"Tell me about it," said Dan.

Dan paused and gazed at Jack. He was starting to get used to hearing Claire speak with a different voice but still found it creepy to be conversing with a dead man. "This is weird, you know? Having you here, inside Claire, I mean," said Dan.

"I can appreciate the disorientation, but you should remember that, in reality, I am not Jack. I am just another facet of Claire's personality, loaded with different information. There is no Jack inside me, just information that Jack has given me to use during these switches. Jack is dead."

"I'm sure you mean well, but you're only confusing me more. I need time to digest all this."

"Understood."

"Meanwhile, how can I get Claire back? We need to figure out what to do now. We can't wait for Rafik's friends to return," Dan said.

"That's simple. All I need to do is relax. When I'm ready, I'll sit down here and do some breathing exercises. You'll have Claire back in no time."

"And if I need you to switch?"

"That's more complicated, but trust me, I'll be back when I'm needed. But before we do that, I need you to tell me everything. It will be better for us both if I am well-informed when the need to switch arises again."

Dan nodded and started to recount the events from the beginning without enthusiasm. "That's what happened until we went to sleep," he said at the end of his report. "Anything else that you need to know?"

"I'd like to know what you're going to do now."

"Hell...I've no idea. I'll talk to Claire, and we'll figure something out."

"That's a poor plan, my friend. You need to have a plan before you speak with Claire. May I suggest something?"

"Go ahead. I'm clueless anyway."

"You need to hide the body somewhere and then get as far away from here as you can."

"That's a creative idea," said Dan sarcastically. "Do you have any more useful suggestions, or can I have Claire back now?"

"None. Keep quiet and let me relax, and then Claire will be back in no time. And by the way, I suggest that you get some blood on your clothes, or you'll have a hard time explaining to Claire how you killed Rafik and remained immaculate."

"Wait!" said Dan. He picked up the dagger and smeared a little blood on his shirt and trousers. "Now you can go," he said.

Jack closed his eyes and started to breathe long, rhythmic breaths. Two minutes later, Claire opened her eyes, a look of confusion on her face. She got up and scanned the room, taking Rafik's body in. She fixed her eyes on Dan.

"Dan..." she said, her melodious, sexy voice returned. She threw herself into his arms, shaking.

CHAPTER 25

Claire stood at the far end of the room, unwilling to go near Rafik's body in its pool of congealing blood. Once Claire's sobs had subsided and she had stopped shaking, she had pushed back from Dan's embrace. After a few moments of silence, she had moved farther away and turned her head, and Dan had kept silent, respecting her need to pull herself together on her own.

"You killed him," she said at last.

"Yes," said Dan, keeping up the necessary lie. It embarrassed him to take credit for saving her, but he felt he had no choice.

"So what do we do now?" Claire murmured, sounding completely confused.

"We need to get away. His friends will be back tomorrow, and they will kill us when they find out what happened here."

"I don't understand," said Claire, shaking her head in disbelief. "I thought we would be safe until we found the cave with the box...It doesn't make sense killing us now."

"I don't think that he meant to kill us now, at least not me. He could've done that while I was asleep instead of locking me up."

"You're right, but Rafik would never have done anything

contrary to Bshari's instructions, which means that Bshari never meant to keep his end of the deal. Just as I feared," said Claire.

"But they were risking losing my cooperation, and they still needed me, don't you think?"

"Quite the contrary. They would have gotten your cooperation using fear as an incentive once you knew they had no scruples. I guess they wouldn't have killed me right away, though. All they needed was to show that they were in command and that we shouldn't play games with them."

"Now it's a different story. They still need me, but you are fair game. I'm sorry that I put you in danger," said Dan, hanging his head.

"You shouldn't worry," said Claire, for the first time sounding bitter. "A nice choice I had, between being raped and killed or being a fugitive. I prefer the current option."

"You are something, you know?" said Dan. "Five minutes ago, you were in shock, trembling like a leaf, and now you're turning all logical."

"It's just the way I've learned to deal with stuff. I told you I've had only myself to rely on for as long as I can remember."

Dan gazed at her with open admiration, a little chagrined she wasn't factoring him in much. After all, as far as she knew, he had just killed a man for her. "Now, you can rely on me," he said.

"I know," she said, but without sounding too convinced. "And that's good because I'm clueless on what to do now."

"Now, we take what we need from the Jeep and put as much distance as possible between us and this place. We can hide until night," Dan said, getting practical. "I need to check the map, but if I remember correctly, once we are off the mountain, we are about nine miles from the outskirts of Suez. That's walking distance. Once we reach the city, we should be safe from Rafik's friends."

"You forget one thing," said Claire.

"What is that?"

"We are murderers. If Rafik's body is discovered and linked to us, the Egyptian police will be after us. In that case, God help us. We can't just walk into Suez as if nothing happened."

Dan stepped out of the building, followed by Claire. He needed to think, and he needed fresh air.

The Jeep yielded a rich assortment of useful equipment: Rafik's Kalashnikov with three full magazines, a highly detailed map of the area in Arabic, plenty of water, some food that included canned Moroccan hot *chraime* fish, pita bread, and assorted cooked vegetables.

They had to leave the rest of the equipment behind, but leaving their bags with all their belongings was out of the question. They would have immediately connected them with the killing.

"We must get rid of the Jeep," Dan said.

"How?"

"We need to push it off that cliff down the wadi."

"But won't they go down the valley and find all our stuff anyway? How is pushing it off the cliff going to help us?" Claire objected.

"Listen," said Dan. "I have a plan. We need to destroy the evidence that may link us to Rafik's death, and the best way to do it is by fire. Pushing the Jeep over the cliff isn't going to be difficult because this area slopes downward so that I can do all the pushing myself. Before we start pushing, I'll use one of these spare gasoline cans to soak the Jeep's inside. Your part will be to start the fire when I move away, just before it jumps off the cliff. Do you think you can do that?"

"If it must be done, then I'll do it," said Claire without hesitation.

"Now, the hard part," said Dan softly. "I want to put Rafik's body at the wheel of the Jeep, but I can't manage it all by myself. I would if I could, but I can't. I need your help to do it."

Dan had avoided looking Claire in the eyes as he spoke. Now, he glanced at her, trying to gauge her reaction. She had lowered her head and closed her eyes. She was drawing short, quick breaths through her nose, and Dan felt a pang of pity for her. Touching dead bodies was nothing new to him—he had done it several times during the war—but he knew how hard it would be for her. But Claire was brave and intelligent enough to understand they had no choice. "I guess that's the right thing to do," she said, speaking in a high-pitched, thin voice. "And it's better done quickly."

"Good girl," said Dan, nodding in appreciation.

"Don't patronize me, okay?" she snapped.

"I'm sorry, I didn't mean to," Dan said. The tension was taking its toll on Claire, and he was afraid she might break down and become useless when he needed her the most. "Here," he said, speaking in his best conciliatory tone. "I've collected all our stuff, including all the documents I could find. I'm taking my sleeping bag with us. Yours is full of blood and must go into the Jeep."

"I assume we won't get much sleep anyway," Claire said. "Why don't we get going?"

"We still have about three hours until daylight. We can't get rid of the Jeep while it's dark because the fire will be seen from a distance. Also, we can't get off the mountain in broad daylight because we don't know who will be down there looking for us. This means we need to hide during the day, and while we're hiding, we may as well get some sleep."

"But won't it be dangerous? Rafik's buddies will be searching everywhere for us."

"I think I know where to hide. Here, look at this map—forget the Arabic. I can't read most of it but can read a map. If we take this trail here, which runs at first parallel to this dirt road we've been driving on, you can see that it takes us to a small hill later on. You see this sign here about midway up the hill? The word written beside it is *kahf*, which means 'cave' in Arabic, if I'm not mistaken. If I'm right, that could be a good place to hide until night."

"Well, I don't have a better plan. We have a lot of work to do, so let's get going," said Claire, walking toward the building. Dan watched her with satisfaction. She had clearly pulled herself together. Now all he had to do was avoid some stupid remark that would make her bite his head off again.

Moving Rafik's body to the Jeep was a grim job. Dan lifted the body under the armpits and could not avoid getting some of the caked blood on his hands. Claire lifted him from the legs, helping him carry the considerable weight. Seating him at the wheel required another great effort. Claire did her best to help while averting her gaze from the body as much as possible.

"What about the blood inside the building?" asked Claire.

"I'll soak it with these blankets, which are going into the Jeep. What is already dry and I can't remove, we will have to destroy with fire. We'll pour some gasoline on the floor and light it up. That's the best we can do. I don't know if it will destroy all the evidence, but at least it will make it more difficult to figure out what has happened. It may buy us some time."

Claire nodded without commenting. They took some of the water left in the Jeep, washed the blood off their hands, and then drank a little.

"We have a couple of hours before light. Let's rest some," said Dan.

They returned inside and sat on Dan's sleeping bag, their backs to the wall, too tired to sleep or talk. After a minute, Claire said, "I'm cold." She leaned her head on Dan's shoulder and closed her eyes. He put his arm around her waist and pulled her a bit closer. Sleeping was out of the question, but at least feeling close offered some comfort.

CHAPTER 26

"My friend!" said the general, kissing Leskov three times on the cheeks. "It's been a long time—five years, I believe."

"I think you're right," said Leskov. "We should see each other more often."

Karim watched the exchange in awe. The general held a powerful position in the military caste, and Karim couldn't believe the ease with which Leskov had gotten access to him. All it had taken was a simple phone call from the airport.

"So what can I do for you, my dear friend?" asked the general. An attendant brought in coffee, and Leskov waited until he had left.

"I need help finding two of my employees who have disappeared," he said. "I guess they will be crossing the canal soon into Sinai if they haven't done it yet, and I need some support from the police in Suez and Ismailia."

"Hmm...Do you think they are traveling of their own free will, or perhaps they were forced to go?"

"I couldn't say. It could be either," said Leskov.

"If they were forced, it could be more difficult to find them...

and what would be the purpose of their crossing into the Sinai desert? Are they planning to smuggle something into Israel? Drugs, perhaps?" The general eyed Leskov with a smirk on his face.

"No, no, my friend. That's not the case. I can assure you that no illicit activity is involved—no smuggling of any kind. Still, I suggest that you don't inquire further. Some things are private and better not discussed."

"I see...That will make it more...how should I say...complicated," said the general.

"Leave us alone, Karim," Leskov ordered. Karim got up without a word and left.

"Money won't be a problem," Leskov said curtly after the door closed.

"I understand. I know you. But I need to know a little more... to make sure that there is no danger to the state. My first interest is the security of the Egyptian Republic."

"I know. I'm aware of your devotion to the republic and to Rais Mubarak. I can tell you that my employees had instructions to recover something that belongs to me, which is hidden in the desert. I know that a certain third party, whom I prefer not to name, would like to steal it from me. I believe that this third party may be responsible for the disappearance of my employees."

"This thing, it is quite valuable, yes?" asked the general, cocking his head.

"To me, it is," said Leskov, "because of its sentimental value. It has no monetary value whatsoever, but still, I want back what is mine." He knew that he was treading on thin ice and that awakening the general's cupidity would cost him a lot, but he also knew that the general wouldn't believe that he was being sentimental.

The general laughed a hearty laugh. "I never knew you as a sentimentalist, my friend. How much sentiment can you get this time?"

"A hundred thousand Euros of sentiment," said Leskov.

"Placed in the Swiss bank account you used five years ago?"

"As usual," said Leskov.

"In that case, I'll give you a letter for the police chief in Suez and one for that in Ismailia. I'll also let them know that you might be calling on them and that they should cooperate. It will be hand-delivered to your offices in a few hours."

"Thank you, my friend," said Leskov. He got up to shake the general's hand. He knew he had gotten off lightly without the general inquiring too much into the matter—some of the questions he could have asked would have been awkward to answer. *The general must be getting old,* he thought as he departed.

"Ra'id Hassan," the general cried, and a door behind him opened to admit a handsome man of about thirty, wearing the rank of Ra'id—major.

"Yes, General," said Hassan.

"I assume you have heard the conversation."

"Yes, sir. Except for the last few sentences that I missed due to noise from the street," he said, keeping a straight face. There were things you didn't hear if you wanted to make a career in the army.

The general acknowledged the last statement with a hint of a nod and continued. "Then you will know what to do. Something is going on under my nose here in Cairo, and I don't know anything about it. That is unacceptable. I rely on you to find out."

"Of course, General," said Major Hassan. He saluted and walked out. That was what the general liked in Major Hassan—he didn't need to be told twice and could be relied on to deliver.

CHAPTER 27

Dan blinked, saw the early morning light coming through the missing door, and realized he had dozed off. "Claire..." he called softly, touching her arm. He watched as she stirred and opened her eyes.

"I fell asleep," she said.

"So did I," said Dan, getting up. He felt stiff and tired from sitting with his back against the cold wall for a long time. "We must get going."

Claire pushed herself up, too, slowly and without enthusiasm. "My shirt is stained with blood," she said. "I was too tired to notice before, but now..."

"My clothes are stained too. We need to change—I assume you have a change of clothes in your bag?"

"As you can imagine," said Claire.

"All right. Let's change now. We'll throw the stained clothes into the Jeep." He took his bag to a corner of the room and turned his back to her. "No peeping," he said, trying to lighten up the atmosphere, but no repartee came from Claire.

Early mornings are cold in the desert, regardless of the time of year. Dan took off all his clothes and dressed up again, shivering.

"Can I turn around?" he asked.

"I've been ready for ages," was Claire's response.

Dan turned to face her and saw that she had dressed in new clothes that looked the same as the ones she had before—khaki Bermuda shorts, shirt, and sneakers. She had tied her hair in a ponytail and looked beautiful despite her haggard face.

Claire had already made a bundle of her old clothes, and they took them to the Jeep and threw them in with Claire's bloody sleeping bag.

"Now?" she asked, and Dan nodded.

He took a gasoline can and went back to the building. Inside, he poured a liberal amount of fuel onto the dark brown stain where the blood had dried up on the floor and then some more around it. Then he carried the can back to the Jeep and returned to the building one last time. He took one of the several matchboxes they had found in Rafik's belongings, lit the matches inside, and threw the burning box into the building. A strong whooshing sound, followed by flames that burned for less than a minute, told him the task was completed. Dan took a quick look to ensure that the fire had charred the blood, and then he returned to the Jeep. Starting the fire had given him a sense of urgency, and he felt it throbbing in his head.

"We must hurry," he said to Claire, who waited in silence.

Dan took his old clothes, tore away a piece of cloth, and wrapped it around a stone. He made a knot to ensure the stone would stay cradled in it, leaving two long dangling cloth tails.

"I'm leaving the tailgate of the Jeep open," he said, handing it to Claire. "You must run after the Jeep as I push it toward the cliff and stay close to the tailgate. When I say so, you must throw this stone into the Jeep through the tailgate. As soon as I'm finished spreading the gasoline inside the Jeep, I will soak the far ends of the stone cloth with it, and then we'll set fire to them. Make sure not to burn your hand. If you drop the stone, we're in trouble because once I start pushing, there's no way I can stop the Jeep from going off the cliff. Questions?"

Claire shook her head and swallowed without speaking. Dan took the can and climbed into the Jeep from the passenger's door, spilling the gasoline on their belongings and Rafik. He took a quick look at Rafik's body, seated behind the wheel. Rigor mortis had set in, and the body had taken a peculiar angle against the seat, but that wouldn't matter if everything worked according to plan. He shifted the gear into neutral but left the handbrake on.

Standing beside Claire, Dan took the can and tilted it; then, he pushed the long tails of the stone cloth into it, pulling them out wet with gasoline. He gave the stone to her and threw the can into the Jeep through the tailgate.

"Let's leave all our stuff here. We'll come back for it later," he said.

He took a matchbox, lit a match, and put it to the stone's tails, which immediately caught fire. Then he jumped onto the Jeep from the driver's side, reached across Rafik's body to release the handbrake, and jumped back down and started to push. At first, he encountered strong resistance, but once the vehicle began moving, it accelerated on its own, and he found it difficult to keep its pace. He had to keep his right hand on the wheel to ensure that the Jeep would take the correct course while using the left to keep the door from slamming against his body. He glanced back now and then to make sure that Claire was following, but the Jeep's body made it hard for him to see her. He had to believe that she was there, though. He didn't want to think of what would happen if she wasn't.

The Jeep was careering toward the precipice, and Dan realized the time had come to jump or go down with it. "Now!" he yelled, abandoning his hold on the wheel and pushing himself away from the vehicle. "Now! Now!" he continued screaming until he saw blazes coming out of the Jeep and understood they had made it.

He fell to the ground with a thud just as the blazing Jeep disappeared over the cliff. The fall injured his shoulder, and for a moment, the pain made it impossible for him to get up. Then he saw that Claire, pulled by the momentum of her run, was skidding on the gravel toward the cliff's edge. She was trying to stop her sliding motion but appeared unable to slow down. Dan wanted to shout, "Drop down!" to her, but the impact of his own fall had taken his breath away. They were only a few feet from the cliff's edge, and he had to stop her at all costs. There was only one thing he could do: pivot himself and put his body in Claire's path, which he did with his last strength.

Claire's foot collided with Dan's head, and he lost vision for a moment—but instinctively, he grabbed her as she fell on her back, pushing him toward the precipice with the force of impact. When their motion finally stopped, they both remained to lie down for a long minute, panting and hurting, only a couple of feet from the precipice.

At last, Claire lifted herself up on her elbow and gazed at him. "Are you hurt?" she asked, the concern evident in her eyes.

"Only broken in a few places," he tried to joke, but the pain on his face contradicted his answer. He managed to come to a sitting position, and there he remained for a moment, catching his breath. Claire offered him a hand and helped him to his feet. They both approached the edge of the cliff and looked down. The Jeep was burning in the valley below, and judging by the flames, nothing would be left to identify in it.

CHAPTER 28

Claire hadn't cried in public for as long as she remembered. The last time that someone had seen her cry was at her father's funeral. She had cried at her mother's, too, but then she had made sure nobody besides her brother Tim could see her tears. Being strong, independent, and self-sufficient was almost a religion to her. The years had gone by, and the pain of her father's death had dulled, but she'd dealt with her mother's mood changes and then nursed her through her illness. She was eighteen when her mother passed away, and then she found herself charged with keeping her family going. Their hardware store provided a small income, with Claire and Tim working there and using a hired hand in the high season. Her father's insurance money had also helped a little, although their little capital dwindled over the years.

Then there was this boy, Rob, whom she had gone to school with and on whom she'd had a major crush in junior high school. He was popular and a great skier, like her father had been—which perhaps was, at least in part, why she admired Rob so much. Rob had ignored her during their school years, and she had gotten over him. But one day, at an open concert in town, they had gotten to talk. The encounter had turned into an unplanned date that swept her off her feet.

Those were her happiest days. She was twenty-one years old, she and Rob were in love, and they were going to get married. Sweet Rob would live with her forever in their little nook in Colorado. He would work hard as a ski instructor in the winter, and as the gifted carpenter he was, all year round, he would feed the little family they would grow together. But Rob was too handsome for his own good and couldn't keep his hands off some rich tourist with whom Claire had caught him fooling around.

She hadn't made a scene. She merely turned her back and walked out. The moment she discovered his betrayal, he was as good as dead to her. She refused to see him or speak with him and put all her energy into finding a buyer for her store and home and getting out as soon as possible.

She split the little money they had evenly with Tim, and he enlisted in the army and left. She loved her brother very much, and they spoke every now and then on the telephone, but she was in New York, and he got himself stationed in Europe, which was OK with her since she hoped he would be safe there.

Rob sat under her window for days and tried to speak with her in the street, but she ignored him, although her heart ached.

Moving to New York was her rebellion against the bad luck that had been her lot until then. New York was the city of unlimited opportunities, or so she thought—until she learned that being a graphic designer in a big city was no recipe for wealth. She had dated a little in New York, but after Rob, those quick relationships felt hollow, more like a temporary sanctuary from loneliness than something to cherish. Besides, she had grown proud of her independence and knew how to make the best of being alone.

Claire was an adapter, swift to identify new trouble and find ways around it. She prided herself on never feeling sorry for herself. *So why am I feeling so miserable?* she wondered. Then she looked around her and considered her situation. She was sitting on a cliff in the middle of the desert, a fugitive from murderous Egyptians and an accomplice in a killing. She had all the right in the world to feel wretched. She wiped the tears from her eyes with the backs of her hands and got up. It was time to get going.

CHAPTER 29

The cave where they hoped to hide until dark was not very far, but the distance seemed insurmountable to Dan. He dropped his bag, his lips twitching with pain. They had been walking for only a couple of miles, but the pain in his shoulder was growing with every step. It felt like a stab in the back, running all the way from his shoulder to his kidney, and it was so intense that he could no longer carry even the lightest weight without unbearable pain. All he could do was to hold the Kalashnikov in his hands. He sat down on a stone and breathed slowly and deeply, trying to chase away the nausea that had accompanied him from the beginning of their journey. The early morning's cold air added a layer of discomfort to the tender flesh that felt every rub against the fabric.

"What's the matter, Dan? Aren't you feeling well?" asked Claire.

"I'm afraid that I may have broken a bone or something. The pain in my shoulder is excruciating, and I don't think I'll be able to continue carrying the weight of this bag. We'll have to abandon some of the stuff."

"I can carry it. I'm fine," said Claire without hesitation.

"No, you can't. You're already carrying the water, which is more important than the rest," Dan objected.

"You forget that I'm a mountain girl. I'm used to carrying backpacks. Besides, we're getting off the road right here, down into the trail that leads to the cave. We can leave half the weight hidden along the road, and I can return for it later."

"You can't go alone. If they catch you…"

"You're no use to man or beast right now. I can take care of myself. Let's get going." Dan was happy to let her take command, if only for a few hours. He was hurting too much to be able to think straight.

The side trail went for a mile and a half, at thirty feet or so below the dirt road level, before making a sharp turn. Claire found a natural recess in the stone wall along which the trail ran. There, she hid Dan's backpack, which he had insisted on dragging for part of the way. Another mile brought them to a narrow, winding path leading up to the cave entrance in a hilly area to their left. The bad news was that the cave was visible from the dirt road, and Rafik's friends might see them unless they hid well. The good news was that even if someone spotted them from the road, there was no direct way to get from that point to the cave, making a surprise discovery unlikely.

They climbed the short distance to the cave. Claire pushed the water supply as far as it went, then helped Dan to climb inside and lie down near the entrance in the shade. "I'll go and fetch your backpack, okay?" she said. Dan nodded, too exhausted to speak, and she climbed down.

Half an hour later, Claire was back with the rest of their supplies. "We have a first aid kit in here. I'm sure it has something I can use to bandage your shoulder," she said.

She went through the kit, which was quite basic, and found some painkillers. "Here, take a couple of these," she said, handing them to him along with a canteen filled with water.

Dan swallowed the pills without even looking at them. "It's

time for us to catch some sleep," he said. "At night, we will have a long walk ahead of us, which isn't going to be easy. We must rest as much as we can. Here, take the sleeping bag. I'll sleep right here."

"No way!" said Claire. "This cave is freezing. You're already half an invalid, and I don't need you to catch pneumonia as well. Jump inside. The sleeping bag is big enough for the two of us."

"Are you sure?"

"Listen, my friend," said Claire, without patience. "There are times when being a gentleman is cool. This is not one of them."

"You're right," said Dan, but he just kept looking at the sleeping bag.

Claire watched him. "Let me see your shoulder," she said. "It may need to be adjusted."

"No, no. It's nothing. It'll be all right after I get some rest."

"Okay," said Claire. She was not convinced, but there was little she could do if Dan wanted to be mulish. "I don't feel like sleeping yet. You go ahead, and I'll join you in a little while."

Dan nodded in assent and finally moved. He kicked off his shoes and climbed into the sleeping bag. The painkillers began to work, and fatigue took over. Two minutes later, he was sound asleep.

Claire woke up and chased away a fly that had selected her nose for a landing ground. She opened her eyes and squinted against the light coming from outside. Judging by the sun's position, it had to be early afternoon. The still air in the cave, which had been frozen cold in the morning, now felt heavy, hot, and chalky. She turned her head from the cave opening and the bright light. She was sweaty, and the inside of the sleeping bag was moist to the touch. She unzipped it and pulled it down toward her feet as far as it would go. That didn't seem to disturb Dan's sleep.

Seeing Dan lying next to her suddenly made her think of Rob. Claire sighed. Dan looked different from Rob, she realized—quite the opposite character. He was not as handsome but radiated rugged masculinity that made him interesting. Still, as she watched him sleep, he looked more like a peaceful child than the mature man he was. He was resourceful. She had to hand him that. She wondered how Rob would have reacted had he needed to get rid of a body in the middle of the desert. The image of a scared, spoiled, and childish Rob dealing with that made her smile. But then, why was she drawing comparisons? Dan was nice, and she liked him in a fuzzy sort of way, but they were not involved, nor were they going to be.

So what are these flutters I feel in my stomach? she wondered, but immediately, she chased the thought away. *What are all these thoughts I'm having?* She was always more demanding of herself than of others, but under the unusual circumstances, she felt she didn't need to be too hard on herself. *I'm not my usual self now, and who would be in my shoes?*

A noise awoke her from her musings. A vehicle was coming their way, and she realized that daylight had exposed them to view from the dirt road because they had placed the sleeping bag near the cave's opening. Anybody who stood at the turn of the road and looked their way with binoculars would be able to see them.

She jumped out of the sleeping bag and started dragging it toward the back of the cave, away from the sunlit area. Dan stirred and opened an eye. "What...?"

"A car. Coming," Claire said, speaking urgently.

Dan sat up and listened. "You're right," he said. "It must be them. If they didn't see Rafik's Jeep down the wadi, they must wonder what became of us."

The cave wasn't deep, and they had to push their backs against the wall to stay out of the puddle of light that the sun had cast on its floor. They waited, speaking instinctively in whispers.

"The Kalashnikov?" Dan asked.

"Here," said Claire, pulling the gun from behind her. Dan

gestured for it. "Are you going to shoot? They don't know we're here."

"Only if they find us. Now, stay back. I need to look outside and make sure they're not coming on foot the same way we came."

"But they may see you if you go out. And your shoulder is hurt. Maybe you should let me do the shooting."

"I'm fine now. The painkillers and some sleep were all I needed. The wound was not as serious as I feared. And I have to take the risk because if they corner us here..."

He crawled out of the cave, keeping low and hidden to view by the rocks near the trail. He looked fearless, and Claire felt her heart flutter again.

CHAPTER 30

Leskov sat in the back of the company's black stretch Mercedes and ruminated about his employees' impotence. He was lucky to have such great connections in the Egyptian government, but it was frustrating that he had to do everything himself if he wanted it done right. During his KGB years, he became obsessed with the great Italian general Garibaldi. He had the maxim that Garibaldi used to quote engraved on a piece of granite on his table. It said, *"Chi vuole, vada, e chi non vuole, mandi"*: "He who wants it goes to get it; he who doesn't want it sends for it." After Karim had taken a whole day to obtain the letter from the general's office, the proverb had never seemed more appropriate than today.

He was lost in thought about what he would do to Dan and Claire if they had double-crossed him when he sensed a change in the noise of the car engine that dragged him back to the present. "What's the matter, Karim?" he asked, seeing that the car had slowed down. "Why are you stopping?"

"This is the checkpoint on the Cairo-Suez road, sir. We need to stop for inspection."

Karim stopped the car at the roadblock and opened the

window. The time was approaching nine p.m., and nobody was around except for them. An army officer, a lieutenant, made a formal salute, pushed his head inside, and inspected Leskov for a few seconds. Then he turned back to Karim. "Documents," he said, speaking in imperious Arabic.

The lieutenant inspected Karim's documents and then ordered, still in Arabic, for them to open the trunk. He signaled two of his men to check it and turned again to Karim. "The passenger's documents, please," he said.

Leskov wouldn't have any of it. Who was this lieutenant anyway, he thought, to get in the way? He understood enough Arabic to follow the simple conversation but not enough to argue himself. "Karim," he ordered, "tell him who we are and under what authority we are traveling."

"Lieutenant," Karim started to say, but then the soldiers who were inspecting the trunk approached and whispered something to their officer's ear. The lieutenant took a step back, and the two soldiers positioned themselves at his two sides with their guns well in evidence.

"Get out of the car," the lieutenant ordered. "Now!" he barked.

Leskov knew better than to argue with stupid soldiers with guns, so he opened the door and climbed out. Karim was already standing by the driver's door. The lieutenant, so it turned out, spoke some English. "Why you have guns in trunk?" he asked point-blank.

"We have a permit. Here," said Leskov, fishing the general's letter from his pocket. "Read this."

The lieutenant read the letter without haste and didn't give it back to Leskov. "The letter does not say about weapons," he said. His body language made it plain that he wasn't liking Leskov a bit.

Leskov realized he had blown it by not asking Karim to tell him what the letter said. He had trusted the general too much and was now angry at himself for it. That wasn't like him at all.

"He must have forgotten to mention the gun permit," he told the lieutenant. "I asked him to make that clear in the letter. I don't read Arabic, so I wasn't aware..."

"Weapons are forbidden. You come with me," said the officer, unimpressed.

"We can't stop here," said Leskov. "We must reach Suez immediately. Call the general, and he'll tell you."

"I call him tomorrow morning," said the lieutenant.

"Call him now! Right now!" Leskov shouted in frustration.

The officer signaled his two soldiers, who got behind Leskov and Karim and pushed them with their guns. "No disturb general at night. I call him tomorrow," said the lieutenant, unruffled. "We will find out if letter not forged." His tone made it clear that he expected it to be a fake.

"That's nonsense," said Leskov, which only earned him another encouraging prod in the back with the muzzle of a gun.

The soldiers led them into a small room with a bed and a table. "I let you have this hospitality room for night," said the lieutenant. "A soldier will bring water." He slammed the door after him and locked it.

"You have done well, Lieutenant," said Major Hassan, who was waiting in the small checkpoint office. "Tomorrow, the general will be busy, and you won't be able to reach him."

The lieutenant kept a serious countenance and nodded with understanding. Hassan continued. "I'll let you know when you can let them go and if you need to confiscate their weapons."

With that, Hassan made a loose salute. The lieutenant saluted back with perfect military precision, and Hassan departed.

CHAPTER 31

"What?" Bshari barked into the telephone. He heard what his man, Muhammad, was saying, but the words were not making sense.

"What do you mean, 'disappeared'? They can't vanish in the middle of the desert. And are you sure that it's Rafik in the Jeep?" Rafik was his wife's brother's wife's nephew, which made him sort of family, and that was why Bshari had given him a job despite Rafik's being a moron. But even Rafik, in his infinite stupidity, shouldn't have gone and landed himself dead in a burned-up Jeep at the bottom of a wadi.

"We have searched everywhere. Allah knows where they have gone." Muhammad was the brighter of the two and the most trustworthy. Bshari did not doubt that if he said they had searched everywhere, that was what they had done.

"Here's what you'll do," said Bshari. "Get off the mountain and take a position in the plain where you can see the road. If they are hiding in the mountain, they will have to come out at some point. You have enough food and supplies for two days, right? If you need to stay longer, I'll send someone with more supplies. Understood?"

"Understood," said Muhammad.

"Good," said Bshari and hung up.

"Let's make coffee," said Muhammad to his companion, a big grin on his face. He liked chores he was good at, and he was good at waiting.

Bshari was beginning to feel that the universe was against him. Things that should have gone smoothly were going wrong. He wasn't usually prone to anger, but he felt the urge to hit the wall with his fist. The pain in his fingers brought him some satisfaction, and he sat down, calmer, to think.

A knock on the door arose him from his brooding. "Come in!" he yelled. A servant opened the door with hesitation.

"Mister Schmidt has arrived to see you, sir," he said. Then, he moved aside to give way to the guest.

The door was thrown wide open, and a tall, lean man walked through it with open assurance. He had blond hair that was getting white under his close haircut. His age could have been anywhere between fifty and sixty. If he had a first name, nobody, not even those close to him, had ever heard it used. His official title was business manager for Europe, in charge of Bshari's many interests there, but his main job was fixing things when the going got rough. He had acquired his skills during his years in the Stasi—the hated and feared security bureau of Eastern Germany. His innate diplomatic ability made him a welcome guest in government and commerce circles, and he made it his business to know everything there was to know about influential people in Europe who might become helpful to his employer under the appropriate circumstances.

Schmidt had run intelligence inside Leskov's organization and knew everything about the staff project, among other delicate assignments. Although he had voiced his opinion more than once that all the fuss around the staff was insane and childish, besides being unworthy of his time and talent, Bshari made it clear to him that he was paying him—and handsomely at that—to give him practical advice on how to achieve what he wanted, not on whether he should want it.

Hearing Schmidt's name brought Bshari back to his optimistic self in a second. He got up and shook hands with him. "Herr Schmidt! I'm so relieved that you could come. I'm tired of having to rely on a bunch of idiots for the simplest chores."

"I came as soon as I managed to get away. Do I understand that the project has hit a snag?" asked Schmidt, lifting an eyebrow.

"You could say that. The Israeli and the American girl have disappeared, and the chief idiot I sent to look after them got himself killed. On top of that, I know that Leskov is in the Suez area, maybe with them, and I don't have enough men to look everywhere for them. What do you think I should do?" he asked.

"Let's look at the map and consider the options. And..."

"Yes?"

"A beer would help. This weather is infernally hot."

"A beer...you know that we, good Muslims, don't drink alcohol."

"I know, and I won't tell anybody," said Schmidt.

Bshari was tempted to insist on a soda instead but decided against it. He needed Schmidt at the top of his faculties, and if a beer helped...He made a resigned gesture with his hand and then clapped for his servant. They waited in silence for him to return with the beverage. Once he'd gulped down the beer, Schmidt placed the palm of his hand on the map and leveled his gaze to Bshari's.

"If the mountain won't come to Muhammad," he said, "then Muhammad must go to the mountain."

"And what do you mean by that?" asked Bshari. The German's patronizing attitude annoyed him.

"It's simple, Mister Bshari. You don't have to run around looking for them. We know that they must go to the Sinai desert and that they have to take the Mitla Pass. So all we have to do is go there, find a good observation point—here on this ridge, for instance," he said, pointing at a place on the aerial photo of the pass, "and wait for them to show up. That shouldn't take them too long, and then we will be able to deal with them after assessing their number and strength. Don't you agree?"

Bshari was finally excited but also a little annoyed that he hadn't thought of this simple idea himself. Still, he was fair enough to give credit where credit was due.

"That's why I pay you," he said. "I wish the idiots who work for me had the same presence of mind."

Schmidt acknowledged the compliment with a brief nod. He didn't care what his master thought of him; he only cared about the payment that came with his admiration.

CHAPTER 32

The late afternoon was casting shadows around their cave, and Dan and Claire wrapped up the remains of their frugal meal. Dan's brief reconnaissance had revealed no danger, and the engine noises had stopped, giving room to the rumbling of their stomachs. They had allowed themselves to relax and eat for the first time.

"My reign for a cup of coffee," said Claire.

"Lighting a fire would be too dangerous," said Dan.

"I know. It was just wishful thinking. You know," she continued, with a dreamy look, "it is strange how we take things for granted when we live our regular, boring lives. We don't realize that simple things like coffee aren't always available when we want them."

"Are you getting philosophical?" Dan gazed at her with an amused smile.

"Perhaps...don't you feel like musing on life sometimes?" Claire answered seriously. Dan kept trying to lighten up the atmosphere. He wanted to keep her from brooding on their situation at all costs.

"Quite often, actually," he said, "but most of the time, I

indulge in philosophy when I'm having a drink on the beach at sunset. Not so much when murderous maniacs are chasing me in the middle of the desert."

"You're funny," Claire said. She laughed and patted his shoulder.

"Ouch!" Dan cried out, pain contorting his features.

"Oh, I'm sorry! Is that still hurting so much?"

"Uh-huh..."

"Take off your shirt. Let me see it," she ordered.

"It's nothing; forget it."

"No, I'm serious. I have a way with bones. People often got hurt skiing and climbing where I used to live. Let me see it."

Dan unbuttoned his shirt, but the movement was too painful when it came time to take it off. "Sorry, I can't seem to manage," he said.

"Let me help you," said Claire. She got on her knees behind him and pulled the shirt off him, careful not to apply pressure to the flesh. Dan's left shoulder was swollen, with purple streaks that extended to his chest, but it looked better than she had expected. She moved forward to face him and touched the flesh carefully, looking for signs of pain in his face. "I know you're tender every-where here, but I need to find out how serious it is. If it hurts too much, just tell me."

Dan nodded, and Claire started touching the back and front of his shoulder and chest. At one point, Dan grimaced in pain, and she stopped, but he relaxed, smiled, and said, "Go ahead. If it weren't for the pain, I would say this is rather pleasant."

"Sure," she said, smiling back. "It doesn't look serious to me, but it needs fixating. We have an elastic bandage in the first aid kit. That and some more painkillers are what you need now. Be patient with me for a couple more minutes, okay?"

"Yes, doctor," said Dan. He sat there, keeping still, while Claire bandaged his shoulder and then helped him with his shirt. Dan swallowed a couple of painkillers with a bit of water. "You're useful to have around."

"So are you. I haven't forgotten that you hurt yourself to keep me from going off that cliff. That was very chivalrous of you, and I haven't thanked you. Thank you."

"Don't mention it. My pleasure. Anytime you need someone to keep you from jumping off cliffs, just give me a call," Dan said, grinning.

"You may yet regret the offer. It seems that I'm getting us into trouble all the time. Let's hope that you won't have to kill anybody else on my account."

"Well, let's see how we get ourselves out of this particular trouble now," he said. "It's getting dark, and I think we should rest a bit more and then hit the road to Suez. Okay with you?"

"Okay, but it's getting cold again. This cave is like a freezer. Let's get into the sleeping bag and keep each other warm until it's time to leave." She got into the sack and kept the flap open, inviting him to join. He got in and zipped it halfway up. The sleeping bag was large but not big enough for two people to feel comfortable in it. It wasn't too awkward when they were asleep, but now he had to assume an uncomfortable position, lying on his side and putting up with the pain in his shoulder, or share some space with Claire. And on top of that, he didn't know what he would do if she switched again to Jack while they were in that awkward position.

Claire watched his embarrassed maneuvers to find a comfortable position without rushing him, but after a while, she took his hand, pulled his arm straight, and nestled her head in the hollow of his shoulder. "Like this," she said, turning on her side to give him more room. She doubted she would sleep, but Dan didn't need to know that.

. . .

Getting back on the dirt road was easier than they had anticipated. Following the trail that had taken them to the cave, they continued for less than a mile until it joined the road. Following the road was dangerous because if anybody were looking for them, they would likely take that route—but Dan and Claire had no choice. It was clear from the map that it was the only way to get off the mountain without climbing down dangerous slopes. They walked in silence.

The dirt road ended some five hundred yards ahead into the plain where the Cairo–Suez road ran, and Dan stopped when they reached that point. "It's time to get rid of the Kalashnikov," he said. "I feel much better with it, but if the Egyptian police catch us with a weapon, we run the danger of being thrown in jail forever."

"You're right. Let's not take chances," Claire agreed.

Dan took the Kalashnikov and its magazines and hid them behind a rocky formation at the side of the road. Then they continued to walk on the road that unwound with a light slope down toward the plain. They had barely emerged from the mountain when they saw on the right a vision that stopped them in their tracks—a Jeep standing a mere four hundred yards from them. Next to the Jeep, two figures sat beside a fire.

"Bshari's men!" Dan whispered. "Let's go back."

They retraced their steps until they were past a bend in the road and sure to be out of sight of the Jeep. They kept whispering.

"What do we do now?" asked Claire, a ring of despair in her voice.

"I can run back to get the Kalashnikov and give them a fight," said Dan, but his voice lacked conviction.

"And get ourselves killed? There must be another way," Claire objected.

"Wait here for a minute," said Dan, "I want to take a better look. Stay hidden from the road behind this rock, just in case."

"Be careful, okay?"

Dan nodded and walked away, disappearing after the road

bend. Ten minutes later, he was back, a look of satisfaction on his face.

"I think I've got it," he said. "The rocky formations by the side of the road—like this one—continue in the plain below. We can't go to the left and try to circumvent the Jeep because it's all flat ground. They would spot us in no time with the moon as bright as it is. But if we keep close to the mountain and circumvent them from the right, we will be low against the rocks, and our silhouettes will be much less visible from where the Jeep stands. Plus, we can do part of the way behind rocks and keep low in between. I believe we can make it. If we don't make too much noise, that is. In the desert, every noise carries, so we must be careful."

"What time is it?" asked Claire.

"Almost ten; why?"

"Because we should wait until they go to sleep before doing all that stealthy stuff you're planning," she said, smiling. "What are they doing now?"

"There are two of them that I could spot. One climbed into the Jeep while I watched them, and the other sits by the campfire."

"Let's give them another couple of hours and see," said Claire.

Dan nodded in assent, and they went back a little more until they found a place to sit behind a rock hidden from the road. There, they sat in silence to wait.

CHAPTER 33

Claire had been right. The campfire dwindled, and the guard stretched beside it, hugging his Kalashnikov. Dan and Claire stood fewer than a hundred yards away from the Jeep, watching for any sign of movement, and the guard hadn't moved at all. The loud snoring coming from within the Jeep left no doubt that the man inside was fast asleep. They started walking at Dan's sign, keeping low and passed a mere forty yards away from the Jeep. They tiptoed, careful to avoid making any noise until they felt they had put a sufficient distance between them and the Jeep. Then Dan stopped and whispered to Claire, "We've made it past them, but we still have a long way to go. Here, let's sit down in this cranny for a few minutes."

They sat and rested for a short while before Dan got up. "We have a three-hour walk ahead of us; let's get going."

The walk toward Suez was uneventful, and it was still dark when they reached the city's outskirts. A bunch of one-story Arab houses that seemed made of mud was the first they saw. Farther on the horizon, taller buildings loomed ominously.

"What do we do now?" Claire asked in a whisper.

"It's almost four a.m., and in an hour or so, people will start to get up. We must find a place to stay—perhaps a house where we can pay for hospitality until we figure out our next steps. Look!" Dan said. They had been walking in the maze of streets, and he was pointing to one of the houses that looked pretty much like its neighbors. "That sign in Arabic says '*Funduq.*' That means hotel."

"It doesn't look anything like a hotel to me," said Claire. "It's a dump, just like all the others."

"All the same, it offers lodging if the sign is right. Let's sit here and wait for signs of life, then we'll go in and try to get a room."

They sat on a stone bench under a solitary olive tree from which they could see the hotel entrance. Claire laid her head on Dan's shoulder and dozed off. *This is too weird for words,* Dan thought. *Please, God, don't make her switch again now.* He fought the desire to close his eyes by concentrating on their next steps. The exercise kept him busy and awake until the first light when the hotel's door finally opened, and a middle-aged man came out to empty a bucket of water in the street before going in again.

"Get up," he said, pushing Claire's head up gently. "The hotel is open for business."

Claire shook herself awake, and they went inside. The man with the bucket was behind a small, dirty desk. He raised his head as he saw them.

"Good morning," said Dan, producing his best smile. "We need a room for one night."

The man returned a blank stare. "Eh?" he said.

Dan forced his memory to remember the little Arabic he knew. *"Nuridu Ghurfa,"* he said at last. He wasn't sure that *ghurfa* meant room, but he hoped so.

The light of comprehension came into the man's eyes, and Dan felt relieved. *"Ah, ghurfa!"* he said, the light of understanding now in his eyes. *"Wahid?"* he asked.

"Wahid," Dan confirmed, nodding in assent. One room was all they needed. He would not get separated from Claire while they were in danger.

146

"Miayat junayh," said the man, putting out a hand, palm up.

"What?" asked Claire. "What is he saying?"

"He wants money. A hundred pounds. Give it to him."

Claire fished into her pocket and found two fifty Egyptian pound notes, which Dan handed the hotelkeeper. The man took a key from behind the desk and motioned for them to follow. A narrow corridor running from the entrance led to four doors. He pushed the last one, revealing a small room with a queen-size bed and a few accessories, including a washbasin and a pitcher full of water. No sign of running water. The hotelkeeper handed the key ceremoniously to Dan and left. Dan hastened to lock the door and then seated himself on the bed.

"I'm dying for a shower," said Claire with a sigh, "but I guess it's not to be."

Dan shook his head. "Not now, at least. Let's catch some decent sleep. We need our strength. When we wake up, we will hunt for food and shower."

"Well, *decent* is a relative word," said Claire. "This room smells, and the bed sheets haven't been changed since they built this place. How you can sleep at all beats me."

"That's something I learned in the army. You sleep when you can, wherever you can, and for as long as you can, even if only for a minute because you never know when you'll get a chance to sleep again. I agree this is not a five-star hotel, but we have shelter and are in no immediate danger, which is what we need for restful sleep now. Good night...or morning. Whichever," he added. He kicked away his shoes, followed by his socks, released his belt, and lay down on one side of the bed. A few seconds later, a light snore made it clear that he was asleep.

Left to herself with little else to do, Claire took off her shoes and lay on the bed, back to back with Dan. She envied his ability to adapt with ease to every environment. With all the thoughts racing through her mind and the room's smell, she felt sleep was out of the question. When it came, it was a surprise.

CHAPTER 34

The general lay back in his upholstered office chair, eyes closed. His jaw muscles worked right and left as he ruminated over the report Major Hassan had just finished giving him. Hassan stood at ease before the desk, waiting for his superior to speak. He knew him so well that he could almost see the thoughts forming behind his brow. At last, the general straightened himself up and opened his eyes.

"You did well, Hassan. So my friend Leskov is now held at the checkpoint. He must be mad as a wet hen by now. Aha!" he guffawed. "It will serve him right! It was a good idea to omit the weapon-carrying permit from my letter. I like the way you think."

"Thank you, General. I'm flattered."

"Something is going on behind my back, and I don't like it. Leskov is not being candid with me, and I like that even less. I want you to keep after him and find out what it is that he is scheming."

"Do you want me to tail him when he's released?" asked Hassan.

"No, I have a better idea. When is the checkpoint commander going to call?"

"I'm not sure, but I can call him now if you wish."

"Do that," the general ordered.

Hassan picked up the phone on the general's desk and barked a few orders into it. A minute later, a voice came through the line. "The checkpoint commander is on the line, General," Hassan announced.

"Tell him to put Leskov through."

Hassan waited five more minutes with the receiver in his hand and then handed it to the general. "Leskov," he said.

"My dear friend," said the general, "how are you doing?"

"How am I doing, you ask? A stupid tin soldier who can't read orders right has kept me here at the Cairo–Suez checkpoint. I'm wasting precious time. That's how I've been doing. And that's beside my complaint at being locked up like a criminal."

"I'm so sorry for the inconvenience, my friend. It's a pity that important state affairs kept me away, and they couldn't reach me sooner. I apologize."

"Well, it doesn't matter now. Will you please tell this bozo to let us go?"

"Certainly, certainly. But I'm concerned about your safety, you know. I hear rumors...and I feel responsible."

The general's voice was mellow, which was out of character, and the nuance didn't escape Leskov's attention. "Don't worry. I can look after myself," he said.

"Yes, sure," the general agreed, sounding even more friendly, "but I still feel responsible for your welfare, and I won't spare efforts to ensure you are in no danger. You know me: There's nothing I wouldn't do for a friend."

"What are you saying?"

"What I'm saying is that I will send my personal aide, Major Hassan, a competent officer, to accompany you on your journey. He will guard you against any harm, and if the need arises, he will be able to summon the help of local authorities. He will have ample authority from me."

"Yes, but…"

"I know what you're thinking," continued the general, speaking in an even sweeter tone. "You think it will be a sacrifice for me to part from Major Hassan, my most trustworthy aide, but I will be happy to do that for you. Besides, it will only be for a few days, right?"

"Really, my friend, I appreciate your offer, but I can manage without him. I don't want you to sacrifice—"

"Don't mention it," said the general, preparing for the punch line. "We will see in due course how this sacrifice can be…how should I say…compensated. Meanwhile, hold tight until Major Hassan gets to the checkpoint and releases you and your equipment. Don't thank me. It is my great pleasure to help such a good friend as you are. Let's have some coffee together when you return to Cairo. Goodbye now."

The general handed the receiver to Hassan, who replaced it on its hook.

"So you see, it's all set. Whatever Leskov is after, you now have a front-row seat to it, and I trust that you will look after the interests of our great Egyptian Republic."

"Of course I will, General," said Hassan. He saluted with a perfect, rigid salute, turned on his heels, and left.

CHAPTER 35

"I can't believe we slept until now," said Claire. "It's late afternoon already."

The shadows of the houses—which they could see from the small window of their room—were already long, and the sun was low on the horizon.

"I can tell by my hunger that it's quite late," said Dan. "Let's ask our host where we can go for grub."

Claire had already washed her face in the washbasin, and Dan used the little water left to wash away the sweat from his sleep. The room was like a furnace, but they had been too tired to notice. They left the room, locking the door behind them. The hotel-keeper was nowhere to be found, nor was any other soul in sight.

"We'll have to find food on our own. Watch out for a sign that says *Mateam*."

"You forget that I can't read Arabic...and I didn't know that you spoke the language."

"I don't. It's just a little that I remember from studying it in school. It was such a long time ago that I'd forgotten almost all of it. Still, when you are in trouble, your memory works miracles. I haven't used those words for decades."

"Good for you," she said. "Now work another miracle and get us some food and a shower. First, the shower, please."

They had just walked into a narrow street out of sight of the hotel when excited voices and shouts made them stop. The noise came from the hotel and was growing in volume. "Stay here," Dan ordered, and he walked back to the corner of the house they had just passed. From there, he was able to see the entrance to their hotel. Two police cars were parked in front, and several men, some in uniform and some not, were arguing at the door. Deciding that he had seen enough, Dan ran back to Claire.

"They've come for us," he said, panting. "We must get away before they broaden their search. Let's move."

"But...how? And Who? Bshari? How did they know we were there?"

"It must've been the damn hotelkeeper. He must have told the authorities that he had two strangers in his hotel. Maybe he is obliged to report foreigners. That's why he wasn't there. I don't think that it's Bshari's doing. He would have come by himself. It might simply be the police taking an interest in two suspicious visitors."

"But all our stuff is in the room...the maps, the sleeping bag... everything," Claire objected.

Dan had lost all the gear he had brought from home during the war when his first tank caught fire. He had hesitated near the tank, debating whether to try to salvage something of his belongings, when his tank commander had dragged him away and said something he had never forgotten: "The only thing you can't replace is your life." He knew how Claire felt now, losing whatever few amenities they had taken with them, but he had to shake her out of it. "I know. There's nothing we can do about it," he said. "Now, save your breath for getting away."

They ran through the mazes of narrow streets, trying to take less crowded alleys and ignoring the surprised gazes of passersby. At an intersection, a battered, old black Volvo stopped with a screech of brakes in the middle of the street and blocked their path. When the Volvo's back door opened, Dan and Claire backed away and turned to run, but a voice behind them stopped them.

"*Tikansu maher*—get in, quickly," the voice said.

Dan stopped and turned around.

"What is that," Claire asked. "Why are you stopping?"

"That was in Hebrew—he's an Israeli."

"It could be a trap!"

"Will it take you all day?" the voice shouted again in Hebrew.

"No, the accent is right. He's Israeli," Dan said with confidence.

They approached the car. "Who are you?" Dan asked in Hebrew.

"Save your questions for when we are out of danger," the stranger responded in English. "Now get in the back and keep your heads down. We have no time to waste."

Dan and Claire did as instructed, and as soon as the door closed, the car raced forward at a speed ill-suited for Suez's narrow, busy streets.

"By the way," said the stranger in English, "my name is Albert. Just so you know, if we get killed."

"But how—" Claire started to say, but Albert interrupted her.

"Miss Williams," he said, keeping his eyes on the road and slowing down a little, "please keep quiet."

He spoke in a neutral tone, but the mention of her name was enough to silence her. She looked inquiringly at Dan, who shrugged and motioned her to go lower in the backseat. After what seemed to Dan like an eternity but must have only been five minutes, Albert turned under an arch that led into a backyard and cut the engine.

"Is this our destination?" asked Dan.

"No," Albert replied. "The car is recognizable, and we need to get away from it. Our hiding place is three minutes from here...if we move fast enough, that is. Get out and follow me. If we meet anybody, do as I do."

The streets in that part of the town were empty. Albert led them at a brisk walk through another maze that looked pretty much like the one near their hotel—so much so that at one point, Dan started to wonder whether they had been moving in circles. Then he realized that he had no cause for being paranoid. It was apparent that Albert was on their side, and anyway, they had little choice but to trust him. They walked as much as possible in the shadow of low buildings, keeping near the walls and stopping at every junction to let Albert check all directions before crossing. Five minutes later, they reached a door painted in blue, which Albert ushered them through. The small foyer behind the door ended in a stairway, and they climbed one floor after him until he reached an apartment door, produced a key, and opened it. They went inside, and he bolted the door after them.

"Uhf!" he said. "I hate the commotion..."

"Where are we?" Claire asked.

"This is my humble apartment—not mine, as a matter of fact, but I have the use of it. You must forgive me if I don't have many amenities here, but I'm sure you'd like a cup of coffee as much as I do."

"We'd love some food as well," said Dan. "We had just gone out to look for some when the police came. How did you happen to be there?"

"And how do you know who we are?" added Claire.

"I'll explain everything in a minute—but first, coffee. Here, go into the bedroom and take a seat. Unfortunately, I don't have any chairs, but you can sit on the bed. Stay away from the window," Albert admonished them.

From where they stood, they could see part of a small kitchen and a door to a bathroom, which pretty much amounted to the entire apartment. Since there was little point in standing there, they went into the bedroom, which indeed was bare except for a bed and a cupboard. Their getaway had been an unnerving experience, and Dan and Claire sat on the bed in silence, each lost in thought.

Albert arrived a few minutes later with a circular tray. He carried a coffeepot with three small glasses and a brown paper bag.

"Here," he said. "I've found pita bread and some decent goat cheese. Help yourselves."

Albert put the tray on the bed, and Dan passed the brown bag on to Claire, who opened it and divided the pita bread and cheese into two equal pieces. She stopped and asked Albert, "Do you also want some?"

"No, thanks. I've eaten. That's all for you."

Dan and Claire ate avidly and drank the strong Turkish coffee that Albert had made. When they finally felt satiated, Claire turned to Albert with a severe countenance.

"Now it's time for you to explain. Of course, we are thankful to you for helping us to escape, but we need some explanations," she said.

"Of course. My name, as I said, is Albert. That's not my real name, but it will do. I am a cultural attaché at the Israeli Embassy in Cairo."

"You're Mossad," Dan stated.

"I am, as I said, a cultural attaché. We at the embassy take a keen interest in what goes on in Cairo, and, of course, we were quite keen to learn what an Israeli, accompanied by a charming lady like Miss Williams—"

"You can call me Claire," she interjected.

"Accompanied by a charming lady like Claire," Albert corrected, nodding in agreement, "was doing in Cairo in a hotel booked by Leskov Industries. You should know that Leskov Industries is involved in some armament negotiations with certain countries in the region, in which we also take an interest. So it was decided that we should keep an eye on you, but then you disappeared and baffled us. Until we got information that Leskov was heading to Suez..."

"Leskov is here?" Dan nearly yelled. "How did you get this information?"

"Do you really need to know, Dan? Of course, you don't. Anyhow, when we learned that he was coming this way, we assumed we would find you here as well, so I came to Suez. Does that explain it to you now?"

"Some, but not all," said Claire. "How did you know where to find us today?"

"Ah! You see this little gadget," said Albert, fishing a small device from his pocket. He pushed a button on it, and the voices of four or five people speaking in Arabic came from it. "Police wavelength," he said. "I heard your description and where they were going to pick you up. I hoped to be able to get there first and warn you. It was lucky that you had already gone out."

"What are they saying now?" asked Dan.

Albert listened for a few seconds and then turned the receiver off.

"They are looking for you. We need to lie low until they tire of searching. I guess they'll give up by tomorrow morning. Before we leave here, I'll listen to their radio to make sure they are not around."

"Leave? Where to?" asked Dan.

"Okay, this is the plan. I'll take you to a friend's home—he's not there, but his servant is, and he is as reliable as they come. You'll need patience because you may have to hide there for a few days. Once you're settled in, I'll go back to Cairo to plan a way to get you out of Egypt. It won't be simple, and we can't make mistakes, so please don't rush me."

"Why are you going to all this trouble?" Dan asked.

Albert acted puzzled. "Why, we Israelis always look after each other. You know that. We have strict instructions to aid the nationals of our country, so I have to get you out of this mess."

"But Claire is not Israeli, and I'm not going anywhere without her."

"Hmm, we'll make her an honorary Israeli until this is over. Besides, you also must do something for us."

"What?" Dan asked.

"Tell me your side of the story. Leskov's involvement, his plans, all of it."

"Claire, you know all the details better than I do..." said Dan.

"All right," said Claire, "I'll tell you everything I know, but I warn you that you'll find it hard to believe."

She collected her thoughts and began their story.

CHAPTER 36

The night passed slowly, with Dan and Claire catching some crowded sleep, half-sitting, half-lying on the narrow bed, and Albert on a heap of clothing he had thrown on the floor. It was already light outside when Dan woke up at the sound of Albert moving around. Claire was still fast asleep, and he had no heart to wake her up.

"Coffee?" Albert inquired.

"Oh, yes!" said Dan.

He got up and went to the tiny toilet cell that passed for a bathroom. A microscopic sink that delivered cold water was all he had to freshen up, but it did the job of shaking away the mists of sleep. He had slept a little over four hours by his watch, which pointed to six a.m. Claire's relation to Albert, who had kept interrupting for more details, had taken a long time. Afterward, Albert had gone out to buy some food, and they had waited, on edge, for his return. Returning after almost two nerve-wracking hours, Albert told them he had done some reconnaissance in the area and was confident that the police had abandoned the search in Suez. The word on police radio was that the foreigners had fled in a black car and had to be far from Suez by now. Searches were ongoing in the north on the road to Fa'id and Ismailia and in the south in Al Adabiyah.

After the improvised dinner, they had sat together and talked. There was nothing else to do. Albert, who was ten years Dan's junior, had been a child during the 1973 war, and Dan's stories about the battles in the Sinai desert enthralled him. He kept asking for more and more details, and his questions jogged Dan's memory to a point where he recalled events that he had nearly forgotten or that he had perhaps preferred to forget. Now, in the sobering light of the morning, it occurred to him to wonder if Albert was, in fact, interested in the history of the war or perhaps wanted him to talk to test the veracity of his account. *Whatever*, he thought and shrugged it off.

"Do we need to wake Claire up already?" he asked, standing at the kitchen door and speaking in an undertone.

"I'm awake," Claire's voice came from the room. "I need to pee," she added unnecessarily, entering the bathroom.

"Coffee will be ready in a minute," said Albert.

"Do you have any toothpaste?" Claire asked.

"Sorry, no toothpaste," Albert apologized.

He brought the coffee on the tray into the bedroom, and they sat to drink it. He had also conjured up more pita bread and a little labneh cheese, which they wolfed down. As soon as he finished drinking, Albert got up, picked up two bundles of clothing, and threw them on the bed.

"Dress in those," he ordered. "We must leave in a little while before the streets become too populated."

"But those are Arab women's clothes," Dan objected.

"Exactly. The police are looking for two European foreigners, not for two Arab women in traditional clothing. With the veils covering your faces, nobody will know you're not local women if you behave as I'll tell you."

"Meaning?" Claire asked.

"Meaning that you will walk behind me in silence and keep a

distance of six to seven feet from me. If anybody speaks to you, don't look at him, and let me handle it. And you, Claire, forgive me for saying it, but try not to shake your tush too much, if you can. Good Muslims consider it impure. Understood?"

"That's easy enough," said Claire, "but where are we going that we need this masquerade?"

"We can't use the Volvo now. That car is hot. I have a white Toyota pickup truck that is perfect for this trip, but it's parked far from here, and we need to walk there. It's okay as long as we don't attract attention, but since the city is on edge because of all the unusual police activity, we must be extra careful."

"But Albert," asked Dan, "wouldn't it be easier and safer if you were to go and fetch the truck instead? We could wait for you here and wouldn't need to dress up."

"First, you'll need to dress up no matter what because you can't drive around in your clothes. I had considered bringing the truck here, but that's dangerous too because, in this densely populated quarter, where everybody knows everybody else, and the most sophisticated means of transportation is a donkey, strangers driving around in a pickup truck may attract attention, and someone may alert the police. The truck is hidden in a much more commercial area and in a better location for getting out of town. So that's what we are going to do. It'll take us about twenty minutes to get there at a normal pace. Drink water before we go, use the bathroom, and get ready for a hot walk. It's almost seven a.m. now, and the sun is already high in the sky."

The trip to the truck turned out to be uneventful. Dan and Claire walked behind Albert, and after a while, Dan started to enjoy his disguise. Behind the impenetrable woman's clothes, he felt as though he was in a game in which he could see but was not seen. Claire, in contrast, had to concentrate on repressing the feminine walk that Dan so admired—the walk that made her look like she was flowing rather than stepping. She studied other women who passed by in the street and soon fell into the same ungraceful walk.

Twenty-five minutes later, they reached the gate of a low building in a busy street that housed many machine shops. Cars and trucks crowded it from every direction. Albert opened the gate with a big, old-fashioned key and stepped inside, followed by Dan and Claire. The white Toyota pickup truck waited there, and the three climbed inside. Albert started the engine and drove out without bothering to lock the gate after him.

"Where are we going?" Dan asked.

"We are going north to a suburb of Suez called El Ganayen. It's a bit risky because we need to take the Al Sweis-Ismailia road to get there, but I have listened for quite some time to the police radio this morning, and it seems safe. My friend's home is in the government district, not far from the El Ganayen district presidency and its police department, the last area where they will be looking for you."

"Clever," Claire commented.

"It will be clever if we get there without incident," Albert concluded with a smile.

CHAPTER 37

The drive to the safe haven was nerve-wracking for Dan and Claire. Albert drove recklessly "to be in character," he explained, and every turn seemed to be a recipe for collision. Just outside the city, they ran into a police truck that was setting up a checkpoint, but since the equipment was not yet in place, the two policemen who were downloading it from the vehicle only gave them a bored glance when Albert passed them, slowing down as he did so.

"Don't stop!" Dan whispered from behind his veil.

"I'm not stopping," Albert whispered back. "We are invisible local people to them, but if I drive by too fast, they may think that I have something to hide. Then they'll take an interest and stop us."

To Dan's surprise, Claire grasped his hand and squeezed it. She had been so quiet up to that point that Dan had come to envy her relaxed attitude. Now, he was almost relieved to see she was as tense as he. He squeezed her hand back to comfort her. "I may need this hand to function again in the future," he whispered from under his veil, extracting a giggle from Claire just as the truck picked up speed again.

After a few minutes, they reached the gate of an imposing villa, set a little apart from other houses that all had the unmistakable appearance of luxury. The street was clean and green with vegetation; each house had ample ground around it. The one they were about to enter had a high stone wall, and its discreet main entrance was at a wide angle with the gate so that little was visible from the outside. Albert spoke in Arabic into an intercom, and the gate opened. He drove to the side of the house, killed the engine, and stepped down, beckoning them to follow him. They circled the building, and the door opened as they reached the entrance.

"Mister Albert," said the man on the mat. He was tall, lean, and dark-skinned, of an undefined age but well over fifty. He dressed in simple khaki trousers and a white shirt with wooden sandals.

"Omar," Albert answered. "Good to see you."

"I've been waiting for you. Please come inside," he said, speaking with a perfect British accent. He turned his attention to Dan and Claire and added, "You may want to get rid of those rags."

Inside, the foyer was pleasantly dark and cool, and Dan and Claire immediately stripped themselves of the heavy disguises.

"We have lost our baggage," said Dan, who felt the need to apologize for their appearance. "What we wear is all we have. It's pretty dirty, I'm afraid."

"I'm sure I can find something for you in my master's rooms. He and his wife are abroad but have plenty of good clothes. Meanwhile, I have prepared a light meal for you if you wish."

"You're a savior!" said Claire. "Bring everything you have. It feels like I haven't eaten in a month."

Omar led them to a spacious dining room with a table that could seat at least fifteen and left, promising to return in a minute.

"What is the deal with Omar?" Dan asked Albert.

"Oh, he likes to play the humble servant, but he is more like a right hand for my friend and runs much of his business. He got his education in England—I believe he has a master's degree in economics—and has many other hidden qualities."

"As long as he brings food, I don't care about his other qualities," said Claire, cheerful for the first time in days.

"I was wondering about his English. He doesn't sound like an Arab at all," said Dan. "If you brought us here, I assume that we can trust him?"

"You can trust him with your life. He, his boss, and I go a long way back. He'll take good care of you...oh, and here's the food," said Albert, ending the conversation for a while.

Twenty minutes later, Dan lay back, his belly full. He gave a deep sigh of contentment and turned to Albert. "So?"

"So now it's time for me to return to Cairo and work on getting you out of here."

"How long do we have to stay in this house?" Claire asked.

"I don't know, but it might take a while. A week or so, I guess. Is that okay with you, Omar?"

"No problem. I have sent the servants away for the rest of the week, and if we need more time than that, I'll tell them to stay home. Nobody will know that you are here, and we can take care of basic needs between the three of us. The house has supplies that can support ten people for at least a month so you won't starve."

"That's great, Omar. I don't think the police will bother you, but it would be best to be ready if someone shows up here. We don't want the neighbors to know that you have company."

"Don't worry. The safe room is in order, and I'll show them how to use it later. It's a room with a concealed entrance," he explained, turning to Dan and Claire. "You can hide if anyone comes snooping around."

Albert got up and shook hands with Dan and Claire. "I'll be leaving now," he said. "Dan, please come with me to the car. I have something I want to show you."

As they got outside, Albert switched to Hebrew. "I wanted to ask you about Claire. Do you trust her?"

"Of course, I trust her," said Dan, perhaps a bit too emphatically.

"Because we will need to do some things to get you out of Egypt that may be dangerous. We don't want to discover that she has an agenda we don't know about when we are in a tight spot."

"She doesn't. She wants out just as much as I do."

"Well, I had a feeling..." began Albert. He hesitated. "But I assume that I was wrong. I trust your assessment. Take care and be patient until you get word from me, okay?"

"Okay," said Dan, and they shook hands again.

Back in the dining room, Claire and Omar waited for him in silence.

"What did he want to show you?" Claire asked.

"Nothing important. He wanted to make sure that I wouldn't get impatient and do something stupid while he was gone. I guess he felt that telling me that in Hebrew was more convincing."

Omar got up and spoke, still keeping up the humble manner of speech that contrasted with his forceful personality. "If you wish now, I could gather some clothing for you and show you where you can take a shower," he said.

"Shower!" Claire cried. "You said the magic word. Lead me to it!"

Dan jumped out of bed and realized that it was already evening. He felt fresh and rested after a long nap in a cool room, coming on top of a long, luscious shower. The room, located on the house's second floor, was the first of a row of three placed on each side of a corridor. A dim wall light was the only illumination available. Standing at the top of the stairs, Dan listened to the house noises, trying to hear activity sounds. But everything was silent. He descended the stairs and saw a note on a low, round table that said, in big, block letters, "I HAVE GONE OUT FOR A COUPLE OF

HOURS TO GET SUPPLIES. WILL BE BACK SOON. OMAR."

That explained the silence, at least in part, but where was Claire? Walking toward the back of the house, he saw an open French window leading to the inner garden enclosed within the property's high walls. The sound of sloshing water filtered through the French window, and Dan walked toward it. A small swimming pool, no more than five feet deep, was in the middle of the garden, only a few paces from the house. In the middle of the pool, Claire was splashing like a kid. She was wearing a white T-shirt and blue shorts and stopped frolicking upon seeing him.

"Good morning!" she said jokingly. "You've caught up with your sleep, haven't you?"

"Yes, I just got up."

Dan felt embarrassed at the sight of Claire's wet shirt sticking to her breasts, leaving little to the imagination, but she didn't seem at all self-conscious.

"Come on in, then. The water is cool and feels amazing," she said.

Dan was wearing orange shorts and a light blue T-shirt that he had selected from the pile of clothing Omar had left on his bed. After a brief hesitation, he took off the T-shirt and jumped in. "It's bloody cold!" he protested.

"Oh, don't be a wimp. The whole idea is to be cool in this infernal weather. You'll get used to it in a minute."

He started sloshing through the water to keep moving until his body got used to the temperature. As soon as he was comfortable, he perched against the pool wall.

"We must keep our voices down," he cautioned. "We don't want anybody to know that this house has guests."

"You're right," said Claire, turning serious. She waded toward him and spoke in an undertone. "Isn't this beyond surreal?" she said. "I mean, just a little while ago, a smelly brute was about to kill me. And now we're here, guests of a mysterious, magnificent host, cooling off in his swimming pool while the whole Egyptian police are looking for us elsewhere. If it weren't for you..."

"What?" Dan asked when she stopped speaking.

"Things might have taken an altogether different turn," she said. "They still might...We've run away from both Leskov and Bshari, and I expect that either one would skin us if he caught us. At this point, we can kiss the reward for the staff goodbye, which means that all this trouble has been for nothing. The best we can hope for is to make it home alive."

"Don't be pessimistic. We have Albert and Omar in our corner, and we've managed fine so far."

"And I have you in my corner," Claire added. Her expression softened as if to emphasize her words.

"You sure do," said Dan.

He forced himself to look away from Claire's face. She was close to him, and he felt electricity in the air. Her right hand touched his shoulder, startling him into gazing straight into her eyes.

"Your shoulder is healing," she said, moving her fingers around it in a caressing touch.

"Much better, yes. Thank you. Things looked bad for a while, but as you see..."

"But you know that things could turn bad. It could happen tomorrow or two minutes from now, and then goodbye to poor old Claire." She stopped again and bit her lower lip before continuing. "That got me thinking. In fact, I've done a lot of thinking lately."

Dan didn't like the sound of it. Overthinking their situation could lead down an unhealthy road—to fear and despair, not to speak of stress that could bring Jack back again. "That's only natural," he said. "You have every right to be nervous after all you've been through."

"That's not what I meant. I started to think about what I'd miss if I died now. I asked myself what I had already missed because I put it off for later or because I and people around me are conditioned to follow rules that sometimes don't make sense and make us go against our will. Don't you ever think about it?"

Claire's eyes were now gazing straight into his, and the world seemed to him to be moving in slow motion around them. He searched his head for a good comeback, but all he managed to articulate was: "And?"

"And do I have to spell it out for you?" she asked, getting closer, so the erect nipples under her wet shirt now touched his naked chest and sent a shiver along his spine.

He shook his head, and his lips formed a voiceless "No."

"Good," said Claire. Her hands went up to the back of his neck and pulled his head toward hers. She kissed him hungrily, pushing her body against his with strength.

When she released her hold and Dan could breathe again, he felt as if a strange power was surging in him, giving him an insatiable desire for Claire and the strength to satisfy it. It was as if she had passed a drug on to him with her kiss. His head swam, his heart pounded, and he had to find what to do with his hands before something in him exploded.

"Let's go up," he whispered, hugging her with strength for emphasis.

Claire pushed him gently back with a mischievous smile he had never seen on her before. "Your place or mine?" she asked.

CHAPTER 38

Dan awoke from a nightmare, panting, and he sat on the bed, trying to chase away the unpleasant feeling left by it. For the past two nights, Claire had snuck into Dan's room so as not to embarrass Omar. Although the Egyptian had received a European education, the country was still puritanical, where nonmarried couples were concerned. They preferred the inconvenience of being discreet over the need to canvas Omar's opinions on the subject. Dan was in heaven. While he had always felt attracted to Claire, he had also thought it was not reciprocated and repressed his aching need for her. He had learned as a teenager not to fret over things you can't have. How wrong he had been! But then, he had misread her time and again. She was different from every other woman he had known before—more mysterious and, at the same time, more forthcoming. He had a lot of work ahead of him if he wanted to learn to understand her.

Despite his happiness, Dan had one worry he could not share with Claire—that she might turn into Jack Jones while they were intimate. That led him to look at her and examine her in what he could only imagine she thought was a weird way. True, Jack was not supposed to emerge except in times of extreme and immediate danger. Still, he had surfaced in Portofino during a nice and quiet dinner without any particular reason. That could happen again. Little wonder, then, that he had nightmares in which Claire would reveal herself as a bearded old man.

That was what had woken him up now. He checked his watch, which said it was past two in the morning. Coming out of the mists of sleep, he realized that he was in bed alone and wondered where Claire was. He waited a few minutes, and when she didn't return, he concluded that she had not gone to the bathroom. He got up and went out into the corridor. Voices reached him from below, and he walked down the stairs gingerly, trying to locate the origin of the voices. At least two men were speaking, but there shouldn't be more than one man in the house. The voices were coming from the living room—a cozy room dotted with comfortable armchairs—and the words were unclear from the outside. He opened the door. The spectacle that awaited him left him speechless. Leskov and Claire sat in two armchairs, chatting, while two dark men stood by without participating in the conversation.

"Ah, Dan. Good to see that you're up," said Leskov in a friendly manner.

"What...why...what's going on?" Dan asked, addressing the question to Claire.

"Hi, Dan," said Claire, speaking in the deep, masculine voice that Dan dreaded. "Take a seat, and we'll explain."

"Jack?"

"Of course. It was lucky that Andrey was in the area, although it took me quite a while to get the word to him. The only phone number I had was that of his New York office. By the way, this is Karim, whom we were to meet in Cairo before Bshari's men kidnapped us. Last night, I came down and called Andrey's office. You were sleeping so well that I didn't want to disturb you, but we'll need to get going soon. It took some work for me to explain to Andrey what was going on with Claire and me, but fortunately, he is familiar with the technique that I have used on Claire and doesn't think I'm going off my rocker."

"Where is Omar?"

"Don't worry about him," said Leskov. "He's resting in his room. We gave him a shot that will keep him dreaming for at least twelve hours, and by the time he comes to, we'll be gone. Now for the plans. I want to introduce Major Hassan to you."

Hassan made an almost imperceptible nod with his head, acknowledging the introduction. Dan gaped at him.

"Major Hassan works for a dear friend of mine, who has been so kind as to place him in charge of our security. He is in civilian clothes because we don't want to advertise that the Egyptian army is taking part in our project, but his credentials will keep us safe, particularly since we know that Bshari's men are armed and dangerous. Jack has given me the details. Any questions?"

"Questions? I have a whole swarm of questions, but right now, I'd like to know what we are going to do next. You know that the police are looking for us..."

"No more, Dan. That was taken care of," said Leskov.

"That's a relief. So what is the plan?"

Dan was having trouble adjusting himself to the new situation. On the one hand, it seemed that being with Leskov was the safest bet—not that Dan had a vote—because at least he didn't seem to surround himself with murderers as Bshari did. But on the other hand, Bshari would not take their defection lying down, and he had already demonstrated how dangerous he could be. And then there was Claire.

In the last two days, she had infected him with a particularly virulent kind of teenage love. He needed her achingly, physically, just like a drug. Watching her and listening to her speaking like an old Irish professor was more than he could take.

"We leave in the morning at sunrise," Leskov concluded. "We still have three or four hours of sleep, so go back to your room because tomorrow may be a long day. We'll wake you up in time to get some food and organize a few necessary items. You too, Jack. Good night."

Dan and Jack climbed the stairs together, but Dan kept a safe distance from him. "Why did you go to Leskov behind my back?" he asked pointedly.

"Well, you were asleep, and by the time I finished my call and came up, it was time for Claire to be back again. She knows nothing about all this. By the way, it surprised me to find you sleeping in the same bed."

"Did you...?"

"No, of course not," said Jack. "I never intruded on your privacy, and I couldn't even if I wanted to. Now it's better if I come to sleep with you, so Claire wakes up in your bed in the morning. You'll need to start explaining about me to her first thing. It may come as a shock to her, so please be gentle."

When they reached Dan's room, Jack stretched himself on the bed.

"Go to the edge!" Dan commanded. "Keep your distance."

"Don't be so edgy, Dan. I'll be Claire again in a minute, and then you won't wish me so far away. Now let me sleep."

CHAPTER 39

Dan barely managed to rest. He woke up every few minutes to check on Claire, who was peacefully asleep. A bright first light filtered through the window, and Claire stirred. She turned from one side to the other, now facing Dan, who was resting on one elbow and watching her.

"Good morning," she said, smiling.

"Hi," he answered. He dreaded the moment he would have to tell her of the uninvited dweller in her brain, which had come too soon. All his energy was going into finding a way to start.

Claire sat up and leaned forward to kiss him, to which he responded mechanically.

"Stop brooding and greet me with a proper 'good morning,'" she demanded.

"Honey...there is something I need to tell you," Dan answered, not looking at her. "Something complicated. Do you want to go and wash your face first?"

Claire jumped out of bed and gave him a piercing look. "You're too serious for this time in the morning. What is it? No, wait! I'm in no shape to hear bad news before I brush my teeth. I'll be back in a minute."

She ran away, and Dan was grateful for the respite, brief as it would be. At least now she knew that something unpleasant was coming. The room had two comfortable armchairs facing the bed, and he sat in one of them, waiting. Five minutes later, Claire was back, and after a quick glance at him, she sat in the other one.

"What?" she asked.

"It's kind of complicated, but I'll try to explain. Please be patient."

"Will you stop beating about the bush?"

"Yes, sorry. You told me how Jack Jones used techniques he had learned at the KGB academy to impress information on you. Do you remember him doing anything else besides the key that he showed you?"

"No, I don't. There were preparative sessions when he hypnotized me or something like that...he induced sleep and injected me with some kind of drug that he said I needed to create the hidden neural paths—that's what he called them—so part of the time, I was asleep. Besides that, nothing."

"That was enough." Dan paused, still debating how to break the news to her. "You said that Jack was dead," he said at last. "Well, the fact is that he is not quite dead yet."

"This is hogwash. He's dead and buried. *I* buried him."

"I know. He may be dead in the flesh, but he's left his personality behind." Dan paused again, struggling. "He has found a way to go on living in somebody else's body. He injected his personality into someone so he could go on living—kind of."

"Are you saying...are you saying that he did that to me?"

Dan took her hand and looked into her eyes. She was taking it well, but he was afraid that she would snap once she realized what it all meant.

"Yes, he impressed his personality into your brain, and it now resides there. You can't see or feel it, but it's there."

"How do you know?" Claire jumped up, pulling her hand away and taking a step back. "Since when have you known?"

"Please sit down, Claire."

"Forget 'sit down'! How do you know this, and since when?"

"Since that night on the mountain. He revealed himself to me then. He explained that he had done it to watch over you because he loved you like his own daughter. He only surfaces when you are in danger. And you two cannot be conscious at the same time."

"Why didn't you tell me before?"

Claire's rage was mounting. Dan searched for a way to soothe her.

"Didn't you have enough cause for stress and worry? Was I supposed to add to that with this uncanny situation? I was trying to shield you as much as I could. I care about you so much," he said, almost choking on the words.

"I'm not a baby, okay? You don't need to shield me from anything. You need to be honest with me, or I won't be able to trust you anymore."

"I agree, a hundred percent. I didn't mean to keep it from you. I was biding my time, waiting for the best time to tell you. And I have told you, haven't I? Please come here," he said, extending a hand.

Claire's rage seemingly evaporated. "Apology accepted," she said, coming to sit on his lap. "But next time you keep something from me, there will be hell to pay. Understood?"

"Yes, sure. But you haven't heard the half of it."

"Now, I'm worried. Keep talking."

"It wasn't me who killed Rafik. It was Jack. I took the credit to spare you the shock, and that was Jack's idea."

"So I killed him! I'm not sure if I should feel happy or freak out."

"It wasn't you. It was Jack, using your hands. You bear no responsibility."

"So why are you telling me this now, before breakfast?"

"I'm afraid that breakfast won't be the usual happy hour," said Dan, looking apologetic. "Jack has pulled a fast one on us. He surfaced last night, and without letting me know, he called Leskov, who is now sleeping in one of the other rooms. He has a couple of bad characters with him. He wants us to leave early this morning for the Mitla Pass."

"The son of...It's a pity I can't give Jack a piece of my mind. What did he do it for?"

"I must tell you that I don't think that Jack has all his marbles. But at least he didn't get us in trouble with Leskov. Leskov thinks we couldn't wait to hitch up again with him, and he's all friendly. If we had to choose between the two, I think he may be better than Bshari, as long as we are pals and cooperate. Besides, one of the thugs he has brought along is an army officer who works for some influential Cairo general. He's called off the police search after us, so at least we have that off our minds."

"What else should I know about Jack?"

"A few more things."

Dan relayed everything Jack had said, and Claire considered the news for a long minute before speaking again. "This is a mess, you know? How do I get rid of Jack? I don't want any piece of him in my brain!" she said desperately.

"Frankly, I don't know—but since what he did was KGB stuff, we could ask Leskov to help after we find the staff."

"If we find the staff," Claire qualified.

"*When. If* is not an option here."

They both became silent, and Claire stroked the back of Dan's head. Then she gazed straight into his eyes.

"You know, when you said that you had something serious to tell me, I thought you were going to tell me that we don't belong together. I don't think I could have taken it. Does this Jack thing... if I can't get rid of him, will it get between us?"

"Please don't worry. Nothing will get between us. I promise we will get rid of him, but even if we don't..."

"Shh..." Claire placed her index finger on his lips. "Don't make promises you may not be able to keep. What we have is enough for the time being." She kissed him fondly and then pulled back. "Now, let's go and get some breakfast. I'm starving."

CHAPTER 40

Breakfast was a somber affair, with Leskov eating in unusual silence. With Omar not there to cook, Karim was functioning as the host—and his kitchen talents were rudimentary. Even so, Dan and Claire ate the overcooked eggs and drank the reasonable coffee on the table. As soon as the food had disappeared, Leskov came out of his silence.

"Ready to go?" he asked.

"Yes, Andrey," said Dan. "But what is the plan for today?"

"Let's look at the map."

Leskov spread a large map of the Sinai Peninsula on the table and studied it.

"As I understand it, the place we are looking for should be in the Bi'r el-Hasnah area, right?" he asked.

Dan considered the map at length before answering. "That is what I remember. It should be somewhat southwest of it. That area is full of caves, and the one we are looking for should be west of this road here, the one that the map names Sadr Al Haytan-Al Hasna. I can't be more specific than that. It has been a long time since that one day."

"So what do you think that we should do? Which way to go?" Leskov asked.

"We should cross the Mitla Pass on Road 50, just until Sadr Al Haytan-Al Hasna Road branches out," said Dan, pointing to the location on the map. "Then, we should follow it, hoping I'll recognize the place."

"Where did you abandon your tank?" asked Claire.

"It was more or less here," said Dan, pointing to a place east from the branching roads.

"Then we could take Road 50 until Nekhel and then go north on Road 55," suggested Hassan.

"That would get us to Bi'r el-Hasnah faster, but I wouldn't be able to find my way to the cave," said Dan. "I never got so far east. I didn't follow the road and never crossed it, so it must have been on my right...I mean, east of me, all the time."

"So, what do you suggest?" asked Leskov.

"The first step is to find where my tank got hit and then retrace my steps. I can see no other way."

"That means that we won't be able to make it in one day," Leskov concluded. "We will have to stay the night somewhere near the pass. No problem, though. We are equipped for it. Let's get ready."

They all got up and walked out. Claire and Dan each had a little bag with clean clothes taken from the owners' walk-in closet. Dan had felt bad about taking them, but Claire had pointed out that there was nowhere else they could get clean clothes, and she was sure the owners, knowing the circumstances, wouldn't mind. Dan was not so sure and only took the least elegant outfits he could find.

"Close the door," Leskov said to Karim as they left. "We don't want any bad characters to find their way into the house." He laughed at his own joke.

A portable radio emitted indistinct Arabic words from one of the Jeeps. Hassan picked up the receiver and spoke into it. A response came over a lot of static, and he threw the receiver back into the vehicle.

"Bad news," he said, turning to Leskov.

"What now?"

"I just got word that Bshari is in the area and is not alone. He has men with him, and I bet he is armed."

"That's good news, I think," said Leskov. "Just as your men stopped me at the checkpoint, you can have the police arrest him."

"Bshari has powerful friends," Hassan objected.

"I understand, but if he and his men carry weapons, you can arrest them and at least confiscate them, right?"

"You don't understand. You don't arrest a man like Bshari. We can't do it."

"Are his friends more influential than your general, then?" asked Leskov.

Hassan shook his head. "They are influential persons in Cairo. Powerful. We won't step on their feet."

"So what can we do?" asked Leskov.

"We will have to get an armed escort to keep Bshari away. We'll go to the checkpoint, and I'll commandeer an escort from the soldiers there."

"More waste of time! That will take us at least two hours," Leskov complained.

"It can't be helped," said Hassan, climbing onto the Jeep.

Leskov had two long-chassis Jeeps with him. He motioned Dan to the first one and sat in front, with Hassan at the wheel. Karim drove the second vehicle, on which they loaded the heavier equipment. Leskov sent Claire to sit with him. Two AK-47 Kalashnikov machine guns were perched against the front passenger's seat of the first vehicle, and Leskov patted them affectionately.

"Still the best gun to use in the desert. Never clogs, always shoots. Best Russian industry," he added with pride as if he had manufactured the guns himself.

"Mmm." Dan felt obliged to agree with the man. He wasn't in

the mood for conversation, but he didn't want Leskov to think that he was brooding.

Leskov had been too optimistic. Commandeering an armed escort took much longer than the two hours he had complained about. They waited for Hassan to return, seated in the same room where Leskov had spent the night at the checkpoint. Strong coffee and some tasty date-filled pastries were the only redeeming feature of the place. But the hospitality did nothing to placate Leskov, who paced the floor like a lion in a cage. It was almost three p.m. when Hassan returned.

"We have the escort waiting for us. We can go," he said.

"We have wasted the whole day," Leskov snarled.

"So, what do you want to do about it?" Hassan enquired.

Leskov made a dismissive gesture, and they got up and left. Outside, an army vehicle waited, one soldier at the wheel and another standing behind a machine gun. Everybody mounted their Jeeps, and the army vehicle followed as they drove away. They drove south and soon reached the entrance to the Suez Canal Tunnel. A couple of bored policemen watched the entrance without apparent purpose and paid no attention to them.

At the exit from the tunnel, they drove on the main road, then turned left until they reached the junction with Road 50, where all signs of human presence ended, and the majestic, yellow, and monotonous desert began. Dan couldn't help but feel excited seeing the places that had witnessed a war that had changed so much in him. He kept staring right and left, trying to identify areas where he had stood or through which he had traveled, but everything was so empty that once the Suez Canal was no longer in sight, orientation was next to impossible.

· · ·

Hidden behind a small hill at the Mitla Pass opening, Bshari watched the little procession of Leskov's vehicles moving toward the pass.

"They got the army involved!" he cried in anguish.

"So?" asked Schmidt, who watched the scene through giant binoculars.

"So it's hopeless! You can't get in a fight with the army. Besides being better armed than we, the army is strong, and I would never dream of confronting them. To get such an escort, Leskov must have pulled strings with high brasses."

"Do you mean to say that you give up?" asked Schmidt.

"Do you think that I want to? I don't have a choice."

"How much was the bonus you promised me for getting you the staff or destroying it?"

"You know very well that I promised you one million euros."

"Double it and leave me one Jeep with your best man as a driver, and I'll get it for you."

"You are crazy! You can't do it. They are many, and you would be alone."

"That's my problem. Double it!" Schmidt insisted.

"I'll double it. But if you get caught, I've never seen you, and I don't know you."

"It's a deal," said Schmidt.

They walked back to the side road where the Jeeps were waiting, and Bshari took Muhammad aside and spoke a few words to him. Then he got into his Jeep and drove away toward Suez.

CHAPTER 41

Leskov's Jeep stopped where the path joined a small dirt road. He jumped down, and the others did the same.

"We are three-quarters into the pass," he said, addressing Dan. "You need to lead from here."

"We were stationed there," said Dan, pointing north, "and our task was to cover the pass and stop Egyptian troops from crossing it. I think I can see the exact place where my tank stood, but the sands have shifted over the years, and the dunes have changed their shapes, so I'm not sure. I will have to find the spot and then go on foot, trying to retrace my steps. That's the only way that I can find the cave."

"Mister Leskov," Hassan intervened, "if that is what you want to do, I suggest we camp near here and start early tomorrow morning. It is almost five in the afternoon now, and we won't be able to go far in the dark. And if we start following at walking speed, by dark, we may be in a place where setting up camp won't be easy. I recommend we follow this side road a little and camp off the main road."

"What you say makes sense, Major," Leskov agreed. "I hate to wait, but I agree that we will need a few hours to locate the cave, and we don't have enough light for that today. Let's go and set up camp, as you suggested."

They turned into the dirt road and drove until the pass was no longer in sight, then they stopped and started to unload their equipment. The escort took position a little farther away from them. Karim approached Dan.

"Please give me a hand erecting Andrey's tent," he said.

The tent was big and had a heavy-duty aluminum frame, pegs, wooden mallet, canvas bag, and pole bag. It took them half an hour to erect. As soon as they finished, Karim brought from the Jeep a folding table complete with two chairs and a small generator, which he connected to a lightbulb that hung at the center of the tent. Then, he inflated a mattress and placed a sleeping bag on it. Leskov walked into the tent and nodded with approval.

"I'm surprised you don't have an air conditioner in this tent," said Dan.

"Not enough room for it in a Jeep," said Leskov. Sarcasm was lost on him, as usual.

The temperature dropped by the minute, and Hassan lit a portable gas stove and filled a pot with water. "I'll make coffee," he said, "and I suggest we eat now."

Karim brought a box with sandwiches and water bottles, which he handed out to everybody except for the escorts. They sat around the stove, eating silently, while Leskov had dinner in the tent. Later, while Karim passed coffee around, they got into a conversation. At Hassan's request, Dan spoke briefly about his war experience as Claire and Karim listened.

"It is time to sleep," Hassan said at last. "Tomorrow, we will start early. Karim," he added, "my tent has room for two. I invite you."

"Thank you very much," said Karim.

"I'll sleep in the Jeep," said Claire.

"I'll take the other one," said Dan.

"Good night," they said to each other, and Hassan stopped the gas flow to the stove and extinguished the fire.

Dan's watch showed the time as two a.m. when Claire shook him awake.

"Oh, I'm glad you're here," he said. He placed a hand around her shoulder and pulled her to him, but she resisted.

"This is not a good time," she whispered. "Look here," she added, handing him a piece of paper. On the paper, she had traced a straight line along which she had written numbers that looked like hour notations.

"What is that?" Dan asked.

"That is trouble. It started as we left the tunnel. At one point, I noted that the surroundings had changed from a moment before, and when it happened again, I understood what was happening: Jack was surfacing for a little while, and I was losing the feel for part of the trip."

"That's weird. Jack only surfaces in times of danger when you are tense or stressed. There was nothing of that during the trip."

"That's not completely true," said Claire. "You told me that he surfaced for a minute in Portofino when we were having dinner."

"You're right. I thought that was a fluke because it never happened again."

"You don't know that," Claire pointed out.

"But what are these notations here?"

"I kept looking at my watch and marked every time I saw a time jump—a gap in the time I was following, which meant that Jack had taken possession during that interval. Besides, I had these jumps in the landscape, which confirmed the switch."

"But...according to this, he switched twelve times in three hours."

"That's what it is...I'm scared, Dan."

Dan pulled her toward him, and this time, she let him hug her.

"We'll deal with that, don't worry. Tomorrow, it will all be over. As soon as we are back, we'll get rid of Jack."

"How?"

"What was done by artificial means can be undone. Jack himself told me so. The doctors will find a way."

"And if they don't?" Claire's eyes filled with tears, and Dan kissed them, then kissed her lightly on her lips. "They will. We will," he said.

"Do you love me? No, don't answer that!" she said. "It's not the right time for this kind of question. I'm sorry, I shouldn't have asked."

"You know I do," said Dan, speaking with fervor. "I can't bear the thought of a single day without you. You're bright, funny, warm..."

"And I keep making stupid mistakes that get us into trouble," she interjected.

"You're real. Real and human, that's what it is." Dan was having trouble controlling the emotion in his voice. "So don't doubt for a second that I love you."

Claire stopped the flow of words by kissing him, and he felt the tears on her cheek. They sat in silence for a minute, united in an uncomfortable embrace in the backseat of the Jeep, and then Claire straightened up and wiped her eyes. "I'd better go back to my Jeep. We don't want to fall asleep together."

"Actually, we do want it, but we can't," said Dan, attempting a smile.

"You know what I mean," she said, giving him a weak smile.

She slipped out through the Jeep's door and away. It took Dan a long time to go to sleep again.

CHAPTER 42

Karim shook Dan awake at a quarter to six. Everybody was up and about, and coffee was cooking on the gas stove. Dan went to wash his face and brush his teeth and then joined the others for a cup of coffee. A repeat of the previous night's sandwiches was their breakfast, and in half an hour, they were organized and ready to move.

"You need to direct me now," said Hassan.

"Do you see that red streak beside that dune?" Dan asked, pointing in the direction. "Drive there."

Hassan nodded, and the Jeep bounced forward. Once they reached the place he had indicated, Dan jumped down and started to look around. He walked right and left of the Jeep until he finally stood and signaled Hassan to approach.

"This is where my tank got hit. This place is etched in my memory. I recognize these rocks here. I remember thinking that that one looks exactly like the profile of my physics teacher. I'll start walking. Come after me but not too close in case I need to change direction."

"Understood," said Hassan, and Dan started to walk.

They went on for three hours before Dan stopped and approached the Jeep.

"What's the matter? How close are we?" asked Leskov.

"I need to fill my canteen, and I'm getting hungry. Why don't we take a break and get some food?"

"How close are we?" Leskov insisted.

"I think that from this point, it should take us two hours, maybe less, to get there...if I don't miss a turn, that is."

It was sandwiches again, which they ate in the little shade offered by the nearby rocks. Claire sat by Dan and got close enough to speak without being overheard.

"How's it going?" Dan asked, speaking in an undertone. "Any surfacing?"

"A couple," Claire answered in a whisper. "Less than yesterday."

"Good, good. Maybe yesterday was because of all the commotion you had..."

"Hmm, I don't know. Are we getting near it?"

"I think we're close. Unless my memory is playing tricks on me. Do you see that dune over there?"

"Yes?"

"The cave must be behind it. I recognized that rock over there," he said, pointing to it. "The one that looks like a sheep. We should be there in twenty minutes, but I needed this break, so I estimated a couple of hours."

"How do we know that the box is still in there?" Claire wondered.

"We are in the middle of the desert. Nobody comes here for fun. Besides, there must be a hundred caves in this area. And if someone found the box and tried to open it without the key, we'll find him or what's remaining of him there."

"I just want this to be over," said Claire.

"It will be. Leskov will get his stupid staff today, and tomorrow, you and I will be free agents again. And if Leskov makes good on his word, there will be enough money for us to take a long vacation. Just you and me."

"Oh, Leskov always keeps his word and is not stingy with money. I have to hand that to him. He will pay up. And then it's you and me...and Jack."

She took his hand and squeezed it with anguish. Dan squeezed it back, trying to infuse optimism into it. "Screw Jack," he said. "We'll get rid of him."

"Dan!" came the imperious call from Leskov. "You have rested enough. Now let's move."

Dan got up and started to walk toward the dune on the horizon. When he reached it, he signaled Hassan to approach its left edge.

"I think this is it. I climbed the dune to get to the cave, but the Jeep will never make it that way. If I remember the topography correctly, we can climb it this way from the left. Let me in."

Dan got in the Jeep, and Hassan drove as directed, followed by the other two vehicles. The path on the left was rockier, and the Jeep got a good grasp on the ground. Two minutes later, they stood on an esplanade bound by the dune on their right. On their left was the opening of a cave.

Getting inside the cave and finding the box, which was on an elevated ledge and looked in good condition, only took a few minutes. It was an ancient burial cave like many others in the area. Sarcophagi had been laid on ledges like those that had hosted the box, but they were long gone, ravaged by grave thieves. Hassan and Karim lifted the box using the handles provided at the edges. It wasn't heavy, and they carried it out without great effort. Leskov, Dan, and Claire stood beside the cave entrance in the shade of the rocky formation. Dan let his mind wander to that day during the war. The esplanade on which the Egyptian BMP-1 had stood was empty, but he could almost see the vehicle with the soldier as he had seen them at first, crawling up the dune.

"What is that noise?" Claire inquired.

"It's the helicopter I rented to take the box safely to the airport. It followed the radio beacon we activated in the Jeep," said Leskov. "My private airplane is waiting there for me to take it back to Russia."

A few seconds later, a small R44 helicopter appeared in the sky. Karim triggered a smoke signal that he had placed at the center of the esplanade. The helicopter landed without difficulty, and the pilot got out and approached them.

"I'm ready to go back as soon as you wish," he told Leskov.

"Good. We will be departing in a matter of minutes," said Leskov. "Go back to the helicopter and get ready."

The pilot nodded and returned to his seat. Leskov turned to Claire.

"I can't wait to see it, Claire. You need to start studying the dial on the box."

"Ehm..." Claire responded in Jack's deep voice. "I somehow switched in without intention, and you need Claire for it."

"So, go away!" Leskov barked with ill-concealed annoyance. "Let Claire back."

"In a moment, Andrey. I'll sit down for a minute and relax, and she'll be back."

Jack sat with his back to the wall and closed his eyes. Three minutes later, he reopened them, looking embarrassed. "She isn't coming back. I'll need more time to relax," he said.

"What is that?" Dan asked. A noise like that of a whip had broken the silence of the desert.

"Look there, on that ridge!" Hassan cried. "Someone is shooting at us. He's too far away to be precise, but he still might hit us by chance."

The flash of a gun was now clearly visible on the distant ridge, and there was a sound of broken glass as the side window of the helicopter shattered. Hassan yelled orders to the military escort, and the vehicle disappeared down the dune. The pilot, frightened by the shooting, had turned on the engine and was getting ready to lift off. Leskov turned to Jack.

"There is no time for that. Karim, Hassan, take the box to the helicopter! It has room for three more, so Jack and Hassan, you come with me. Karim, you and Dan can take the Jeeps back to Cairo."

"No, Andrey. Claire is not going anywhere without me," Dan announced.

He grabbed an AK-47 that was propped against the wall and pointed it toward Leskov. Hassan had his own gun pointed at Dan.

"Don't be stupid," said Leskov. "We will proceed according to plan. If you don't stop pointing that gun at me, Hassan here will think nothing of shooting you. Get out of the way!"

"I won't. You can take the box, but Claire is coming with me. She'll open the box for you later."

"Dan," Leskov started to say.

"I'm sorry, Dan," were the last words Dan heard Jack's voice say, and then everything went black.

CHAPTER 43

The shadows were long when Dan came to. The place was deserted but for himself and one Jeep that Leskov had left behind. He brought himself to a sitting position with no little effort and remained there for five minutes, collecting his thoughts. His half-full canteen was next to him. He drank avidly from it and used a little water to wash away the dust his eyes had collected while he was out.

He felt stupid that he had not taken into account that Jack would take Leskov's side. He had acted on an impulse, and the situation had gotten out of hand. He realized that he had no time for recriminations—that time would come soon enough—but now he had to decide what to do. He got up and inspected the Jeep. There was no water or food in it and, of course, no weapons, but the key was in the ignition. He weighed his options and immediately discarded the idea of going after Leskov and back to Cairo. By now, Leskov would already be on his way to Moscow, and on the road to Suez, Dan could run into the maniac that had shot at them before. He didn't relish having to fight his way back when he didn't even have a pocketknife. No, he had to go east, toward Israel. Eilat was not much farther than Suez from where he was, and the border between Egypt and Israel was wide open there.

Although he knew the way to Eilat, he was glad to find a map in the Jeep that confirmed his memory. Eilat and Suez were more or less equidistant from where he was. He switched on the engine and started to drive. He wanted to make as much progress as possible before dark.

Nights in the desert can be pitch-dark if there is no moon, as was the case tonight, but driving by headlamps was dangerous because you never knew to whom you were advertising your presence. He had driven for about two hours on a trail that hadn't been traveled for a long time when he started to feel the strain of driving alone in the dark. Coupled with the fact that his head still ached with a dull, pulsating pain, it was too much. He stopped and closed his eyes, trying to wish away the pain. By time traveled, he judged that he was only about twenty miles from Eilat and wanted to get there as soon as possible, but prudence prevailed. By experience, he knew it would be easy to fall into a hole or off a cliff in the dark.

Dan woke at first light, feeling stiff and with the pain in his head that had extended to his neck. He took a gulp of the little water left in his canteen and started the engine. Five miles later, the engine began to splutter and then died. He had run out of gas, and the Jeep had no reserve tank. If one existed, Karim had taken it for his own vehicle. Left with no choice, he abandoned the Jeep and started walking in the general direction of Eilat.

Yusuf was always attentive to what went on around him, a habit he had acquired as a Bedouin scout in the Israeli army. He was on his way to an abandoned metal dump left by the military a few years back. He sold metal scraps for a living and knew he would collect enough copper for the day, so he did not need to hurry. Driving past what looked like a small heap of garbage in the desert that morning, he sensed something wrong. He stopped and put the gear in reverse until he reached the garbage again. His instinct had been right as always: It wasn't garbage; it was a body. He jumped down from his pickup truck and knelt beside it to inspect it. The man was still alive, but he had clotted blood on the back of his head and was running a fever. Yusuf didn't waste time asking himself questions. When the man failed to react to his calls, he lifted him up and carried him to the truck.

At the Yoseftal Medical Center in Eilat, the ER physician only needed to take a glimpse to see that the man was in critical condition. He wanted to know what had happened to the patient, but Yusuf didn't know. He also couldn't give a specific location where he had found him. "On the hills" was the best they could get out of him.

"The police will be here soon to write a report," said the ER nurse to Yusuf. "Wait here for them."

Yusuf nodded and watched as they took the wounded man from the ER to the intensive care unit, and then he left without leaving his name. He had his business to look after.

CHAPTER 44

Leskov was a man of his word. Returning to his Tel Aviv home from the hospital after a two-week recovery, Dan found a thick envelope from his lawyer with a note that told him that all his company's shares had been returned to him. He tossed the envelope on the kitchen table. Despite the news brought to him by his partners, who had visited him at the hospital to tell him about all the new deals they had signed, his mood was gloomy.

The company was finally doing well. Although the deal with Leskov had included buying his partners out, Dan had insisted on giving them some of his shares to keep them in the company. His generosity was paying off with the new deals they were bringing in. Between that and the money paid him by Leskov for the original agreement, his financial problems were over—but his mind was far from at rest.

His apartment felt cold despite the oppressive, humid heat of the late summer. He picked up the phone and dialed the only number that, at the moment, he felt like calling. "Hello," said a deep, welcoming voice at the other end.

"Zigi, it's me, Dan."

"Oh, hi. I meant to call you. Where are you?"

"I'm home. I need to talk. Can I come over?"

"Sure. My last patient has left, but I have some paperwork to do. Why don't you come to the clinic?"

"I'll be there in half an hour," said Dan.

Sigmund Froind—Zigi to his friends—was the only friend he had made during the war he had kept in contact with. The other two, who had been with him on the stolen Egyptian truck, had been killed just two days after returning to the army lines. With that name, given him by Austrian parents with a distorted sense of humor, it was almost inevitable that he should go on to become a psychiatrist. Besides working in a hospital, he had developed a lucrative private practice and kept an elegant office in a building in the center of Tel Aviv. By the time Dan got there, the secretary had left, and Zigi himself opened the door.

"Hi. You look good," he said. Zigi always looked like he was piercing your outer shell with his eyes, but Dan had grown used to it and didn't mind it.

"I'm okay now...at least from the physical point of view. Do you have time for a long story?"

"Listening to stories is what I do for a living," said Zigi in his usual soft-spoken manner.

They moved into Zigi's private office, and Dan sank into a comfortable armchair. "It all began when a Russian billionaire proposed to invest in my company."

Dan narrated the bare essentials, omitting the Claire–Jack double personality and Rafik's killing in the Egyptian desert.

"That's the general picture," said Dan at last, "but I've left out quite a few important details...I don't know if I should tell you the whole thing..."

"I'm here to listen to anything you want to tell me. So far, it sounds like a nice mess that you let yourself into. But now it's all over, right? I mean, you don't believe that nonsense about Moses' staff..."

"I no longer know what to believe, but I couldn't care less. Staff, shmaff, that's not the problem."

"I understand that it was a harrowing experience for you, particularly since you almost died in that desert. You did the right thing coming to me to get it off your chest, Dan. You know I'm a good listener."

"It's not just a matter of getting it off my chest. I don't doubt that you're a great shrink, but I didn't come here to get analyzed. I may need your help."

"Sure. You know you can count on me," said Zigi emphatically.

"There are some things that I didn't tell you that would get me into trouble if they became known...and I might be getting you into trouble by telling you. So, before I do, I need to make sure that you're okay with it."

"Oh, give me a break!" said Zigi. "I hear uncanny stuff every day. I'm sure that I can bear to hear it from you. Everything you tell me will be strictly under doctor-patient privilege. Go ahead and shoot."

"All right, here's the full story," said Dan. He filled in the remarkable tale of Claire's alternate personality and how it had nearly gotten him killed in the Sinai desert.

Zigi listened without interrupting. When Dan ended the story with his waking up in the hospital in Eilat, he said, "That's a pretty amazing tale. It would be hard to believe it if I didn't know you so well. Still, you got out of it okay, and I think that now is time for you to put it behind you."

"I wish I could."

"What...ah," said Zigi, with a grin. "We have a thing for the girl?"

"That's a hell of a way of putting it, but we do."

"Although she almost killed you, and she left you to dry up in the desert?"

"It wasn't her."

"Oh, yes, it was the Alter, you say. But are you sure? Patients with dissociative identity disorder sometimes behave erratically and often lie. How can you know that it was the Alter and not Claire herself?"

"I'm sure of that. I know she has feelings for me. She was trying to protect me as much as she could."

"Yes? Is that why she hasn't called you yet? It's been three weeks now."

"That's why I'm worried sick. Something must have happened to her, and I don't know what to do."

"You know, from what you are telling me, this Alter of hers was getting stronger. He may have become the dominant personality. That would explain why she hasn't got in touch with you."

"But is that possible? Jack Jones only surfaced in times of danger and then only briefly."

"It is possible. The literature well documents that in several cases, the Alter with a more dominant personality took over and repressed all other Alters, who were then pushed into the background. In some cases, they even disappeared forever."

"What do you mean 'disappeared forever'?" Dan asked, growing agitated.

"Let me check that my recollection is right. I have a book here..." Zigi got up and approached one of the shelves of his office, which sagged under the serious-looking books. He picked one and opened it, flipping through the pages until he reached a particular point and read for a while. "Here, I was right," he said at last. "I have multiple personalities case studies in this book, and here is one where the therapist was no longer able to evoke Alters who had previously manifested themselves. For all practical purposes, the patient had switched from multiple personalities to a single personality. However, the others were still in the background and made themselves known for short periods at times."

"But that's terrible! I don't know what to do. I was hoping to find Claire and bring her here—if I do, will you be able to help her?"

"I might, although that's not my specialty. I know better specialists than I in that field. But you don't know where she is. I suggest we weigh the therapy options after she gets back in touch with you...if she does. You know I'm your friend, Dan, so I must ask you to consider the possibility that this Alter—Jack as you call him—has already taken control. We can't rule that out."

Dan nodded in silence, deep in thought, and then he thanked his friend and left.

CHAPTER 45

Another week passed without a sign of life from Claire, and Dan started to think that he would have to make peace with her never coming back. If she didn't contact him soon, he resolved to find a way to contact Leskov and learn what happened to Claire from him. But his expectation of Leskov's willingness to help was low. That was going to be the last resort. He didn't want to believe that she would simply disappear and kept chasing the thought away, but he had to recognize the possibility that he would never see her again. Every time the phone rang in his apartment, which didn't happen often, he jumped up, hoping to hear Claire's voice. One evening, another familiar voice spoke at the other end of the wire.

"Dan?" said the voice.

"Is that you, Albert?"

"Yes, it is. It's good of you to recognize my voice."

"Where are you?"

"I'm in Tel Aviv. How are you doing, Dan?"

"I'm...okay, I guess."

"We need to talk," said Albert.

"What about?"

"Some things that need winding up."

"Okay, ask away."

"Not by phone. Let's meet. I know this nice and quiet café. We can have a coffee and chat. What do you say?"

"You know, I don't feel like it."

"I understand you have gone through difficult times, but I still need to meet you."

"And what if I don't want to?"

"You want to."

"Why?"

"Because. We can't leave loose ends, and neither can you."

Dan sighed and stared at the phone cradle as if it held the answers.

"All right. Give me the address," he said at last.

The café was small and crowded, and Albert waited at a small, round table. *Is this where we should be talking about confidential matters?* Dan wondered. Albert looked completely different in jeans and a polo shirt than the Arab-looking peasant he had met in Suez, but he immediately recognized his cheerful face. They shook hands and sat down.

"So, what do you want to know?" Dan asked.

"Straight to the point, ah? No small talk. All right. I just got back from Egypt, or I would have called sooner. I want to know how you ended up almost dead in Eilat. And I want to know who killed Omar."

"Killed? Are you sure?" Dan whispered in shock. "They told me that they had drugged him to sleep for twelve hours."

"Who's they?" asked Albert.

"Leskov. He had two men with him. One was the Egyptian who works for him, Karim, and the other was an army officer named Hassan."

"Omar, rest his soul, will sleep forever," said Albert. "They cut his throat."

"Bastards!" Dan exclaimed.

"Bastards is right. So you didn't know about it?"

"I told you I didn't."

"And how did Leskov find you? Did you call him?"

Dan hesitated. Telling Albert the truth might put Claire in danger. Nobody would believe the double personality story on his say-so. "I don't know," he said at last. "I think the police may have found out where we were and told that officer, Hassan. Anyway, they came in the middle of the night and took us with them."

"So, where is Miss Williams?"

"I don't know that either. Leskov kidnapped her after we retrieved the box, and that's when I got clubbed on the head and left to die in the desert. Somehow, I managed to get to Eilat—don't ask me how, exactly, because I can't remember—and here I am."

"That's a neat story, Dan. It doesn't square out in my view, but it's neat. For now, I'll give you the benefit of the doubt, but don't play with me, okay?" Albert got up and handed Dan a piece of paper. "If anybody connected with this story contacts you, call this number and ask for Albert. We'll be keeping an eye on you."

"Keep as many eyes as you want. I couldn't care less," said Dan.

"Take care," Albert said and left.

CHAPTER 46

The days passed. Dan tried not to think about Claire. She could be anywhere, with or without Leskov. He kept himself busy working hard and keeping long hours, so much so that he was always the last to lock up the office. On the third Thursday night after his return to work, the office phone rang.

"Yes?" he answered in his characteristic curt manner.

"Dan..." Claire's unmistakable voice said at the other end of the line.

"Claire? Claire, where are you? Why haven't you called me until now?"

"Dan, please come take me. Please come. Come now. Please..."

"Where are you? Tell me where you are, and I'll come right away."

"I'm in Lausanne, Switzerland. Please come..."

"The address. Give me the address!"

"Rue...Rue Gaston. I don't know the number. It's a big house. Red-brown door. Lots of geraniums in the windows. Black Mercedes. Please come..."

Claire's voice sounded weak, and she only mumbled a few words.

"I'll be there as soon as I can. Give me the phone number."

"The phone number..."

A long silence followed, and a deep, masculine voice said, "Who's that? Who's calling?"

"Jack?" Dan whispered into the phone.

"Yes. Who's there?" came the answer.

Dan held the phone away from his ear, uncertain about what to do next. He stared at it until he heard the click on the other end.

In the three hours after Claire's call, Dan paced the room, drank Coke, and tried to decide what to do. Several plans raced through his mind, and he picked up the phone twice to call Zigi and share them with him before realizing that each plan had a fatal flaw. A knock on the door brought him back to the present. On the mat was a tall, dark, lean man whom he immediately recognized.

"Good evening, sir," he said, "my name is Hamid, and—"

"I know who you are," Dan interrupted him.

"Mister Bshari sends his regards."

"Tell him to go to hell," said Dan. He started to close the door, but Hamid's shoe was already in.

"You need to listen to me," Hamid continued in his quiet, low voice. "I won't take up too much of your time, and it will be to your advantage."

"You don't have anything that I want."

"I believe I do," retorted Hamid. "It is about the phone call you received tonight."

"Which phone call?"

"You know the one to which I refer. The one that matters. May I come in? We can't have this conversation at the door."

"How do you know about the call?"

"Please, Mister Ze'evi. I'll answer all your questions, but not here."

Dan hesitated for a moment. "Wait here," he said. He closed the door and bolted it. He owned a gun he never carried, but this time, he needed it—if not for protection, then for comfort. He retrieved it from his bedroom and opened the door again.

"Come in," Dan said, moving aside. He pointed at the two facing armchairs in his living room, keeping the gun well in evidence.

"Who told you that I received a phone call?" Dan asked.

"Nobody," said Hamid.

"So how do you...wait a second! Is my phone bugged?"

"Please, Mister Ze'evi, don't get excited. None of my employer's interests contrast with yours, and, in fact, I believe that they are aligned."

"You work for Bshari."

"I do."

"And you also work for the Egyptian Embassy."

"There is no conflict between my different employers. Let me ask you something, Mister Ze'evi: What are your feelings about Moses' staff?"

"Feelings? I don't have any feelings. I wish I'd never heard of the damn thing, and I don't believe it is more than a hoax, anyway!"

"That's good. Then we can understand each other. Let me tell you how I see it. It is my understanding—but correct me if I'm mistaken—that you would like to find Miss Williams, who, as far as we know, is being held against her will by agents for Andrey Leskov. Am I right so far?"

Dan said nothing, giving only a slight nod.

"My employer, as you know, is eager to recover the staff—which Leskov holds captive, so to speak. We believe cooperating is in our mutual interest since Miss Williams appears to be a good link to the staff. Do you agree?"

"Why?"

"Because Miss Williams has the key that opens the box that holds the staff, so at some point, they will have to bring her to it. When they do, we will kill two birds with one stone: You will have found Miss Williams, and we will have found the staff. Then you can take her, leaving the rest to us."

"And you won't shed any tears if Claire is not there to open the box, and the staff gets blown to pieces, right?"

"I'll be frank with you. Our preference is to get possession of the staff and expose it for the fake it is. Failing that, we would be happy with its destruction. Of course, we would need Miss Williams for the better option, but not for the second."

"So, what do you want from me?"

"Mister Bshari would like to cooperate with you in this operation. He holds you in great esteem."

"Bshari is a lying, double-crossing son of a bitch!" Dan's voice betrayed his anger. "Holds me in great esteem, bah!"

"I don't think that being abusive will get you far, Mister Ze'evi. I suggest you take a realistic view of the situation."

"Practical? I'll be practical," Dan said, raising his voice and gesturing with the gun. "Get the hell out of here. Tell Bshari to stay away from me."

"Please don't be theatrical, Mister Ze'evi. That might have unfortunate consequences for Miss Williams," said Hamid, still speaking unctuously.

"Leave her out of this! This is between Bshari and me."

"You're wrong, and you will see it if you think straight. Suppose you can work with Miss Williams to help us locate and take possession of the staff. In that case, everybody will have a happy ending, except perhaps for Andrey Leskov. But if you don't...well, you understand."

"I don't," said Dan.

"You are obstinate, Mister Ze'evi. You appreciate that we can't allow Leskov to keep possession of the staff. Now, should anything happen to Miss Williams, something irreparable...there would be no way to open that box without blowing it up. You see?"

Dan jumped to his feet and stood, his face near Hamid's, red with anger.

"Don't you dare threaten Claire, you hear me? I'll show you..."

"I'm not threatening, Mister Ze'evi," Hamid said quietly. "But accidents happen, and I am not in a position to prevent them. I'm here as your friend, believe me—not your enemy."

Dan felt emptied of strength. He sat back in his armchair and took his head in his hand, thinking hard about all he had heard and trying to find something to do or say—but his mind was a blank.

"What do you want me to do?" he asked at last.

"It's simple. We had information that Miss Williams was in Europe, but our informant couldn't tell us exactly where and why. We now know that she is in Switzerland. I assume you were planning to go and find her even before my visit, so that's what you should do. We will keep an open communication line with you and be ready to help you once you find her and can get her to cooperate. We assume that we should stay away until you have reached an agreement with her. She may distrust us."

"She should. But what is she doing in Switzerland, and why do you think she hasn't opened the box yet? Maybe she did and *then* went to Switzerland."

"No, she didn't. As you know already, we have someone in Leskov's organization. He's reliable and close enough to Leskov to know that the box is still unopened but not enough to find out why. He heard vague talks about 'preparations' needed before opening it."

"So you need me to solve your problem for you."

"*Our* problem. As I said, our interests converge. And we will be ready to help when you need us. I'll give you phone numbers in Zurich and Geneva to call if you need help or when Miss Williams is ready to work with us."

"But what if she doesn't want to?"

"She will have to. As long as the staff is in Leskov's hands, she's in danger. Please don't do anything stupid, like trying to get away from us. She will be in danger wherever she is until the staff is disposed of. From Leskov and others, as you understand. There is no other way out but to do away with the staff, once and for all."

Dan realized, with a feeling of doom, that Hamid was right. Whatever the reason for the delay in opening the box, Leskov would likely lose patience soon and get hold of Claire, doing what it took to force her to open it. And if Leskov didn't do it, Bshari would make sure that the box's key would be gone forever. Bshari and Hamid were unaware of the Alter's existence and the problem that Jack presented, which worried Dan the most—and he wasn't going to tell them about it. Claire wasn't in Russia yet, so there was a chance to rescue her. But time was running out.

"All right. I'll work with you," said Dan at last. "Give me the details."

"Here, I have all the phone numbers you need on this paper," said Hamid, handing it to him. "Including my private number here in Tel Aviv. Feel free to call any of those if needed."

Dan nodded. He was too troubled to speak. Hamid got up and left with more unctuous words of farewell.

CHAPTER 47

Dan sat in his tight airline seat, holding a bag between his legs. There was a good reason for keeping his bag within reach: two small flasks filled with precious liquids.

"This bottle here contains hydroxyzine," Zigi had explained. "You should try this one first, injecting five milliliters. If, and only if, that doesn't work, you should switch to the other bottle that contains diazepam. It's very potent, so don't inject more than five milliliters, at least for the first time, and see how Claire reacts to it. The maximum recommended dose is thirty milliliters in twenty-four hours. And make sure to inject it deep into a muscle. The buttocks will be your best choice, or the thigh if that's not possible. Can you do that?"

"I took a course as a volunteer paramedic. It was a while ago, but I still remember how to give an injection."

"Good. I'll give you a few disposable syringes. Keep the stuff refrigerated whenever you can. If you get stopped with it, you must say you are epileptic and you need the drug on you at all times to inject if you feel you are about to have a seizure. Understood?"

"Yes," Dan had said, hesitating. "I appreciate this."

"I hope so," Zigi said, "given that if you're caught, and they trace this back to me, I would lose my license and very likely go to jail."

"I won't forget it," Dan said.

"Actually, try to forget I was ever involved. And now get the hell out of here, or you'll miss your flight."

So now Dan was on his way to Geneva on a Swissair flight, fighting the unreasonable fear that a flight attendant might snatch his bag from him and expose him at any moment.

"Have a nice flight," the pilot's voice had wished over the loud-speaker system. Dan didn't think he would.

Dan's fears proved unjustified, and after an uneventful flight, he got off the plane and out of Geneva's airport. He had rented an anonymous blue Audi and was now driving at moderate speed toward Lausanne. His head felt empty, and all he could do was drive mechanically until he reached the city limits and needed to start paying attention to the map.

Reaching his destination—a small three-star, family-owned hotel—turned out to be easier than he had thought. His room was so clean and smelled so good that, for a moment, he almost believed he was there on a well-deserved vacation. But time was working against him, and he had to move fast. He ate a quick sand-wich washed down with a Coke at the small hotel bar, dropped off the room key with its massive key ring at reception, and sat in the car to plan his route. The map of Lausanne that he had bought at the airport was on a large scale, and he had no trouble locating Rue Gaston—a winding street that ended at the city's edge. He still had to figure out which house was the right one, but he hoped that Claire's details would be sufficient to find it.

It took Dan fifteen minutes to reach Rue Gaston. Once there, he drove up the steep street at a slow pace, examining each house. By his third passage, he had narrowed down his choice to three houses clustered toward the top end of the street, so he parked his car at a small esplanade where the street ended onto a country road to continue his inspection on foot. The first villa he checked had many geraniums, a red-brown wooden door, a red Fiat, and three young kids playing in the yard. He discounted it and moved on. The next house, sunken in a sloping meadow with the entrance at a bend of the road, had to be it. He checked over the fence and saw a black Mercedes parked on a gravel path hidden from the road. Most of the window shutters were closed, and the house had an abandoned look, belied only by the car.

Looking for a vantage point from which to watch the house, Dan scouted a small grove some five hundred feet higher in the sloping meadow leading to it. The vegetation was tall at some points, and he had to walk through a nettled patch that left him itchy, but at last, he made it to the grove and positioned himself in a shady part from which he had a good view of the house below.

Everything was still and quiet around the house. In contrast, in the grove, mosquitoes and various other winged insects seized the opportunity to have a ball in his ears, nose, and hair. Dan ignored them and settled down to watch for signs of activity in the house below.

The distant sound of a slamming door woke Dan from a reverie. He was awake, but his mind was elsewhere. He saw a big man walking fast from the house toward the Mercedes. He got into the car and drove away. It wasn't much of an event, but at least it was some sort of activity. Dan checked his wristwatch and realized he had been sitting there for over four hours. The watch said five past six, and the long shadows of the trees left no doubt that it was late afternoon. Little wonder that his butt was hurting.

Another hour passed before the Mercedes returned and parked in the same spot as before. This time, the passenger's door opened to let out another man—or so Dan thought at first. The almost military short haircut and the man's clothing kept the illusion for a few moments, but something in the walk and the general appearance betrayed that a woman was under that disguise. Dan kicked himself mentally for not thinking to bring binoculars with him, but even with his naked eye, he was sure that it was none other than Claire. Still, his long watch had paid off, and he now knew that this was the correct house. He watched as the two went into the house, then made his way back to the street and walked to the villa's main entrance.

He hadn't budgeted for the presence of a second man. That could get in the way of injecting Claire with the drugs he was keeping in his pockets, which he hoped would induce a state of relaxation and bring Claire back to the surface. But perhaps he could get her by himself for the few moments needed to inject her —and, anyway, he had no other plan. He rang the bell and waited. The sound of heavy steps came from within, and the man he had seen driving the car opened the door. He was a full head taller than Dan and twice as broad at the waist. He gave him an expressionless gaze and said, "Yes?"

"I'm here to speak with Claire," said Dan.

"Who's there, Boris?" someone asked from within the house, and Dan felt a shiver running along his spine as he recognized Jack's voice.

"He says he wants to speak to Claire," said the man with a bass voice and a heavy Russian accent.

Lighter steps came from within, and then Jack appeared at the door. Seeing her transformed into a different person, wearing a man's clothes and deprived of her femininity, was harder for Dan to bear than he had imagined.

"Dan!" he exclaimed. "Well, well...good to see you in good shape. I had wondered..."

"What? If I had made it out of the Sinai desert alive?"

"More or less. You know I did my best to save you. I'm sure that Hassan would have shot you. That's why I had to hit you—

for your own good. I kept wondering if you made it out all right."

"You could have taken my side instead of knocking me out, but I'm not here to argue."

"So why are you here? What do you want, Dan?"

"I want to speak to you. In private," said Dan, glancing at Boris. "Can we go inside?"

"Jack," Boris started to say, but Jack's raised hand silenced him.

"It's okay, Boris. I know him. Let's go inside."

Jack moved aside, and Dan walked in. Jack motioned Dan to an armchair and seated himself in one facing him. Boris kept watching over them from the door but out of earshot.

"So?" said Jack.

"You know why I'm here."

"I can guess," said Jack with a sigh.

"I want Claire back."

"Not going to happen, Dan. You'd better make peace with that."

"But I don't understand you, Jack. Were you lying when you told me you loved Claire more than your own child and would always watch out for her happiness?"

"I said that, didn't I? No, I meant every word, and I still do."

"Well, then..."

"And that's what I'm doing. What you don't understand is that I *am* Claire. We are not different persons. I'm just another facet of her personality—an older and more mature one, who knows what's best for her—and I'm doing what is best for Claire, for me."

"I disagree because Claire never consented to be given a split personality, and I don't think that what she wants is to morph into an old man."

"Listen, Dan. When you're as old as I am, you will understand that life has to have meaning. Few people live a meaningful life, and even fewer can do the great feats that Claire will do soon. I'm sure you understand what it means, unraveling the secrets of the staff."

"Ah, yes, Moses' staff. That bullshit," said Dan, dismissing it with a wave of his hand.

"It's not bullshit at all, Dan. It's real, and it's within our grasp. The staff is in Russia now, well guarded by Leskov, and all we need to do is to bridge over a few missing pieces of information before we can open up the box to harness its power."

"What information? Claire never mentioned anything like that to me."

"What I didn't have the time to research back in '73 was the danger of damaging the staff and its power by taking it out of the protective sheath and exposing it to ambient air without taking the appropriate precautions. After all we've done, it would be stupid to spoil it by being rash. What a letdown it would be to hold the staff in our hands and to discover that it has lost all its powers and is nothing more than a piece of wood."

Dan had no interest in Jack's tale. He was letting him speak, hoping that Boris would go to another room for a few minutes, but the Russian didn't move.

"I put all that to Leskov, who understood the matter and agreed with me that we should be careful. That's why I'm here, doing research at Lausanne University. I'm happy to say that I believe I've completed my research, and soon I'll be putting that knowledge to the test on the staff itself."

"The staff is safe in its protective sheath where I understand it was for a long time, yet you haven't opened the box. Why didn't you?"

"Oh, that...a small setback. I don't have the pattern needed to open it. It's only impressed in Claire's mind. When I made room for her to surface and open it, she refused to cooperate and retreated into the background. But I'm sure I'll overcome that hurdle soon."

Despite his cheery words, Jack looked worried.

"Leskov doesn't know that, right?" asked Dan, lowering his voice.

"Let's say he doesn't have the fine details," Jack answered, speaking in an even lower voice. "He knows I needed to do more research before we could open the box, but I haven't told him about Claire's stubbornness—no need to worry him. I'm sure that Claire and I will come to terms. The difficulty is that Claire and I cannot converse directly, so it's a matter of communicating in writing or via tape recorder, neither of which makes reaching an understanding easy."

"So what will Leskov do when he finds out you can't deliver?"

"I will. It's only a matter of time. I'm going to play this straight with Leskov, although working with him is difficult," said Jack, shooting an anxious glance toward Boris. "He doesn't trust me much. That's why he has sent Boris to watch over me. I guess he thinks I might disappear on him."

"This is crazy, Jack. You're placing Claire in grave danger...and yourself, too. If it turns out that you can't convince Claire to cooperate, there is no telling what Leskov will do."

"I told you. Claire and I are the same, and what's good for me is good for her. She's just being difficult with the pattern, but she'll come around soon. We are due back in Moscow the day after tomorrow, and she'll understand that finishing the job is in her best interest."

"Let me talk to her, Jack, please. If she tells me that she agrees with you, I'll go away and never return. That's a fair proposal, isn't it?"

"I'm afraid that isn't possible. Talking to you would destabilize her. She's in an unstable state of mind as it is. I'm sure that you see that, too."

"What I see is that you're stark, raving mad. You are usurping Claire's body to satisfy your madness, and you must be stopped."

"Yes? And how are you going to stop me? I'm Claire Williams, an American citizen. All my papers are in order, and I'm free to go and do what I like. How I choose to act and dress is none of your or anybody else's business. And you know something else, Dan? I don't like your tone and want you to leave now. Boris!" he called. Boris approached. "This gentleman is leaving now and is not welcome back again."

Boris looked over at Dan, who got up. He was trembling with fury but understood that continuing to argue was futile. "This is not the end, Jack," he said.

"Yes, it is," Jack said and turned away.

Outside, Boris put a hand on Dan's shoulder and squeezed hard. "You don't come back, understood?" he said.

Dan made an effort not to wince. He nodded and swallowed, ready to leave. Suddenly, he felt his breath leaving him as he doubled over and fell when Boris' other fist hit him hard in the stomach.

"You don't come back here! Understood?" Boris repeated, kicking him in the face. He kicked him in the stomach and in the kidneys a few more times to make himself clear. Then he lifted Dan without any apparent effort and threw him out the gate.

CHAPTER 48

Getting back to the hotel had taken Dan more time and energy than he ever would have dreamt. He had lain in the grass for a long time, thankful that the street was peripheral and nobody was passing by to see him in that shape. He fought nausea off for a while, then picked himself up and limped uphill toward his car. His body ached in more places than he could count. But the real shock was seeing his face in the mirror. He had a long hematoma under his left eye that turned purple and kept company with a swollen right eye.

His hope to get the key to his room from behind the reception counter without running into anybody was dashed as soon as he reached the hotel. The owner's son was at the reception desk, and he had to go past him to get his key.

"What happened to you?" asked the young man in a disinterested Swiss manner.

"I went for a walk outside the city and fell from a rock I was trying to climb," Dan lied.

"You should see a doctor. Would you like me to call the house doctor?"

"It's nothing. I'm sure that a good shower is all I need," said Dan.

"Hmm...it doesn't look like it to me," said the young man. "Our house doctor is not expensive," he offered helpfully.

"Thank you. I'll see how I feel later, and if I need him, I'll let you know."

"Please do," said the young man, shaking his head as in disapproval.

As soon as he got to his room, Dan threw himself onto the bed, breathing shallowly. Every deep breath sent a spike of pain from his bruised chest to his head. He was dizzy with pain, and lying motionless was all he could manage. A few minutes later, exhaustion took over, and he fell asleep.

Dan got up the following day feeling hungry, which surprised him. The pain in various parts of his body had become duller but more diffused, and the purple signs on his face had taken on a greenish shade. Judging from the pain in his side, he had cracked a couple of ribs. He stood in the shower under a jet of lukewarm water for several minutes. However, even the gentle touch of the water was painful on his bruises. Soon, he felt a little better, then dried himself off and dressed while trying to ignore the pain.

With the help of oversized sunglasses that hid much of his battered face, he was not as conspicuous as he had feared. He walked out, taking the room key with him and skirting the reception counter to avoid having to talk to the owner's son. The hotel was not far from Lausanne's shopping district, and he strolled, scanning the shops to find ways to hide the signs of yesterday's beating. He would have to buy some makeup.

The street was alive with passersby and music. Some events occurred that day because a live band played traditional Swiss songs, and girls in Swiss costumes were pirouetting around. A clown jumped before him and showed him a sign written in French, but he moved on too fast for Dan to read it.

A shop's name attracted his attention. The sign said, "Costumes," and Dan found himself glancing through the window. He looked for a long time as a plan started to form in his mind, and then he pushed the door and walked in.

"Bonjour," an elderly clerk welcomed him.

"Good morning," said Dan. "I wonder if you could help me. I plan to go to a friend's dress party tonight and need a costume. Perhaps you could suggest one to me."

"Certainly. What about this beautiful Poirot? It's approximately your size, and we can make alterations if needed."

"I was thinking of something a bit less conspicuous. More conservative, if you see what I mean."

The clerk thought for a second and then pulled a hanger with a costume from a stand. "Well, then this Charlie Chaplin could do," he suggested, "or I may have a Sherlock Holmes left. Would you like me to see if we still have it?"

"Yes, please," said Dan, and the clerk left, returning a minute later, shaking his head and looking contrite. "I'm sorry, sir," he said. "We're out of Sherlock Holmeses."

"Then I'll try the Charlie Chaplin," said Dan. "Do you also have the mustache and the makeup to go with it?" he asked.

"Of course, sir," said the clerk, looking hurt by the question. "We are a full-service shop."

The Charlie Chaplin worked well because the outfit was almost normal without the hat and makeup, and keeping the jacket unbuttoned, it didn't look too tight. The makeup kit offered a variety of colors that would help him conceal his battered face. Dan paid cash, thanked the clerk, and left. He had brought a lot of cash with him so that the purchase would be untraceable. He didn't know exactly what would happen in the next few days, but he had a feeling that the greater the degree of anonymity that he could maintain, the better.

Back at the hotel, he placed the package with his costume in the trunk of his rented car, then walked in, ready to talk to the owner. He needed to be prepared to leave at a moment's notice but had to avoid attracting attention. The owner was behind the counter and turned his attention courteously to Dan.

"Good afternoon, Mister Ze'evi," he said.

"Good afternoon, sir," said Dan. "I have a question. I have booked my room until tomorrow, but I am waiting for a relative who was expected today and has missed his flight, so I may have to extend my stay. Would it be a problem if I had to stay longer?"

"Not at all, Mister Ze'evi. We have rooms. No problem. Just let us know if you need to extend."

"Thank you, I will," said Dan. "I'll check out if and when he manages to get here today, which might be at any hour since I don't know what alternative travel arrangements he has made. How do I check out if it's late and you're not here?"

"The room is paid for, so all you need to do is drop the key here in this box if my son or I are not around."

"I'll do that," said Dan with a smile that cost him some pain in his eye.

The Swiss Telecom office from which Dan needed to make one last call was just around the corner. He got a phone booth assigned to him and dialed Zigi's number. After an unnerving wait, Zigi's voice said, "Hello."

"Hi, Zigi. It's me."

"Are you okay?"

"I'm fine, sort of, but my meeting didn't go too well. I'm calling about that friend of yours in Zurich that you were telling me about."

"Yes?"

"I may need his help after all."

"When?"

"I don't know. Perhaps even tomorrow."

"I'll call him right away," said Zigi.

The next number he dialed was the one that Hamid had given him.

"Hamid?"

"Yes?"

"It's Ze'evi. I'm checking in. Things are moving, and I may need your help. I'm not sure yet."

"I'm glad you called. Did you see her?"

"In a sense...but I can't go into details by phone."

"I see. What do you need?"

"I don't know yet. Just be available, okay?"

"You can call one of the local numbers I gave you. They will reach me at all hours."

"Fine. I'll be in touch when I can."

"Do that," said Hamid, and Dan hung up.

Dan's next stop was the travel agent's office near the Swiss Telecom building. A polite and helpful agent checked the next day's flights from Geneva to Moscow and came up with two morning and two evening flights. Swissair took off at 9:00 a.m. and 9:15 p.m., and Aeroflot took off at 11:15 a.m. and 9:00 p.m. The morning flights were fully booked, but seats were available in the evening. "Would the gentleman like to book a seat on one of them?" the agent inquired.

Dan explained that he preferred morning flights and would be back to book one for another day. He was met with a puzzled look by the travel agent.

Back at the hotel, he approached the owner again. "My relative has managed to get on a flight and will arrive early tomorrow morning, so I'll be leaving early," he said.

"Then please leave your key at the front desk when you leave. I hope you had an enjoyable stay with us."

"Yes, most enjoyable, thank you," said Dan.

In his room, he unpacked his Charlie Chaplin package and studied the makeup. Having satisfied himself that he had all he needed, he locked his room and strode toward a nice restaurant he had spotted earlier that day. He deserved a good meal for a change.

CHAPTER 49

D an got up early the following day. The hotel served breakfast from six a.m.; at that hour, he was the only guest in the small dining room, which smelled of great coffee and baked goods. He ate slowly, savoring the Swiss butter and honey on the freshly baked bread he had become addicted to.

Back in his room, he spent a few minutes applying makeup to the most colorful bruises on his face, then donned the Charlie Chaplin costume. He decided against the mustache, which looked too unnatural to pass for a real one. Hat in hand, he wheeled his bag to the elevator, which took him two floors down to reception. Nobody was in sight when Dan dropped the key as instructed and walked out. The time was 6:30 a.m., and he had ample time to get to Geneva's airport and familiarize himself with the surroundings.

Dan parked near the exit of the short-term parking lot at the airport and took with him the tote bag that contained his "weapons": two syringes, one filled with hydroxyzine and the other with diazepam. The syringes were of different sizes, so Dan could be sure not to take the wrong one if he had to act quickly. As he had hoped to do in Rue Gaston, he planned to inject Claire first with a small amount of hydroxyzine. Jack's emergence was prompted by stress, so he hoped that the relaxation induced by the first injection would bring Claire back, but if it did not produce the effect he hoped for, he was ready to inject the diazepam. Zigi had said that diazepam could cause personality switches in some patients. Dan had to be careful while injecting it because the syringe held seventy-five milliliters, much more than the five Zigi had instructed upon. And if neither worked...he didn't want to think about it.

And then, of course, he had to find an opportunity to inject the drug, which was another significant hurdle. But this was the only plan he had.

Arriving at the terminal, he realized he had another problem—Swissair flights left from a different pier in Terminal 1 than Aeroflot, so he couldn't quickly check both for Claire. This thought worried him so much that he started patrolling Swissair's check-in area. He continued his patrol until 8:30 a.m. when the check-in for the 9:00 a.m. flight closed. Claire had not shown up, so she wasn't flying Swissair. Dan walked quickly to the Aeroflot check-in area, which only consisted of five check-in counters and was much easier to monitor than the endless row of Swissair counters. The Aeroflot counters were not open yet, which wasn't surprising since check-in wasn't due to begin until 9:30. He had time to rest and unwind a little.

Leaning against a pillar by the entrance, Dan inspected his reflection in the glass window and examined his disguise. It was so effective that even he wouldn't have recognized himself. He grinned at his image, tilting his hat and playing with his jacket. The grin died on his face when he saw Claire walk in through the door with Boris in tow, and seeing him reminded him of the many spots on his body that still hurt. He retreated behind the pillar and watched while Claire seated herself in the middle of an empty row of metal seats next to the dark Aeroflot counters. He kept thinking of her as "Claire," hanging on to his hope to bring her back, although he knew he was looking at Jack right then. Boris said something to her, placed two bags beside her, and walked toward the restroom. On an impulse, Dan followed him, passing behind Jack's seat.

The bathroom was empty except for Boris, who was using a urinal beside a toilet stall. Like little kids often do, he had dropped his pants to the floor and was peeing with vigor. Dan didn't stop to think: His hand went instinctively to the diazepam syringe, which he stuck in Boris' buttocks, pushing hard on the plunger. Boris turned with an animal roar, thrashing the air before him with his hands but missing Dan, who had taken a few steps back. Boris' eyes became cloudy, and his knees started to give. Dan quickly grabbed him, pushing him into the nearest stall and onto the toilet seat. His body was limp, and he didn't resist. Dan climbed on the neighboring stall's toilet seat and leaned down to lock Boris' stall door from the inside, checking on his condition. He was motionless but breathing heavily, appearing to be fast asleep. Dan picked up the tote bag and walked out, breathing through his nose and striving to regain calmness.

Jack was still seated in the same place, reading a magazine. Dan sat to her right, turning his face away to avoid recognition. Jack was reading intently and ignored him. Dan took the small syringe with the hydroxyzine and stabbed her thigh, injecting a small amount into the muscle. He had retrieved the half-empty, now-crooked syringe from Boris but hoped that he wouldn't need to use it. Jack's body jerked at the pain of the needle, and she turned her head to face him with a shocked expression.

"What the hell did you..." she said in Jack's deep, masculine voice but stopped in midsentence. Her expression morphed from one of anger to sheer surprise and confusion.

"Sorry, Claire," said Dan. He watched her closely. After a few seconds, her face softened, and she shook her head as if to clear her thoughts.

"Dan," she whispered.

"Yes, Claire. Are you back?"

"You came..."

There could be no mistake—the voice and the expression were Claire's. Dan was excited, but he knew there was no time to waste.

"Yes. We'll talk later," he said urgently. "How do you feel? Can you walk?"

"I'm a bit dizzy," she said, getting on her feet, "but I'll walk. Which bag is mine?"

"It doesn't matter now. We need to take them both. I'll wheel them. You just walk as naturally as you can by my side. We need to get away now."

The stress in Dan's voice was evident, and Claire nodded and put her hand on the handle of one of the bags. Her walk was wobbly, but on a security camera, she would look like someone who walked out of her own free will, not coerced into leaving the terminal. That would puzzle the police if they ever got involved.

Dan stuffed the bags into the trunk at the terminal parking lot, opened the passenger door for Claire, and seated himself behind the wheel. He switched on the engine just as the realization of the events caught up with him. He began shaking so violently that he had to grab the wheel with both hands and force himself to calm down. Finally, the tremor stopped, and he managed to drive away. Claire simply sat in a sort of stupor, watching him.

Once on the E25, driving toward Zurich, Dan relaxed and glanced sideways at Claire, who kept silent and stared straight ahead. "How do you feel?" he asked, mentally kicking himself at the banality of the question.

Claire kept shaking her head as if to wake up. She spoke in a whisper. "I'm...strange. It feels weird being me again. I've been away for so long..."

"You're okay now," Dan reassured her, not knowing what he meant by "okay."

"No, I'm not. I feel that Jack is trying to retake control. To push me away. He's strong..."

The anguish in Claire's voice almost made Dan despair that she would not be strong enough to resist him.

"Hang on, Claire. We'll make him go away. That's where we're going. To a place in Zurich where the best specialist will do just that."

"Pull over, Dan. *Pull over!*" Claire almost screamed. Dan stopped at a highway emergency parking area and switched off the engine.

"What's the matter, Claire? What's happening?"

"You must tie me up. Do it now! He may take over any second."

Dan took the hydroxyzine syringe and injected three more cc's into Claire's hip. "This will help."

Claire closed her eyes and massaged her hip. She inhaled three times, then opened her eyes and gazed straight at Dan.

"That's not good enough. We don't know how long it will last. It worked only for a short while the first time. And it will be a disaster if Jack switches while you're driving. You must tie me up."

Dan nodded. She was right, and he had to take precautions. He got out of the car, opened the trunk, and fished in one of the bags until he found a couple of neckties with a horrific color scheme. "Yours?" he asked.

"Unlikely," said Claire, "but I wouldn't know. I was completely confined to limbo while Jack was in control. No sound, no vision. Just blurred surroundings. Here," she said, at last, offering Dan her fists.

Dan tied her hands together with one of the ties and then used the second tie to tether her hands to a handle in the passenger's door.

"Is that too uncomfortable?" he worried. "We have almost three hours before we reach Zurich."

"It's all right. Not particularly cozy, but safety comes first."

She had spoken with her usual clear diction and smiled timidly. Dan relaxed a little. He hadn't seen her smile in a long time.

"You're coming back, aren't you? You sound almost like your old self."

"A little...but I'm tired. Perhaps it's the stuff you injected me with. I'd like to sleep some if you don't mind." She leaned on the door and closed her eyes. Dan kept an eye on her to ensure she was all right, appreciating Claire's smooth, delicate face. It seemed to disappear when Jack was in control, replaced by hard, angular features.

The trip to Zurich was smooth. Dan only stopped once, toward the end, to inject Claire with hydroxyzine again for safety when her sleep started to become agitated, and her features hardened.

The Zellinger Klinik, located in Zurich on Witellikerstrasse, was a small building that almost looked like a private residence. It was located in a neighborhood that was home to several private hospitals. After pushing the intercom button, Dan said his name. A few seconds later, a voice with a Teutonic accent filtered through the intercom speaker. "Please drive straight and park in the back," the voice said. "I'll meet you there." The gate opened automatically.

Dan did as instructed and drove on a gravel path that ran along a beautiful building that looked like a big, bright country house with geraniums at the windows, waiting to receive guests coming for a pleasant vacation. He turned right at the house corner into the back area, stopping after a short distance near a door. The door opened, and a lean man of about sixty approached them wearing a business suit with a golden tie.

"I'm Doctor Zellinger," he said. "Doctor Froind has called me and has given me a preliminary idea of the problem. I will need more details. Please come to my office."

"In a moment, Doctor. Pardon me, but I have to untie her first."

"Untie, I see..." said the doctor, raising an eyebrow.

"I know this is unusual, Doctor," said Dan, who had managed to untether Claire from the door and was working on her wrists.

"Unusual is the essence of my work, Mister Ze'evi. Don't you worry. Do you need a hand?"

"Thanks, but I'm managing. Here, you're free, Claire."

"Thanks," she said, smiling weakly.

They walked inside and sat in two leather chairs before Doctor Zellinger's desk. He waited for them, then sat in his chair and leaned back. "Before we start, some formalities," he said. "I am videotaping this, just so you know. Miss Williams, before giving you any treatment, I must assure myself that you are here of your own free will. Are you?"

"I am."

"And you are not under any undue influence, coercion of any kind? Threats? No?" Claire shook her head. "Good. You are aware that the treatments I conduct here are efficacious but extreme and may involve the use of medications, including psychoactive drugs, which may have temporary, albeit severe, side effects. During therapy, I will not have the luxury of consulting with you and of asking your consent to a specific treatment, so you need to give me carte blanche now to treat you as I see fit—of course, in consultation with Mister Ze'evi, if you trust his judgment and that's what you want. While you undergo treatment here, you lose all your civil rights and freedom. I am in charge of those for the duration. Do you agree?"

Claire hesitated and looked at Dan, who nodded. "We have no choice, Claire. I'll be here to look after you as much as I can, but you need to trust Doctor Zellinger. He comes highly recommended by a close friend of mine, so I trust him completely."

"Then I do, too," said Claire.

"Good, Miss Williams. You must also appoint Mister Ze'evi as your proxy because I may need his approval for certain procedures. You must sign this paper confirming your agreement to all the above."

Doctor Zellinger took the signed paper from Claire and turned to Dan.

"Mister Ze'evi, we need to talk about costs now. The treatment will take at least ten days, and the all-inclusive cost is seven thousand Swiss francs per day. If you wish to stay with us, your room's full fare will cost an extra five hundred francs per day. Is that acceptable to you?"

"That's fine. Whatever it costs to solve Claire's problem."

"Good. You should have said that before, and then I would have doubled my price." The doctor bared his yellow, crooked teeth, looking like a stuffed frog. "That was a joke, you understand?" he said in his thick German accent; without waiting for a response, he got up, turning practical. "Let's get started. You stay here, Mister Ze'evi, while I make arrangements for your room. You come with me, Miss Williams. We have work to do."

CHAPTER 50

"Mister Ze'evi, wake up, please."

Dan sat up in his bed, instantly awake. He hadn't been sleeping well since they got to the clinic, waking up at every noise. He blinked to clear his vision and immediately recognized the night nurse Doctor Zellinger had introduced to him on the first day of their stay.

"What's the matter? What's happening?"

"Doctor Zellinger wants you to come," said the nurse. "Please come with me."

"Yes...give me a second," said Dan.

The nurse nodded and retreated to the corridor. Dan jumped out of bed and pulled up his pants, stopping only to push his feet into the slippers neatly placed by his bed every evening. He hurried out and followed the nurse, who walked the corridor without a word. They walked through a maze of corridors until they reached a door on which the nurse knocked. Doctor Zellinger immediately emerged and joined them.

"What's the matter, Doctor? What's happening?" Dan asked. He was agitated, and the doctor touched his arm reassuringly.

"Nothing to be worried about, Mister Ze'evi. Please calm

down. Miss Williams is in no danger, but we have reached a critical stage of the therapy, and I felt I should consult with you before proceeding."

The doctor's explanation did nothing to ease Dan's apprehension. "It's three in the morning, and you're holding consultations? Please, tell me what's going on."

"Miss Williams' two personalities have surfaced at the same time—I am not surprised; this is an expected and positive result of the therapy, but—"

"But what?" said Dan, growing impatient.

"For one, it happened much sooner than expected—four days. I would have estimated it to take twice as long."

"That's 'for one.' What else?"

"The resulting conflict is much more violent than usual," said the doctor. It was apparent that he was trying to be soothing but was himself troubled. "I have never witnessed a conflict as harsh as this one. Come see for yourself."

The doctor opened the door and invited Dan to follow him. The room was narrow, and one wall had a one-way mirror that let them see into Claire's room. She was pacing the room and gesticulating. Doctor Zellinger threw a switch, and Claire's voice came through a loudspeaker.

"I'm me. You go away. Go now. I'd climb that if I only could. Go now," she said in a high-pitched voice. She was spitting out the words and sounded furious.

"What..." Dan started to ask.

"Wait," the doctor ordered. "Listen."

"I tell you. I'm telling you. Listen to me! Sit. Sit down!" This time, the words were spoken in a deep masculine voice that sent a shiver down Dan's spine.

Doctor Zellinger switched the audio off and turned to Dan.

"The nurse woke me up when she heard this. Thank God she was vigilant. We must act immediately—with electroshock therapy. I need you to know that it is generally safe but painful. It may trigger a dangerous physical reaction in a tiny proportion of patients. It's rare, but I need your signature before I proceed."

"What is the danger?"

"It may lead to seizures and epilepsy, memory loss, and rarely, brain damage. In the extreme, it might lead to death, but given that Miss Williams is young and healthy, the danger is infinitesimal."

"But that's terrible!" Dan was shocked at the thought of the danger the doctor had outlined. "Why do you want to do that to her?"

"We have no choice, Mister Ze'evi. Unless we intervene at the right moment, we may not be able to cure her at all. It was expected for her condition to behave atypically—Doctor Froind had forewarned me that it was an artificially induced personality split, something I had never seen before. It's not at all like a common dissociative disorder, and that's why there are many questions we don't know the answers to. What we do know is that if we miss a window of opportunity, it may never present itself again."

"Are you sure that there is no other way?"

"None that I know of," said the doctor, shaking his head for emphasis.

"Then go ahead," said Dan. He felt the heavy burden of responsibility on his shoulders, but he had to rely on the doctor's expertise. He signed the form that the doctor had handed him without reading it.

"Thank you," said the doctor, taking the signed form. "I'll make preparations. Please wait in my study," he added. "You don't want to witness the procedure."

Sometime later, Doctor Zellinger came into the study.

"How is she?" Dan asked, jumping to his feet.

"She's past the procedure and is resting now. We sedated her, and she's sleeping peacefully. From the physical point of view, she seems to be all right, but we have no means to know how successful the electrotherapy has been. We need to be patient."

"For how long?"

"We'll start our assessment tomorrow. If everything is well and the crisis is behind us, she should be out of here in three to five days."

"If…"

"I appreciate how traumatic this must be for you, but look on the bright side: This crisis was an opportunity that gave us a therapeutic window. We must remain optimistic. Now, it's past five in the morning. You or I can do nothing useful right now, and you deserve to get some sleep. And so do I."

"Sleep…I'm not so sure that I'll be able to."

"Here, take this," said Doctor Zellinger, handing him a small plastic vial with a pinkish pill in it.

"I never take pills," said Dan.

"Take it this time," said the doctor, still extending him the vial.

Dan nodded and took it, and then he walked out, trying to keep a straight back despite the weight he still felt on his shoulders.

CHAPTER 51

Dan and Claire were again seated together in Doctor Zellinger's office, but this time, they were smiling.

"It's hard to believe that only five days have passed since the night Claire had her crisis," said Dan.

"Yes," Doctor Zellinger agreed. "You have made an amazing recovery, Miss Williams. I had a hard time keeping Mister Ze'evi from seeing you other than through the one-way window. I thought he would burst at times, but I feared that meeting him could destabilize you."

"Well, from now on, I'm not going to let anybody keep her away from me," said Dan, placing a hand over Claire's.

The treatment was behind them, but the atmosphere was still tense. Dan didn't know exactly what to expect from Claire after all she had gone through and their long separation.

"So, Miss Williams, you did much better than you had hoped, ah?" said Doctor Zellinger with evident pride.

"That's right, Doctor Zellinger. Thanks to you." She spoke hoarsely—the only side effect of the cure. Doctor Zellinger had told them the swelling in her vocal cords was a known side effect of the electroshock and would disappear in a few days. Meanwhile, he said, she would do well to speak in whispers and give her throat a rest.

"And thanks to your strong constitution. You are a remarkable young woman. I hope you are satisfied," he added, turning to Dan.

"I think that 'satisfied' is the understatement of the century," Dan laughed. "You worked wonders! But before we go, I wanted to ask you: Is it possible that Claire will have any other aftereffects of the treatment? Is there any medicine she needs to take?"

"You can always expect minor side effects, such as headaches and dizziness, but nothing serious. She doesn't need medications except perhaps an aspirin every now and then. Miss Williams passed all her physical and cognitive tests with flying colors. She's as fit as a fiddle. Of course, if any question comes up, you should call me. I would recommend staying in the Zurich area for at least a couple of days, just to be on the safe side, although I'm sure you won't need me. Take a vacation. You both deserve it."

Dan and Claire thanked the doctor, shook hands warmly with him, and left. In the car, they sat, savoring freedom. They smiled at each other. The mood was one of embarrassment, though, as if they needed to get reacquainted after their forced separation. They did not touch. Dan thought it felt like an invisible ice barrier existed between them, which might take a while to melt down. He would give her all the time she needed.

"This time, I don't need to tie you up," Dan finally joked.

"Maybe later tonight," Claire joked back coquettishly.

"I have no objection to that," said Dan, beaming at her. "But first, we need to find a place to stay for a couple of days. Any preferences?"

"Let's go outside Zurich to one of those nice holiday resorts they have around here. Maybe we can go to Davos or something like that."

"Davos it is, then," said Dan. He was happier than he'd been for a long time.

They drove in silence outside the city, and after a while, Claire pointed to an uphill side road that passed through a grove. "Look how beautiful that place is. Let's go and take a look!"

She's excited like a child who sees new, beautiful things, Dan thought. He couldn't begin to imagine how much her traumatic experience had scarred her. She needed him to be gentle, and he resolved to do all it took to make her happy again. He slowed down and turned onto the narrow country road. When they reached the first trees, Claire placed a hand on Dan's arm and whispered, "Stop here. Let's get out for a while."

"Why don't we go to Davos first?" Dan asked. "We can find a room, and then we'll be free to take all the time you want to drive around and see things."

"Oh, but it's so beautiful out here...and it's still early. Only five minutes, okay?"

Dan found it hard to resist her happy smile. "Okay," he said and switched off the engine.

They got out of the car, and Claire ran to the nearest tree. She stooped to pick up a flower and then walked around aimlessly. Dan stood by the car, simply enjoying looking at her. She called to him, "Oh, look how beautiful these are!"

"What?" he asked. She beckoned him to come, and he strode toward her.

"Those lilies, up there," said Claire, pointing at a bed of flowers on a nearby hill. "I'm going to pick some." She took a step forward and stopped. "I wonder if it's not too steep...I get so dizzy," she whispered, "but they're so beautiful. I'm sure that I can climb that slope." She took a step forward.

"Wait!" Dan cried.

"Why?" Claire asked, puzzled.

"You shouldn't exert yourself for a while. I'll go and pick them for you. You wait here."

Dan started to climb up the hill without giving Claire time to argue. The climb was easy, and he strode eagerly, looking forward to bringing the flowers back to Claire. Her new childish and engaging personality fascinated him. Her delight at simple things like flowers was captivating.

Two minutes later, he reached the bed of lilies, panting a little. As he stopped and looked back, he heard the sound of an engine and saw the blue Volvo drive away fast with Claire at the wheel.

CHAPTER 52

S tupid! That's what he had been. He should have known it. The whispering was obviously meant to mask the masculine voice, the detached sensation he had felt between them in the car. That was Jack all along. *I should have suspected something,* he blamed himself. Clearly, Jack had allowed Claire to surface, knowing that he would be able to take control when he wanted to. By letting everybody, Claire included, believe that the treatment had exorcised him, he had thwarted the cure. Jack had played him and Doctor Zellinger as well. He had bided his time and had maneuvered Dan into lowering his guard so he could get away to who knew where.

It didn't take Dan long to realize that hitchhiking in the middle of a Swiss highway would not be easy. Perhaps it was because he had no backpack to label him a tourist, or maybe because he was trying to catch a ride in a place where he had no good excuse to be, but countless cars had darted by him without the hint of a thought to pick him up.

Although he was angry and finding it hard to think coherently, one thing was clear: He was in a bad fix. He still had a few hundred

Swiss francs in his pocket, but everything else was in the car that Jack had stolen.

At last, a truck stopped by him, and the driver opened the window and said something in German that Dan didn't understand.

"Zurich," Dan answered, hoping he would be understood.

More German, followed by an inviting sign, was all Dan needed to climb up to the cabin. The truck moved on, and the driver made some more conversation, which Dan could only respond to with a broad smile and polite nods. The genial man didn't seem to mind that the conversation was unilateral and kept chatting. When the truck reached the city, Dan spoke one of the only German words he remembered. *"Bahnhof,"* he said, and the driver nodded with understanding. After a while, he stopped the truck and pointed to an intersection. *"Bahnhof,"* he said.

"Danke," said Dan and climbed down. The truck moved on. A five-minute walk in the direction indicated by the truck driver got him to Bahnhofstrasse and from there to the train station. Twenty minutes later, Dan was on a fast train to Lausanne.

Going back to Lausanne was the only move Dan could think of. He reasoned that Jack would have to go back to find out what had happened to Boris and organize his flight to Russia. He might be able to track him down, but Dan had lost a lot of critical time on the highway. Jack had gained a considerable head start.

The train only went as far as Geneva, and he had to change to a local train to Lausanne. By the time he reached the city, it was already dark. A taxi took him to Rue Gaston, and Dan directed him to the last house at the upper end of the road. He remembered that the house was empty, and he walked past its gate and waited until the taxi disappeared down the road. He moved cautiously, trying to keep out of sight of the house as much as possible. The Mercedes was gone, and his rented Audi was parked in its place.

The house looked deserted, without a light or a sound coming from it. Dan approached the car and looked inside. The keys were in the ignition, and the doors were unlocked. He opened the trunk and gave a sigh of relief when he saw that his bag was still there. The two bags he had taken from Boris at the airport were gone, and so was Jack.

CHAPTER 53

Claire opened her eyes in the semidarkness and looked around her. The room she found herself in looked like a motel room with a simple bed, a small table, and a water bottle next to a half-filled glass. She got up and examined the two items on it: a piece of paper and a pocket tape recorder. Scribbled on the paper were the words "Listen to the recording."

Her throat was dry and felt like sandpaper. She ignored the glass but decided that the bottle should be safe. Taking a drink, she took the tape recorder and sat back on the bed. She stared at it for a whole minute, as if by doing so, she could get a glimpse of what it contained, and then pushed play. Jack's voice came from the speaker, loud and clear.

"Hi Claire, sweetie. It's me, Jack. I hope you're not sore at me for these slight differences we're having. It's a pity that we can't have a real face-to-face discussion, but I haven't figured out how to do that yet, so we must make do with this method of communication. At first, I had a lot of trouble switching back and forth, but now I've got the hang of it, and it's much easier.

"I'm giving you the time to listen to this and to respond, and then I'll switch—so don't get any funny ideas into your head about leaving the room, which is locked, by the way. We need to come to an agreement, you and I, so please be reasonable.

"You know that I could take full control, and then you would never emerge again, but I care about you very much, so I'm willing to discuss a time-sharing arrangement. But first, I need your word that you will open it when I let you out next to the box. Otherwise, Leskov will never let us be. It's in our best interest, and I'm sure you see that. So please record your response to my proposal, and then we can discuss the details. You know how to do that, right? Push the red button and record it. Do it now since the time before the switch is short."

The recording ended, and Claire pushed the stop button. She pushed the red button and brought the recorder to her mouth.

"Fuck you, Jack! Fuck you! Fuck you!" she said into the microphone, and then she threw the recorder onto the bed and sat there, crying, waiting for the switch.

CHAPTER 54

The architect who had designed the Leskov Industries building's lobby had obviously kept his employer's predisposition for grandeur in mind. Inside, he had placed a long wooden desk, behind which sat three receptionists who could have easily been three Miss Russias—except they were not smiling. Dan approached the one in the middle.

"I'm here to see Mister Leskov," he said. He did his best to sound friendly, but she maintained a frigid countenance.

"Document, please," said the ice queen. She inspected Dan's passport for a full minute, typed into a keyboard, and finally said, "Someone will come for you. Please wait on the couch."

Dan seated himself on the couch and went through the speech he had prepared for perhaps the tenth time. Obtaining an audience with Leskov hadn't been easy, but thanks to the fact that Dan's company's name was not unknown at the Leskov headquarters, he had managed to get access to Leskov's secretary after "only" five attempts. It had only taken her one day to make him an appointment, which Dan took as a good sign. He waited twenty minutes on the couch before a young woman approached him.

Dan got up. "Mister Ze'evi," she said, "I am Natasha, Mister Leskov's assistant. Please follow me." She also maintained a severe countenance, and Dan wondered whether smiling was forbidden in the building. He followed her to a gate equipped with a metal detector attended by an armed guard and then to a glass elevator that took them to the eleventh floor. After a brief walk along a corridor and through a large anteroom, they reached an ornate door, which the secretary opened after knocking on it. The room inside was huge, and, again, Dan had to walk what seemed like an infinite distance to get to the big desk behind which Leskov sat. As he approached, Leskov got up, circled to the front of the desk, and rested on it.

"Well, well, well," he said. "I wasn't expecting to see you again so soon."

"Or, perhaps, at all," Dan retorted.

"As you say. But you have me curious so that I can give you five minutes. What do you want?" he asked.

"I believe that you need my help," said Dan.

"Indeed?" Leskov lifted an eyebrow. "With what?"

"Getting your hands on that staff."

"You're not up to date, Dan. I already have it," said Leskov. The smirk on his face was one of triumph.

"I don't think so," said Dan, gazing straight into Leskov's face. "You have a box, which may or may not contain the staff, but without my help, I doubt you will ever be able to open it."

"You're wrong," Leskov retorted. "Your friend Jack is this moment on his way to Siberia to the box, which is at the Leskov Industries Research Center. With the information gathered in Switzerland, he will have your friend Claire safely open the box for me."

"Oh, so he hasn't told you yet..."

"Told me what?" said Leskov, straightening up.

"That Claire is not cooperating. As you know, Claire has the key—or, rather, she is the key. Without Claire, you will never be able to open that box, and she isn't going to open it for you unless I help you."

"Jack will make her," said Leskov, but he didn't sound convinced.

"Jack is mad and growing madder by the day. He thinks that he can control Claire, steal her body, and take her money from you. Are you going to let him?"

"Look here, Dan, I don't care, okay? I made a deal with that person—or thing—if it's not a person. I don't care whether it's Jack, Claire, or the Pope. It has the key to my box and must open it. Don't bother me with your petty problems."

Leskov spoke with disdain, and Dan made an effort to keep his composure. He had to sound like someone in control.

"Are you aware of what happened in Switzerland?" he asked.

"I know you tried to interfere and gave my man Boris a hard time, but that got you nowhere. All you managed to do was to delay us a few days."

Dan knew this was his one chance. He had to be convincing, or Leskov would kick him out. But he had prepared his story and rehearsed it a hundred times in his head. He was ready. "Not exactly," he said calmly and assuredly. "In Switzerland, I took Claire to a specialized clinic where she was treated. The doctor brought her back for a long stretch, and we spent time together making plans. She told me quite plainly that she'd rather die than let Jack live her life in her body as he is planning to do. We agreed that she would open the box only after she was back in full control and rid of Jack."

Dan watched Leskov's expression closely, needing him to believe it. "I know you have the equipment needed to reverse the split of personalities and to rid her of Jack."

"My laboratory has all the equipment, and the best specialist in this area works for me there. But I have no reason to do that for you. When Jack gets to Siberia, all I need is to put him to sleep for a while so that Claire can emerge, and then I'll make Claire cooperate and open the box. And she will cooperate, I assure you. I have foolproof methods to make people reasonable. I don't need you."

"That's where you're wrong. Claire isn't consciously aware of the details, but during her treatment in Switzerland, she received a posthypnotic command deeply set in her mind, which made her forget the pattern. She can only remember it if she hears my voice telling her so with the right words, and I'm not going to do it until I'm sure that you have rid her of Jack for good. On the other hand, I can make her forget the key forever with another command. We took precautions."

"You *are* clever, Dan. Perhaps too clever for your own good, but you have a good card there," Leskov said admiringly. He paused and finally slapped him on the back hard enough to remind him of his tender spots, courtesy of Boris. "So, how much do you want to help me out?" Leskov asked.

"I don't want any money, although Claire will want what was promised her."

"And she will get it. I am a man of my word."

"I know that. You have already proven that to me. And you see, we have a common interest: I want Claire back for my own reasons, and you want her back so she can open your box. Claire and I don't care about the box or the staff. You're welcome to them, and you're spending enough money to deserve them."

"I could make you say the right words to her, you know?" said Leskov as in an afterthought.

"How would you know if what I'm telling her will bring the memory back or cancel it for good?"

Leskov furrowed his brow for a few seconds. "All right, wait," he said at last. He hit the speaker's button on the modern phone on his desk and dialed a number. After a few rings, Jack picked up.

"Hello, Andrey," he said.

"Have you got to Novosibirsk yet?" Leskov asked.

"No, not yet. I made a little detour to rest. I'm not in Russia."

"Where are you?"

"I'd rather not say," Jack said after a brief hesitation.

"My instructions to you were to go straight to Novosibirsk. My plane is ready to take me there for the opening of the box."

"I know, I'm sorry."

"Let me speak with Boris."

"He's not with me," said Jack.

"What do you mean, not with you? His instructions were to stay with you all the time."

"I know, but he couldn't help it on account of the sleeping pills that I put in his vodka. He's fast asleep in a hotel room and won't be around for a day or two. I took all the cash that Boris was carrying, by the way. I needed it for traveling, so he may need you to put him in funds when he wakes up. I hope you don't mind."

"Are you mad?" Leskov shouted. "What are you doing?"

"I'm working in the best interests of the project...and mine. I'm having a little domestic problem with Claire. She's stubborn and threatens not to open the box. I need time to complete what I need to do to take final possession of my body. Once Claire understands there is no way back, she will be grateful for the opportunity to surface now and then. I will make opening the box a condition for letting her share time with me. The negotiation is taking a little longer than planned, but she'll come around. Be patient."

"And what if she refuses? That's too dangerous, Jack. I don't like that you disobeyed my orders. I want you to go immediately to the Research Center and wait for me there. We can work on this together there."

"Sorry, Andrey, no can do. You'll thank me in the end. I'll be in touch with you in a few days, and I'll tell you where to deliver the box for opening," said Jack and hung up.

Leskov turned his head slowly from the phone and stared at Dan. "He's mad," he said in a low voice.

"I told you so," Dan said with anguish.

CHAPTER 55

J ack Jones gazed at the cell phone in his hand. Little had he known how useful it would be when Leskov, with his mania for gadgets, had ordered Boris to take this phone with him. He was not sure that the phone's location could not be traced with the appropriate equipment, though, so he had turned it off and taken the battery apart for good measure.

Jack was sure that Leskov was hitting the ceiling by now, but he was much more intelligent and would play him as he had planned. Making Leskov believe that he was far away from Russia was critical to this stage of his plan. The thought of what Leskov would think if he could see him now, swiping Boris' card at the Research Center entrance, brought a smile to his face. There would be no personnel around at that time of night, and the magnetic card would let him through the Center's corridors without any trouble. He had all he needed in a small backpack.

The special projects wing had a single entrance, guarded by a heavy steel and armored glass door. He swiped the card, and the door opened. The access controls, a control panel connected to a small screen, were inside. In the panel, he selected the Open From

Inside Only option. Now they would have to blast the door open with powerful explosives to get to him.

A quick walk took him to a door marked Clean Room, and he stepped inside. The room had no windows and was fitted with an aeration system that always pushed air out. The box was on a steel table, with the locking system in view. He brought a chair near the box to make the locking system at eye level. Then he took the small tape recorder from the backpack and started recording.

"Dearest Claire," he said softly, "the moment has come to make a decision. The decision is entirely yours, but it will affect me as well. After listening to this recording, I hope you will come to your senses and do the right thing. If you decide otherwise, my sad duty will be to execute Plan B. Let me explain. The pattern that opens this box is engraved in your mind. But through my studies in Switzerland, I have concluded that I can glean some limited information stored in your part of our shared mind despite that limitation. I have done some tests, and I managed to see the key, albeit not clearly, not yet. But I am sure that I will be able to transfer the image of the key to my part of our shared consciousness, although to do it, I will have to repress your existence to the extent that you may never again be able to surface. I don't want to do that, but it's your call. Please understand that we must open this box. We have a deal with Leskov that will allow us to live happily for a long time.

"I want you to understand how much I love you. To me, you are the daughter that I always wanted. I don't want to harm you." Jack stopped the recorder, grimaced, and hit the record button again. "If we stick together and keep working on it, I am confident that we will find a way to coexist in this body in a way that will make us both happy," he said, trying to speak with a calm, fatherly voice. "I will always share our time with you fairly. You know I mean well. When you listen to this recording, please think about how good our lives will be together, and all that you need to do is open this box. "

Jack hit stop and placed the recorder on the box, knowing that Claire didn't need hints to listen to it now. Then he lay back in his chair, closed his eyes, and started to breathe deeply.

CHAPTER 56

"So, where is he?" Dan asked.

Leskov had just come into the room again after a lengthy consultation with his phone specialists.

"I don't know. I don't, damn it!" Leskov's frustration was growing every minute. The phone call with Jack had almost pushed him over the edge, but when he had calmed down, he had become practical again. He was pragmatic—Dan had to hand that to him. As soon as he had appreciated the situation, he had accepted Dan's cooperation as if it had been his idea from the beginning.

"We must think," Dan said. "Where can he go? He intends to work on Claire, so she agrees to his conditions. To accomplish that, he must have a card to force her hand. What is it?"

"How would I know?" snapped Leskov. "Perhaps we should let him. Then, after achieving his goal, he will be more reasonable and come to us. There is a chance then that we could reverse the process and eliminate Jack from Claire."

"What do you mean 'a chance'?" Dan asked with concern.

"I have never taken much interest in all those things. I have people who do that for me. I'm no damn scientist; I'm a businessman."

"We can't take chances! We must get to him before he gains full control."

"Yes? And how do you suggest we do that?" Leskov asked testily. "God only knows where the damn freak is."

Dan realized what the answer had to be. "Wait!" he said, "I told you that Jack must have a card to force Claire's hand. That card can only be the box."

"Why the box?"

"Think. Suppose he tells her that unless she cooperates, he'll open the box and take a chance that they both get killed. In that case, that might be enough to convince her—except that she can't open it without my order," Dan added, remembering that he had to keep up the lie. "God knows what will happen then!"

"What you're saying is that he could be in Novosibirsk, the filthy liar!" Leskov pushed a button on his communication panel and said, "Get me the Research Center."

The following three minutes passed in tense silence, and then a voice came through the speaker on Leskov's desk. "Novosibirsk speaking, sir. I'm the security officer."

"Anything to report?" asked Leskov.

"Actually, sir, I was wondering how you already knew about the problem we are investigating. We only became aware of it a few minutes ago."

"What problem?"

"It appears that the access door to the special projects wing is malfunctioning. It has been reset, so it is locked from the inside, and we cannot access that area. Our record shows that it was opened from the outside by Boris Lenchinsky, but he never checked in at the entrance. We are now turning on the video cameras in the wing to see if anybody is in that area. They were not on," he added, "because the wing is not in active use right now."

"Hook me in. I will supervise this myself."

"What's going on? What did he say?" Dan asked. He had listened to the exchange in Russian, but the only word he had understood was *Novosibirsk.*

"Trouble at the Research Center. It looks like Jack is there," said Leskov. He pushed another remote, and the wall on his right became a large screen. At first, only white noise showed on the screen, but four camera images started to become clear after a minute. The fourth showed the room where the staff was. Claire was lying back on a chair next to the box.

"Enlarge number four," Leskov ordered the officer, and the room came alive almost in full size on the wall before them. "Are the microphones on?"

"Yes, sir. You can hear what goes on in the room. Bidirectional audio is another story. If you want to be heard in the room, you need to tell me, and I'll connect via the audio link we are using."

"Okay. Be quiet now."

Claire stirred, sat up straight, and looked around. Then she got up, picked up the tape recorder from the top of the box, and pushed play. Jack's voice came from the tape recorder. The room microphones picked it up as a faint sound, and Dan and Leskov had to keep entirely still to be able to hear what he was saying. When the recording ended, Claire got up, laid the recorder down on the chair, and stood still for a few seconds. "Son of a bitch!" she said. "Old, demented, dirty son of a bitch!"

"Let me talk to her," Dan urged.

"Hook us in for audio," Leskov ordered.

"You can speak now," said the security officer's voice.

"Claire, honey, can you hear me?"

"Dan? Where are you?"

"I'm far away, but I'm here to help you. Listen to me."

"Yes, but where are you?"

"I'm in Moscow. Andrey and I are watching you via video. We are here to help, but you must listen to me, okay?"

"Okay."

"Jack is out of his mind, and you need to humor him; otherwise, he may do something stupid. When we are finished talking, you'll record an answer for him. I need you to understand and remember it. You must do this right."

"I will. Oh, Dan, I'm so glad to hear your voice."

"I'm glad too, but now listen. First of all, tell him you love him too, like a father—like the father you lost when you were a little girl. Tell him that you want the two of you to be together. Did you get that?"

"I did, but I hate him, and he knows it."

"It doesn't matter. He wants to believe that you two can work it out, and he'll be thrilled to hear you say that. Now, listen carefully. You will need to tell him what we did back at the Swiss clinic, but you must make that completely clear, okay? Tell it to him like this: 'While we were in Switzerland, the doctor instilled a posthypnotic command in me that keeps me from seeing the key unless Dan gives me the right command. I need Dan to be with me when I open the box.' Did you get that? You must tell him precisely as I told you, okay?"

"Yes," said Claire, "I'll tell it just as you said."

Good girl! Dan thought. Until that moment, he hadn't been sure that she would understand his game, but she was bright and would play along naturally.

"Tell him that I'll do anything you tell me and that you will make me release the block and then leave the room. Tell him I am mad about you, but you are not in love with me. Tell him I scare you, and you want to get rid of me.

"Tell him he should contact Leskov and ask him to bring me to you. That's it. You need to be convincing. Under no circumstances can you let him understand that I am already with Andrey."

"I'll do my best. I'm confused, though. And I am tired. But I need to start recording now. I don't want to switch before I'm done."

"I love you," said Dan, trying to keep the emotion from his voice and not succeeding.

"I love you too," said Claire. "Now, keep quiet and let me work."

"Switch off audio from our side," Leskov commanded.

"Audio off," said the voice from Novosibirsk.

"You're not bad, you know?" said Leskov. "I could use someone like you, with that presence of mind, in my organization."

"Haven't you used me enough already?" said Dan.

CHAPTER 57

J ack was happy. Claire had finally come to her senses and had started to see the logic behind his plan. He remained on guard, however. The possibility that she might be trying to double-cross him had not escaped him, but he was ready for it.

One of the things he had experimented with at length while in Switzerland was what he termed "intermittent presence." In practice, it meant that instead of switching for an extended period, he could surface only for a second or two, appraise the situation in the room, and switch back again without Claire knowing it. To Claire, that only meant a momentary loss of concentration and a bit of dizziness. It would result in significant fatigue if he did this too often because it was demanding on the body's resources. He didn't like doing it because he also felt exhausted after a few appearances, but he planned to use it when Dan was in the room to make sure that they were not playing any tricks on him.

He got up and approached a desk with a telephone and dialed Leskov's number.

"Cut the audio!" Dan said urgently when the phone on Leskov's desk rang. The last thing they wanted was to give away to

Jack that they were watching him. Leskov barked an order in Russian, and the audio from Novosibirsk went dead, then pushed the speaker button on the phone.

"Doctor Jones on the line," said the secretary's melodious voice.

"Put him through," said Leskov.

"Hello, Andrey," said Jack.

"Where are you?" said Leskov, with his typical lack of patience.

"I'm in Novosibirsk, at the Research Center, where you wanted me," Jack answered in a conciliatory tone. "I followed your instructions."

"Good. You had me worried. I don't like insubordination, as you know. Nothing good can come of it. We must follow the plan."

"Of course, of course. I followed the plan; I only needed some time to bring Claire to her senses. I'm happy to say that she has come around and will cooperate."

"Wonderful! I'll fly over," said Leskov, his face contradicting his tone. *What an actor,* Dan thought.

"There is only a small snag..." Jack added.

"Yes?"

"She needs her friend, Dan Ze'evi, here to open the box. It turns out that without him, she has a block that won't let her perform. Can you get hold of him?"

"I think so. I used to own his company, so I have all his contact information. If he's in Israel, I should be able to get him over here in a few hours. I'm sure he'll come running when he hears that his girlfriend is calling. Are you using the company apartment?"

Dan gave him a thumbs-up. *He's as cunning as I am,* he thought.

"Not really," said Jack. "For security reasons I don't need to go into right now, I am locked in the staff room. That's where I am calling you from."

"That can't be comfortable. Do you have enough food and

water? Why don't you ask our people at the Research Center to get you some?"

"No, thank you. I'll rough it. I have supplies for a day, and I hope it will all be over by then."

"All right, then. If you change your mind and need anything, just give me a call. Meanwhile, let me track Dan down, and I'll call you when I know where we stand."

"You do that," Jack said, then hung up.

"You played it well," said Dan. *Compliment for compliment,* he thought to himself. Leskov was having a rough day, and oiling him up a bit wasn't a bad idea. After all, Claire's welfare depended on him.

"The little bastard, giving me instructions. Me!"

"Yes, that's impudent," said Dan, "but don't forget that he doesn't have all his marbles."

"Yes, yes. Now we'll wait a little, and then I'll call the little bastard to tell him I got hold of you and that you are on your way. I think we should be in Novosibirsk tomorrow late afternoon."

"Late afternoon sounds about right," Dan conceded.

"Now we sleep," Leskov said, pushing another of the myriad buttons on his desk. Yet another Russian goddess came into the room. "Take Mister Ze'evi to the guest room and wake us both up tomorrow at eight," he ordered, then he left the room without so much as a good night.

CHAPTER 58

Leskov could be counted on to deliver. Jack knew that. The news that Dan Ze'evi would soon be on his way to Novosibirsk meant that this trying process would soon be over. Now, he just had to ensure nobody would trick him before Claire opened the box. Then he would repress her back into the deepest meanders of their joint brain, and she would be gone forever.

He had devoted much of the time he had spent in Switzerland to get ready for it. He had perfected his control technique so much that all he needed to repress her into nothingness was five minutes of quiet and concentration. It wasn't as if he didn't care for her, but he knew that there was no other way if he didn't want to be the one to disappear. She was so gullible that she had believed his promises despite all he had done to her so far.

As long as she could surface, there would always be a struggle for control of the body. No, she had to go as soon as she had done her part and opened the box. Perhaps he would let her surface once or twice a year if that turned out to be possible. He wouldn't begrudge a few moments of happiness to her.

The phone on the desk rang.

"I'm here, and I've brought Dan Ze'evi with me," said Leskov. "What now?"

"Keep everybody away except for Dan. I have unlocked the door to the special projects wing, and he can come in. I will be by the box. If anybody attempts foul play, I'll select the wrong key, and we'll all be blown up, along with the staff, so you'd better make sure that we play by the rules."

"Nobody's planning any foul play. I want that box opened as much as you do," said Leskov.

"All right, then," said Jack. "Let Dan in, but keep everybody else away. From where I sit, I can see the door of this wing, and if anybody gets close, there will be problems."

"Nobody will. I'm sending Ze'evi in."

Leskov nodded, and Dan walked from the control room toward the special projects room. He pushed the door, and it offered no resistance. A short, poorly lit corridor led to the storage room, and from where he stood, he could see Jack sitting beside the box. He walked toward him calmly to avoid alarm. Jack's hand was on the locking mechanism, and any unintentional movement could set it off.

"Jack?" he called.

"Come on in, Dan. Good to see you. I apologize for leaving you stranded on that Swiss hill, but it couldn't be helped. I hope you're not holding it against me."

"You fooled me all right, Jack. I felt quite stupid that I hadn't caught on to you."

"You were easy to fool. It was that doctor who gave me a hard time. I had to let Claire take control most of the time, and I only managed to surface here and there. I thought he had seen through my little stratagem a couple of times, but he was too full of himself to doubt he had succeeded."

"I agree. I'm quite pissed off at him," said Dan. Chatting was putting Jack at ease, and the more relaxed he was, the better.

Jack nodded and made a face as if to join Dan's sentiment.

Then he stiffened. "That's close enough, Dan. Don't get any closer."

Dan was standing some four or five paces from Jack. "How do we do it?" he asked.

"I'll tell you. I'll let Claire surface in a moment, and you will use that posthypnotic suggestion—a clever idea, by the way—to unblock her from remembering the key. Then she'll have to call those lawyers to get the inner key as well. I have a phone right here. When that's done, she'll select the right key and open the box. That's agreed between her and me."

"All right. But I'll need her to confirm that she agrees," said Dan. That would buy him a few more seconds. "Let's do this."

"Not so fast, Dan. First, I want you to understand where you stand if you're thinking of tricking me. Although Claire will surface, I will still be watching and running things. I can control her hand even when she is conscious. Believe me. Any funny business and I'll push the unlock button, and up we'll all go in flames."

"I don't believe you," said Dan. "When Claire is Claire, you're gone. And besides, you haven't come all this way on your quest for a new life only to kill yourself."

"Well, I'll prove it to you. Until I do, be smart and take my word for it. And you'd better believe that I can kill all of us if I want to."

"All right, all right. I wasn't planning any trick anyway."

"Good, good. Now be silent, and let me relax so Claire can resurface."

Jack closed his eyes, and Dan watched in silence. Half a minute later, Claire opened her eyes and gazed at Dan.

"Dan...you're here." She smiled tiredly.

"I'm here, honey. Why don't you take your hand off the switch?"

Claire lifted her hand from the unlock switch, but then she grew rigid, blinked, and put it back.

"Uh-uh, told you," said Claire in Jack's deep voice, and then she blinked again and looked at Dan apologetically.

"I...I feel dizzy. What just happened?"

"It was Jack. He can still control you while you are awake. Let's start the process and get it over with, okay? I reverse the command. Command reversed. Do you see the key?"

"Hmm...yes, it's coming back to me now."

"Great. Now, use the dials on the lock to select it, but don't push the unlock button. You need to get the inner key first."

"I know that," said Claire.

"I'm reminding you, just in case."

Claire had to use both hands to operate the dials that generated the key sequence, so she took her right hand off the button and started working them. After a full minute, she stopped and fixed her gaze on the sequence she had created.

"Is that it? Are you a hundred percent sure?" Dan asked.

"I'm almost sure. Not completely. Perhaps you need to give me your command again. I still see it slightly blurred, and I'm not positive about the last two dials."

"Okay. I reverse the command. Command reversed."

Claire sighed and lay back in her chair. "My God, that was a close call. Now I see that the sequence I created is wrong. I can see the correct one at a distance. It's getting clearer, but not enough. Give me your hand while you say it as we did at the clinic."

Dan took a few steps forward.

"I reverse the command. Command reversed," he continued reciting as he approached and grabbed her hand. Then, he pulled with all his strength, and she fell backward with the chair, away from the box. Without wasting a second, Dan jumped on her and grabbed her hands. He placed his knee on her belly, immobilizing her to the ground.

"Sorry, honey, but I have to do it," he said.

"You tricked me!" Claire bellowed with Jack's voice.

"So I did," said Dan, getting up and relinquishing his hold on the squirming body to Leskov's men, who had run into the room the moment that Dan had neutralized the danger. "And just so you know, I didn't give her the right command either," he added for Leskov's ears.

"Well done," said Leskov, who had joined them.

"I've done my part. Now do yours," said Dan. His voice was still shaking from the effort and the emotional scene.

In the laboratory, behind a large window, Dan watched as people in white aprons strapped Claire's body to a bed. Jack hadn't stopped shouting profanities and threats, but the glass that now separated them was soundproof, and Dan could no longer hear them. Strong white lights made Claire's face look pale, and drugs were streaming into her veins. Her body was now limp, and the shouting had stopped.

"I hope they know what they're doing," said Dan.

"Don't worry," said Leskov. "I have a greater interest in your girlfriend's welfare than you have—well, perhaps not a greater one, but let's say an equal one. Do you see that old man on the right beside her bed? That's Professor Lubich. He invented this system. He's the best you can get. He used to work for me back when... well, you don't need to know."

"How long will this take?" Dan asked.

"The procedure is not long, perhaps one hour, but then she needs to rest. I hope that by tomorrow morning, she'll be up and feeling all right."

"I want to stay with her," Dan said.

"No problem. As soon as the procedure is completed, you can sit by her until she wakes up. Are you hungry?"

"A little."

"Let's go and eat. I had wonderful caviar brought on my plane."

"No, thank you. I want to stay here. A sandwich will be enough."

"You don't know how to live," said Leskov, shrugging his shoulders. "I'll have food brought here." He turned around to leave. "Stupid sentimentalist," he added to himself under his breath.

CHAPTER 59

Dan had dozed off. Sitting by Claire's bed, watching her catch the first signs of awakening had proven tiring. He tried to suppress the fear that she might not be her old self again when she woke up, but his mind needed proof to be set at ease after all the twists and turns he had gone through lately. He shook himself awake as Claire finally stirred. Her eyes were open, and she stared up at the ceiling.

"Claire," he said quietly, almost whispering.

"Hey," she said wearily.

"How do you feel?"

"Drained, but I think I'm okay...thanks to you."

Dan took her hand and got closer. "Thanks to you and your presence of spirit. I worried that you might not play it right and that I couldn't drag you away from that button, but you knew what to do."

"You know that I've gotten past your thorns and can read you like an open book," said Claire, openly pleased.

"Yes, but now..."

"Now, trust me," Claire interrupted. "Now it's my turn to do the right thing."

The door opened, and Leskov walked in. "Ha! Glad to see you are awake, my dear," he said. He was joyous, as Dan had never seen him before. "As soon as they told me you had woken up, I dropped everything and came over." He put it as if he was doing a particular favor, rushing to see her in the middle of his busy day. "So it's time now to wrap this up. I can't wait to hold the staff in my hands. I'm sure that you are strong enough to get up. Let's go and get it."

"No, Andrey," Claire said.

"What do you mean, 'No'? That was our agreement. Now you keep it."

"Our agreement was that I would help you find the box, with Dan's help, and then I would open it for you, and you would pay me as agreed. There was nothing in our agreement about you letting a maniac hijack my body. Perhaps you thought you would save some money that way, but you broke our agreement, so don't come to speak to me about agreements."

"Claire," said Leskov, speaking slowly between clenched teeth, "you will now get up and open that box for me, or else. Do you understand?"

"Sorry, Andrey, but I couldn't even if I wanted to. I need to get the second part of the key—the inner key—from my lawyers, and they will not give it to me unless I make my call to them from New York or Tel Aviv."

"Stop playing games with me, Claire."

"I'm not playing games, Andrey, but I don't trust you anymore. 'No trust, no business.' You taught me that, remember? So I took precautions. The instructions my lawyers have are to destroy the code immediately if the call comes from any other place."

"What do you want?" asked Leskov, who was starting to realize that he didn't have a winning hand.

"As I told you, I need to get the inner key. Before I do that, I need you to send the money to my offshore bank account—you have the details—and get business-class tickets to Tel Aviv for Dan and me today. Once I reach Tel Aviv and confirm that the money has been deposited, I'll get the keys to you."

"You're playing a dangerous game with me, Claire," said Leskov with a piercing stare. He shifted his gaze from her to the wall and thought for a half-minute before turning again to Claire and speaking.

"If I wire the money and don't get from you what is mine, there will be consequences. Dire consequences," he said, preserving a little of his dignity.

"Do you think I'm stupid, Andrey?" Claire asked. "I know very well that if I tried to double-cross you and run with the money, my life wouldn't be worth a dime."

"Yours and that of your friend, here, understand me?" Leskov added.

"That's why I won't be running away with the money. Because I'm not stupid and because I understand you."

Silence fell in the room. Leskov closed his eyes for almost a full minute. When he reopened them, he said, "I agree. As long as everything is clear between us and on the table, we will do it your way. How will you be giving me the key?"

"I can't give the external key to you, but I can point it out to you. We will use the video link you set up between Leskov Industries and Dan's company. I can read the inner key to you by phone. I'll call you when we are back, and the money is verified. Is it a deal?"

"It is. You're too headstrong for a woman, but I admire that. Yes, I do. I'd hate to have to make you pay, so don't double-cross me. Stay here, and I'll get plane tickets for you."

Claire nodded, and Leskov stormed out. He appeared never to enter or leave a room like other people. He had to make entrances and exits.

"Whew, I thought that he would explode," said Dan. "You played him like a pro."

Claire placed a hand on his arm and quieted him, pointing her finger to the ceiling.

Claire kept silent for most of the flight. She was meditative, and Dan didn't force her to talk. The time for that would come. He was happy when the taxi that had taken them from the airport dropped them at his home.

Being back in Tel Aviv felt surreal. To Claire, it felt like it had been ages since she had been there before she knew she had an Alter planted in her head. To Dan, it was a homecoming for which he had hoped for too long. The taxi had just left, and Dan was fumbling around the potted plant where he kept his house key when a dark, tall figure emerged from the street and stood there in plain view.

"Hamid?" Dan said, astonished.

"It's okay," said Claire. "I told him to be here. I called him from the airport when I went to the restroom."

"Why?"

"I'll explain later, okay? Go inside, and I'll be with you in a moment."

"Oh, no. I haven't had the opportunity to tell you, but he was here before and made veiled threats about you. He may be dangerous. I'm not letting you out of my sight again. Not with bad characters like this Hamid around."

"All right," said Claire, "but please stay here and let me talk to him alone."

Dan stood at the door and followed Claire with his eyes as she walked the short distance to Hamid. She approached him and spoke quickly and quietly. He watched as Hamid repeatedly nodded in assent. After a brief discussion, Claire handed him a piece of paper, and he left.

"What was all that about? What did you two talk about?" Dan demanded to know.

"I'll tell you everything, okay? But in a little while, not now. Please be patient and trust me. It's for your own good."

"You aren't planning on double-crossing Leskov, are you? You don't want to get yourself killed!"

"No, don't worry. Hamid presents no danger for us. Only good things." Claire placed a hand on his arm in a clear attempt to reassure him.

"I don't see how," said Dan.

"You will, you will," said Claire, and then she clammed up.

Her casual demeanor wasn't enough to relieve Dan's anxiety. He went to his room and pocketed his gun, determined to keep it handy.

Dan watched Claire as she slept beside him. She looked so peaceful, and it was amazing how well she had emerged from her experience. There were still many unresolved questions—what scars it had left on Claire's soul and his own, for that matter. Had they changed? Were they going to be closer than before, or would they drift apart?

Claire had rejected Dan's suggestion that they might go out for dinner. "I need some quiet, and I need you to stay close to me," she said. That evening, they had eaten a light dinner that Claire had cooked with what canned food they had found in the house. They opened and emptied a bottle of red wine. Watching her move around while cooking and eating had arisen an aching physical desire in Dan, but he couldn't bring himself to take the first step. Claire needed time to readjust, and he would give it to her, no matter how waiting would make him climb walls. The important thing was that she was there with him, safe in his house.

Safe? At least, he hoped so.

CHAPTER 60

Claire closed the laptop Dan had brought home from the company's office and set up for her.

"What's up? You look satisfied," he asked.

"I am," said Claire. "I just checked my bank account, and the first payment has been made. One more, and we are good to go."

"One more? I thought Leskov was going to pay all at once. Is he really wiring two and a half million dollars?"

"He is," said Claire, smiling brightly.

"Then you're a rich woman. Congratulations."

"That's enough money for us to live on, go where we want, do what we want."

"We?" said Dan, raising an eyebrow.

Claire got up and came to sit on his lap. She kissed him lightly and then, when he responded hungrily, gave him a long, sweet kiss.

"Of course it's 'we.' If you think I would let you off the hook after rescuing me, you're dead wrong," she said, teasingly placing her hands around his neck.

"No, no," Dan laughed, wriggling himself out of her hold, "I like the hook! I'm all for the hook."

"Good for you. It's time to check again," said Claire.

She got up and opened the laptop. After a few clicks, she shut the laptop down.

"It's all there. Time to call Leskov."

The expensive video link that Leskov had insisted on installing at Dan's company came in handy. They were now in the company's offices, which at that time of night were empty. They had insisted on postponing the event to after ten o'clock, Israel time, to make sure that they would not be disturbed. Leskov hadn't liked it and was getting increasingly impatient as the time passed, but he had little say in the matter. Dan was amazed, time after time, at how well she had handled herself with Leskov and how unfazed she was by his threats.

A camera gave the image of the box dials, which were visible in high resolution on the large screen, together with Leskov himself. The dials consisted of ten wheels, each allowing a change between ten slightly different shapes. The number of possible combinations was in the billions, so only a person with specific knowledge would get to the right one.

"I can see you; can you see me?" Leskov asked.

"Yes, we see you," said Claire.

"Stas!" Leskov cried imperiously.

A noise behind them made Claire and Dan turn. A man they had never seen before had been lurking in one of the other rooms and now came out of the dark. He silently pointed a gun at them. He was small and thin, but the gun was big.

"What is this, Andrey?" Claire demanded.

"This is my man, Stas. If you make a false move, he will kill your boyfriend, my dear, and then he will shoot you in the leg—in both legs if he needs to. Did you really think that you could impose conditions on me, on Andrey Leskov!? Did you think that I would put up with it? If you did, you are a fool."

"What do you want, Andrey?" Claire asked. Her eyes had narrowed to a slit, but her voice was calm.

"I'll tell you what I want. I want the keys to open this box. Then I want you to wire the money back to me, and then, perhaps, I'll let you live. Perhaps both of you, if I'm in a good mood and you don't make trouble for me. But you will have to beg and convince me."

"Andrey..." Dan started to say, but Leskov checked him with an imperious "Quiet!"

Dan kicked himself mentally for leaving his gun at home. He tried to calculate his chances of getting at the man without being shot but realized that Stas was keeping his distance. He was too far from him and would have all the time to take him down if he took a step toward him. He had to stay alert and find a better moment to attempt to overpower him.

"Now call your lawyers and get the inner key. And put the call on speaker," Leskov commanded.

Claire glanced at Stas, who stood there like a statue, only moving the muzzle of his gun to cover her as she moved to the phone. She dialed a number without lifting the receiver, and a voice came from the speaker.

"Kowalsky," it said.

"Good afternoon, Mister Kowalsky. I hope this is a good time," Claire said, keeping a normal tone.

"Perfect. I was waiting for your call at my direct number as we agreed. What can I do for you, Miss Williams?"

"I'd like you to open the envelope you keep in escrow for me and give me the eight-digit code, please."

"What is the phone number to call you back on?"

Claire gave Dan's number to him, and a few moments later, the phone rang.

"Thanks for calling me back, Mister Kowalsky. Please proceed."

"With pleasure, but first, we need to confirm your identity.

Just one second while I open the envelope...yes. Please give me the PIN."

"It's 7523."

"All right, Miss Williams. I have confirmed your identity. Here is the code. I'll read it slowly to you. Please write it down."

Leskov wrote down the code as Kowalsky read it, then signaled to Claire to end the call. After she ended it, he spoke with a satisfied smirk.

"Now, the external key. You see the dial clearly, yes?"

"Yes," said Claire.

"Start giving me the key."

"All right. Turn dial number one slowly until I say stop."

Leskov did as instructed.

"Stop!" Claire commanded. "Now dial number two."

It took fifteen minutes to go through all the dials. Claire went back and forth between them, making minute changes to the shape that appeared on the display until all dials were in place.

"Is that it?" Leskov asked. "Can I open the box?"

"Yes, that's the key," said Claire.

"Vladimir!" he cried.

A stout man appeared on the screen. Leskov spoke to him briefly in Russian and then left the scene. A few moments later, following another cry from Leskov, the stout man pressed the opening button on the lid and lifted it, then immediately left. Leskov reappeared on the screen and inspected the glass cover. Beneath it, there was no staff but only a few yellowing pieces of paper.

"You scammed me!" Leskov roared. "You filthy...Wait and see what I'll do to you as soon as I've neutralized the explosive mechanism," he added viciously. He pushed the keys of the inner keyboard frantically, reading the code from the page on which he had written it, and meanwhile, he kept mumbling, "I'll take your eyes out for this. Swindling me. Me!"

Claire placed a reassuring hand on Dan's arm, and they watched Leskov's outburst in silence.

"When," Claire whispered to Dan.

Before their eyes, the screen shaped like a white flower and then turned black. A loud noise terminated the video link.

The man, Stas, took a bewildered step forward, trying to see what was happening on the screen. As soon as he came close enough, Dan hit him on the arm, making him lose his grip on the gun that fell to the floor. Another blow made him fly across the room. Dan recovered the gun and pointed it at Stas, who got to his feet and bolted, disappearing through the door.

Dan turned back and took Claire in his arms. They were both shaking. "What just happened?" he asked. He looked and felt bedazzled.

"The inner key was not the right one," said Claire.

"But...but then Leskov is dead."

"May he roast in hell."

"You killed him!" Dan accused her.

"It was him or us. Do you think that he would have let us live? This man, Stas, was a killer."

"A lousy one. Anyway, I don't understand how you did it. The lawyer read the code out loud."

"I'll explain it to you sometime, but not now. I'm still shaking."

Back at Dan's home and a little calmer, they huddled together on the sofa and tried to make sense of the day's events.

"It's amazing that Leskov took a chance at opening that box, knowing the consequences of a mistake," Dan mused.

"If you think about it, what he did made sense. He was afraid I might trick him and make him select the wrong external key or even make a mistake, so he called someone else—Vladimir—to open the lid and be blown up in case of a problem. But he had no reason to doubt the inner key. He knew the process and heard the lawyer as he read the code to me, so he was convinced that the inner key could not be wrong. He didn't know that I had arranged to have the wrong key read out to me in case of danger. Besides, he was so vain that he had to be the first to see the staff. It's amazing how intelligent people can become stupid when their ego gets in the way."

"Speaking of which, the staff never existed. I don't understand it."

"What you don't understand?"

"I can't understand Jack's insistence on attempting to open the box, which would only expose the scam that he had cooked up. It doesn't make sense."

"I figured that out," said Claire. "You told me that Jack didn't have genuine memories. He only knew what had come up in conversation with me. When he recruited me, he couldn't very well tell me that the whole staff story was something he had made up, so he sold it to me as a true story, and that was the only memory to which he had access. That's how he came to believe his own lie."

"But what did he have to gain from it?"

"I guess that the purpose was to perpetuate himself in my brain. He obviously thought that he would be able to take full control of my body quickly, and he planned to end this charade as soon as he did. But the Alter was far from perfect and had lost knowledge of Jack's original intent."

"I think you're right. Your theory sits well because he never attempted to retrieve the box during all these years. He knew there was nothing worth retrieving in it."

"I wonder why he hid the box in the desert in the first place. You saw that it was full of papers. Perhaps those documents had nothing to do with the staff. Maybe his original intent was to hide the documents, and he made up the story about the staff only much later. I don't know."

"We will never know."

"It doesn't matter now, anyway," said Claire. She hugged him and kissed him lightly on the lips.

A thought kept bothering Dan. "How does Hamid play into all this?" he asked.

"Oh, that was a bonus. The idea came to me on our way here. As you remember, Bshari wanted the staff destroyed. So when I went to the restroom at the airport, I called Hamid and asked him to meet me. I put a proposition to him: I would make sure to have the staff destroyed against the payment of a nice sum. He agreed immediately. That was the second payment that I verified before calling Leskov. I'm afraid only one million this time," she added smugly. "In the worst-case scenario, if everything went well with Leskov, I would have given Bshari his money back."

"So you got paid twice for blowing the up box. You're amazing!"

"*We* got paid twice. You keep forgetting," Claire pointed out.

"Much as I look at this from every angle, I can't see a flaw. I assume that the news of the explosion at the Leskov facility and the premature death of the great Andrey Leskov will be in the news tomorrow so that Bshari will know he has got his money's worth."

"And we were four thousand miles from Leskov when the explosion occurred so nobody can blame it on us."

"Not our fault if he played with fire," Dan agreed.

Claire gave a little sigh. "I want to take a long shower, and then we need to celebrate," she said.

Claire was not one for half-measures. They had bought the most expensive Scotch in the liquor store, which now stood half-empty beside the bed. The liquor had taken effect well, and Claire had made him sweat as he had never sweat before. He lay on his back, and Claire lay beside him, her right hand reaching across his body.

"You're better with some Scotch in you," she said, kissing his chest.

"You're the best with and without it," he said.

She pushed herself up and sat on him. She leaned forward, placed her hands on his arms, and pinned him to the bed, kissing him on the neck. She was quiet for a few seconds, and then she stiffened, blinked, and opened her mouth.

"So this is how you do it...sickening," she said in a deep, masculine voice.

"Aahh!" Dan cried. He tried to push her away and get up, but Claire's features softened, and she laughed.

"Just messing with you," she said.

I hope you enjoyed EXODUS '95. If you did, I have other titles I think you would like:

CHIPLESS *- A dystopian action novel (and its sequel, REWIRED);*

ONCE AWAKENED *- A psychological SciFi thriller;*

THE EVELYN PROJECT *- An international thriller with a sprinkle of time travel.*

Please give them a try.

The Author

MEET THE AUTHOR

Kfir Luzzatto is the author of thirteen novels, several short stories, and seven non-fiction books. Kfir was born and raised in Italy and moved to Israel as a teenager. He acquired his love for the English language from his father, a former U.S. soldier, a voracious reader, and a prolific writer. He holds a Ph.D. in chemical engineering and works as a patent attorney. In pursuit of his interest in the mind-body connection, Kfir was certified as a Clinical Hypnotherapist by the Anglo-European College of Therapeutic Hypnosis.

Kfir is a member of the HWA (Horror Writers Association) and ITW (International Thriller Writers). You can visit Kfir's website and read his blog at https://www.kfirluzzatto.com. Follow him on Twitter (@KfirLuzzatto) and friend him on Facebook (https://www.facebook.com/KfirLuzzattoAuthor).

ALSO BY KFIR LUZZATTO

CROSSING THE MEADOW

THE ODYSSEY GENE

THE EVELYN PROJECT

HAVE BOOK, WILL TRAVEL
(With Yonatan Luzzatto)

AN ITALIAN OBSESSION

EXODUS '95

CHIPLESS

REWIRED (*The sequel to CHIPLESS*)

ONCE AWAKENED

The Tessa Extra-Sensory Agent series:

TESSA (Tessa Extra-Sensory Agent Book 1)

THE OTHERS (Tessa Extra-Sensory Agent Book 2)

HUNTER (Tessa Extra-Sensory Agent Book 3)

PHANTOM (Tessa Extra-Sensory Agent Book 4)